Copyright © 2025

2025 Year of First Publication

By: Emily Deymonsup (author)

For permission requests, contact the author at: rp2b2c@gmail.com.

Book Cover by Richard & Natallia Price

Edition Number: 1

Disclaimer of Liability
Whilst I have referred to real life places in the story, anything depicted taking place in any of them has no relation to past or current people and events. The Owner shall not be liable for any direct, indirect, incidental, consequential, or special damages arising out of or in connection with the use of copyrighted materials, including but not limited to errors, omissions, or inaccuracies in the content or loss or damage of any kind incurred as a result of the use of any copyrighted material

DOMINIC PEPPER & THE HIGH PRIEST'S DARK CRYSTAL

(Book 1 of the Dominic Pepper series)

INTRODUCTION

Fourteen-year-old Dominic discovers a divine parchment with the power to protect against evil. At first, he misuses its holy magic for petty revenge at school with hilarious consequences but when a satanic sect learns of the parchment, they set their sights on him. Summoning Lucifer's monstrous messenger, Bestia Terrae, the sect targets Dominic's girlfriend, Miriam, as a sacrifice.

Dominic's attempt to protect her unleashes the parchment's true strength and plunges him and his friends into a perilous struggle against dark magic. Their daring escape marks them as sworn enemies of the sect, and Dominic is forced into his first deadly confrontation with Bestia Terrae.

But his trials are only beginning. As Dominic learns more about the parchment, he discovers his powers are greater than he ever imagined, yet they are equally matched by Lucifer's High Priest, who will stop at nothing to destroy him. With Miriam's life in the balance, Dominic takes the battle to Wilmindor, a breathtaking world in another galaxy, where forests, skies, and lakes are alive in dazzling, magical harmony. The inhabitants of Wilmindor pledge their help, but their alliance comes at a tremendous cost.

Two battles rage: in Wilmindor, where wondrous creatures sacrifice themselves to shield Miriam, and in the satanic temple, where Dominic must face Bestia Terrae alone. To save Miriam, his friends, and himself, Dominic must risk everything, his courage and his powers against Lucifer's most formidable and fearsome High Priest.

TABLE OF CONTENTS

TABLE OF CONTENTS (cont)

CHAPTER ONE

JUST ANOTHER MONDAY

It was the last miserable cold dark Monday morning, before St. David's High School's February half-term break. As usual, Dominic was sound asleep submerged under his duvet and other assortment of his favourite covers. How he ever found comfort having his head supported by four pillows was still a mystery, but it worked for him and he was totally oblivious to the outside world.

"Dominic, I won't tell you again; You're late for school," came a distant shouting, breaking the warm and peaceful tranquillity of his sleep. Dominic just snuggled down even deeper into his cosy and warm world.

"Get up you lazy devil," joined in his slightly older fifteen-year-old sister, India as she passed his bedroom returning from the highly treasured one and only bathroom. But nothing could wake him, he was fast asleep dreaming of a passionate embrace with his favourite girl in the world, Olivia. He could feel her gentle kisses all over his neck and it felt so wonderful and cool. But somehow though, still in his dreamy semi-conscious state he managed to work out that the beautiful wet sensation of Olivia kissing him was impossible. He was after all in bed in his house, and she was a pop star living thousands of miles away. Suddenly the logic of it all flashed through his mind; *Well, if I'm wet then, who, what and how?* and he quickly opened his eyes to see Randolph, his pet bull dog licking away at his neck.

"Randolph, get off," he blurted out quite annoyed that a dog had ruined his beautiful dream.

This time those annoying interruptions to his sleep had worked and he stretched out his arms into the cold freezing air. The reaction was instant and although still only half awake he immediately re-coiled them back into his warm and comfortable world. *Blow that* he thought, *I'm not moving from here today.*

Monday was always the same, getting up in the freezing cold in those horrible dark and depressing mornings. Waiting in the rain for the school bus to trundle along and then facing everyone cheering themselves up by calling him names. Then to cap it all, he had to face first thing double English, his most hated and detested subject.

"Mum, I don't feel well," he faintly uttered down to his mother in his best croaky voice hoping she would fall for his lame excuse. "I think it was all that extra pepperoni that stupid India put on the pizza last night," trying to add a bit more substance to his poor attempt of deception.

"Well, if you can stay up to all hours on that silly computer then you have only yourself to blame," responded his mother who was busy preparing their school lunches. "And if you think you're staying at home in bed all day, you're sadly mistaken. You can vacuum up and clean the bathroom," quickly following it up. That did it, that was even worse than going to school and he rolled out of bed, half-awake and sauntered into the bathroom.

Standing in front of the mirror, he hated how he looked. First that disgusting orthodontist brace around his teeth and additionally now, having to battle nearly every day with the dreadful ever appearing spots. Today was no different and there sure enough, another one had appeared from nowhere.

I just can't go to school looking like this, he thought to himself. Then suddenly remembering something that he had seen his sister using, a sort of makeup which she always uses to cover her blemishes.

He quietly slipped out of the bathroom and tip-toed along the landing to India's bedroom. It was all clear, she was downstairs helping mum getting things ready. *Now where's that make-up bag* quickly thinking whilst entering her room. What a state of total clutter faced him, everything strewn all over her bed as if a tornado had burst in through her window. *How dare she call me untidy when her bedroom looks like this* was going through his mind whilst rummaging through a most bizarre range of girls cosmetics.

This must be it, as he picked up some sort of a pencil with a skin colour lead in it and proceeded to blindly rub it to his spot. It only took a few seconds and he had just finished when he heard the sound of the first stair of the staircase squeak. It was dead give a way that someone was coming up and so quickly replacing the pencil he darted back into his bedroom.

Now he could see his cosmetic skills, looking into his wardrobe mirror to see his handywork. What a mess, he now looked instead like a clown with a slight rosy cheek and decided for the better to quickly wipe it off with his pyjama sleeve.

I bet Asher Angello doesn't have this problem he thought to himself, discarding his pyjamas in favour of his white tee shirt and black V-neck jumper and trousers school uniform. Asher Angello was his username on Facebook which of course was a play on Asher Angel, his hero from the movie, Shazam.

As Asher Angello, he could pretend that he was sixteen and not his real fourteen. He was tall, athletic and of course good looking with a cute smile and all without those dreaded spots. He had his pick of all the girls, they all wanted to communicate with him (er Asher!). His favourite was, Olivia Rodgers who was fourteen too with long dark auburn hair and reminded him of his dream girl Olivia Rodrigo.

She had been his Facebook friend for over six months and they had become very good friends indeed. It was her who consoled him and made his life tolerable at his new school when everyone teased and made fun of him.

He had never really known his father as he had left the family when he was only six, leaving his mum to bring his sister and himself up on her own. She had really tried her best and he knew it, but it was never a substitute for a real dad. He really didn't care about all that now, it was a thing of the past but why on earth did his mum marry someone with the surname, Pepper. How did she never realise that this would be ridiculed by all his class mates. To make matters even worse, someone in his class had realised that if you take the first two letters of Dominic and add them to the first two letters of Pepper, it spells DOPE! Incredulous, parents do not understand what happens at school when they pick stupid names. Pepper was bad enough to have to deal with, all the dozens of jokes around salt and pepper but Dope was one step too far and really annoying.

Once again, the silence was shattered with his mum's voice shouting.

"Dominic, this is the last time I'm telling you, your bus will be here any minute." Quickly finishing dressing, he rushed down the stairs two at a time and burst into the kitchen. Ignoring the bowl of cereals which he always hated anyway, he quickly downed a glass of apple juice before picking up his backpack to dash off out.

"See you later," blurting out to his mother as he slammed the front door shut and before she could remind him to be home early. He could tidy his bedroom which was now in such a state it was totally unrecognisable as something any human could sleep in, let alone do their homework in.

Arriving at the bus stop, he could make out also rushing in the distance was Kelly Maunders, one of the girls in his year. He hated her, she thought she was so grown up as she had since she was eleven been allowed to wear a grown-up bra. She loved parading her chest like a peahen in front of all the boys teasing them, and which always caught their attention and whistles.

One minute later, through the rain and spray appeared his double-decker bright cherry-red bus. Well, it should have been on any decent day but not this one. All the spray and grime from the roads had made it look a depressing dirty muddy-red colour, perfectly fitting for the cold miserable Monday.

Climbing on-board, he was immediately greeted with the now normal jeers and teasers from all the other boys.

"Here's Dopee," shouted a red-haired freckled year seven, emphasising the "ee"; *God* he thought, *does everyone know me now* and quickly sat down in an attempt to calm things down.

St. David's High School was a typical 1960's style building, no special features and no historical past of any substance to make it stand out, it looked just like any other school built in that era. Dominic had moved there a year earlier owing to Mrs Pepper changing jobs and having to move from the other side of Chester.

The staff were pleasant enough but the boys were proving difficult as Dominic's previous school and St. David's were arch rivals in their football teams and which Dominic unfortunately now felt victim to their constant vitriol. The only thing of interest there for Dominic was computer coding which they did on Wednesdays. He loved technology and I.T. and his aim was to eventually become a computer programmer

It was a typical dreary boring day at school but at least it was one day gone of the last week of that term before they broke up. At last, the day was over and at least he could now recover back at home for a few hours before starting all over again tomorrow and so off he dashed.

Arriving back and in keeping with his normal routine, he slung off his backpack and raided the fridge. He was always famished when he got back from school, not that he hadn't had too little to eat, it was just that he was a growing lad and needed extra food intake. Armed with a hastily made ham sandwich and his favourite cherry tomatoes he rushed up to his bedroom to see if he had received any messages from his Facebook friends.

The first one he read was from his best friend Will, who was his closest friend from his previous school and with whom he still kept in regular contact with, visiting each other several times a month. With his bright red hair and freckles, he too had his fair share of bullying when he first started secondary school and probably why he and Dominic were drawn to each other and became such good friends. Will, unlike Dominic was pretty studious and Mrs Pepper loved Will coming for dinner as she would always try and persuade him to keep pushing Dominic to do better at school.

"Sat our mock exams today" the message read; *"It was awful, worse than I had expected"* continuing on. *"Hope yours go better than mine- We are off on holiday to Greece tomorrow for the week, back on Sunday so good luck, Will"*

"Blast," blurted out Dominic. He'd forgotten all about them and rushed downstairs to retrieve his timetable from his bag.

Grabbing his bag, he opened his timetable and there it was, mocks, Tuesday in five subjects with the first starting with English, first period. *I've not done anything* he thought to himself, *I'll be a laughing stock which on top of the names I'm already called, will make my school life impossible.*

He racked his brain for a grain of an answer to his dilemma. He couldn't play ill again, he had just tried that with his mum and certainly not for three days. I know, at last thinking of a plan, *I'll pretend to go to school and wag it. No one will know, I'll set off as normal each day and go to Chirk Castle and come back the same time. Mum will never realise* and so with this plan now formulated he went back upstairs to answer his internet mates.

CHAPTER TWO

THE PARCHMENT

The next morning arrives and without any prompting this time from his mum, Dominic's up and even downstairs ready before his sister. He was thinking that the faster he got out, then the less chance they have of asking him about school and what he had on that day.

"It's nice to see you up early for once," his mum commented, quite impressed by his new found keenness.

"I've arranged to meet a mate at the bus stop and exchange a few ideas about building a web site."

"Well, anything to get you out of bed is fine by me," replied mum and off Dominic rushed out.

Chirk Castle lay almost twenty miles away to the south of Chester where Dominic lived, just a few miles past Wrexham and the only bus that went that way, left from the town centre. So warily ever cautious, of who might see him and tell his mum, Dominic walked via every small back street passageway he could, eventually arriving unnoticed at the bus stop where luckily a bus was already waiting. Dropping onto one of the empty seats, he threw his backpack down next to him and breathed a sigh of relief thinking, *thank goodness that part is over, I should be all right from now*

The impressive medieval castle was built around 1300, initially as a fortress along the English/Welsh border in order to keep the Welsh under English rule following the defeat of the Welsh Prince, Llywelyn the Last. It was widely rumoured to be haunted by two ghosts and stories were rampant about witchcraft and all sorts of covens which had gone on there over the years. The latest sightings of the ghosts had apparently been seen by several workman who had been working on some walled repairs late one evening three years ago. Since all this had attracted unwanted graffiti artists, heavy tall iron gates had been erected across the entrance to prevent any further occurrences. Anyway, none of that was of concern to Dominic and all he was out to do was to hang around unnoticed until 3.00pm, catch the bus home and then just moan to his mum how awful school had been. *Perfect, no one would be the wiser, it was a piece of cake* Dominic thought and smiled about how easy it was all going to be.

He was not into historic structures with their heraldic tapestry of magnificent history, nor how many battles had been fought there; or how they lived. No; none of this was of the slightest interest and indeed just the opposite, he found it all very tedious and tiring but he had no choice now but to persevere until he could catch the 3pm bus back home.

After wandering around for several hours, essentially just passing time, he managed to find a quite secluded corner where he wouldn't be noticed and sat down to rest. Getting up early in the morning never suited Dominic at the best of times and a slight rest was well deserved after this morning's early start and so he settled down to pass the remaining time.

It wasn't too long or so he thought before he woke with a start as his right foot was suddenly pricked by a bout of intense pins and needles. Immediately realising that he'd fallen fast asleep, panic set in.

It was totally dark, there was no noise, no people, he couldn't see anyone nor hear anything. "Oh No!" he screamed to himself and quickly looked at his watch. It was almost 6.00pm and of course he couldn't see anyone as the place closed at 4.00pm. Jumping to his feet he quickly ran towards the entrance hoping beyond hope that somehow the gates just might still be open. *Please let them be open God* praying forlornly in the desperate hope that some angelic being would hear him whilst hurriedly rushing and becoming more scared with every step. "Just let them be open, just this once and I promise I'll go to school tomorrow," Quietly whispering to himself under his heavy breathing hoping that it would help.

Around the corner he turned and there it stood like a sentry standing on guard, was a massive pitch-black morbid iron structure, silhouetted by the outside castle flood lights blocking his route. The gate was locked, all those prayers were worthless.

"NO!" Shouting at the top of his voice, in a fit of temper at the impregnable, uncompromising wrought iron guardian blocking his exit, and not caring if anyone heard him. He would rather be told off than spend the night there.

He reached the gates and shook them with all his might but it was utterly useless. *What I am to do? Mum will now find out what I've done, on top of me having to spend the night here,* was all he could think about. Throwing his backpack down so he could use it as a seat he sat down to weigh up his options and the trouble that lay ahead. "So much for my brilliant simple plan," grumbling away to himself.

He sat down facing the gates and gazed up at the dark sky in some forlorn hope that some divine intervention would occur, when he noticed what appeared to be a gap in the intricate spirals of the design at the top corner of the gates. *Was this a way out?* immediately sprang into his thoughts? And he jumped up to take a closer look; Yes, he was sure it was enough of an opening for him to squeeze through. His heart was thumping madly as this impossible chance of an escape route started to crystallize. By utilising the well weathered mortar joints as handholds in the massive stone pillars that the gates hung from, he could climb to the top and squeeze through it in the corner. He had no time to lose and quickly collecting his bag started his climb.

As he was nearing the top of the gate, he could now see more clearly and breathed a sigh of relief as he could clearly make out that the gap was large enough for him to definitely get through. One last foothold and he was there, as he reached out to grab hold of a small opening at the top of the pillar. As his hand searched for a secure grip, he touched what felt like some rolled up rag. Thinking it was on old hessian type cloth and would be useful to wipe himself down from all the dust when he got to the other side. he decided to hold onto it.

Putting it in his pocket, he quickly made the last effort to the top and throwing his backpack through first, very agilely made quick work of getting through himself. He was delighted with his luck and how clever he had been to spot that opening. "Fat lot of good they are at trying to keep people out" muttering to himself totally forgetting that this incompetence had given him his only chance of escape. Picking up his bag, he slung it over his shoulder and ran off to the bus-stop. Twenty minutes later he was sitting on the top of the bus exhausted by the all the adrenalin he had used up but at least warmed by the knowledge that he was going home.

He dwelled on his exploit for a few moments and how lucky he had been, and now he could see with the light of the bus, realised just how much dust he was covered in and that he better wipe himself down. Remembering the cloth in his pocket Dominic pulled it out and started to unravel it, when something fell out onto the floor. Lying inside had been another smaller, what seemed like a muslin cloth very tightly bound with thread as if for extra protection.

Picking it up and placing it on his lap, he decided to at least try and wipe his hands a bit cleaner first and finished unravelling the larger cloth, and noticed that on the inside of it there was some strange writing on it. It looked like a recipe, no it wasn't a normal recipe that he had seen in his mum's cookery books, it was strange. It seemed to have been written in a very old English style. It seemed genuine enough, not that he would know, but after all he did discover it in a place that used to be renowned for witchcraft. Examining it further it was clear it was page made what to Dominic looked like fine linen and had clearly been roughly torn out of a book as one long edge was jagged and frayed whilst the rest was neatly cut

Studying it even more intently now, he was sure he could make out the heading:

"Last. Blessed by God the divine gift of sense and Protector from evil.

Potion of Eternal Accordance"

The rest of it, appeared to detail amounts and ingredients of what to do as well as some other instructions but it could all wait for now until he got home when he could read it all properly. Even getting told off for being two hours late was all worth it now.

Next, Dominic addressed the most intriguing part of his discovery, the smaller tightly bound parcel but again thought better that if it was something very small, he might just loose it in the dim light of the bus and so placed it back in his pocket to properly look at when he got back.

Sure enough, the scolding he received was as bad as he expected but this time, he was impervious to any harsh words or punishment Mrs Pepper could throw at him. His mind was focused elsewhere now. All he wanted to do was study his parchment and see what was in the small parcel.

Dinner just took the briefest of moments, even the opportunity to ridicule his sister was missed when Randolph jumped up and spilt her coffee over her. No, nothing could keep his mind from his piece of treasure.

I wonder what it means he thought rushing into his bedroom and turning on his computer typed in,

"Blessed by God the divine gift of sense and Protector from evil."

It was obviously a mixture or recipe of some sorts but what did "senses" mean kept flashing through his mind? This is where the computer and internet were invaluable. It was not a complete load of rubbish and time wasting as his mum thought; It was full of fascinating facts and information at the click of the mouse, well, outside of his Facebook friends that is.

It was clear that Last, meant the last process in some sort of procedure but he could do nothing about what was missing and he just had to focus on the sheet he had.

What on Earth does, the divine gift of sense and Protector from evil. mean? Still racking his brain. *Is it something to do with commonsense or sensing something is going to happen? If it's common sense does this mean that I could become great at school.* The possibilities were endless. There was only one way to find out and that was to make the potion and try it out.

Still not opening the small tightly bound parcel yet, believing it must be something really important wrapped separately like that, he put it to one side until he had finished reading the complete instructions just in case.

Putting the stained and crumbled parchment down into his scanner and with the help of his computer and AI attempted to make sense of the potion's words and especially the old measuring volumes that were used. As far as he could make out, it looked like.

"Potion of Eternal Accordance

Take ye eight gills of clear water and set within a stout vessel. Place it o'er a lighted flame and bring to a fearsome boil. When the vapour riseth as spirits from the deep, add thereto eight drachms of olive oil. With solemn hand lay in a lock of thine own hair, bound with thread, and one whole spider's web, gathered with care. Let this stand and gentle to the boil till the space of twenty minutes pass, as the sundial be told, and stir it not.

Now, with utmost reverence, take forth the holy silver needle, which hath been blessed by our Lord God. Touch not the point, for it pierceth more than flesh. Grasp only the blunt end and insert into thy upper arm. Count to five, no more, no less. Then withdraw and wait the turning of half an hour by the sundial's shadow, in stillness and silence, no more.

"That's it," Dominic exclaimed excitedly, "There must be a silver needle in that tiny parcel" and fully understanding that it had something to do with God, extremely carefully but excitingly opened it. Inside the fine muslin material, lay the most beautiful long silver needle. There was no fine intricate design to it, simply plain but somehow it looked incredibly beautiful and serene, and a sense of peace and calm came over him.

Immediately questions flooded into his mind. *I wonder if it really has been blessed by God. How did anyone know?* All flashed through Dominic's mind, but what the heck he had nothing to lose by continuing. He now became extremely nervous and careful about touching it at all as he returned to the instructions,

"From the hand of the arm that hath not been pierced, draw forth seven drops of blood. Let them fall, one by one, into the simmering draught. To this add one sliced bulb of fennel.

Bring again to angry boil for until count of ten and next to gentle boil until the sundial hath marked another half hour. Whilst the fire endureth, place within the vessel:

- *One chicken's liver, cut by four,*
- *Half a clove of garlic, well bruised,*
- *And at the last, one finely diced r******, the measure of a quarter gill.*

Raise the flame once more until the broth doth bubble full strong for five minutes, then abate the fire and suffer it to still yet another half hour.

When the sun no longer cast upon the world, strain the liquor clean, and set aside till the cool of night hath chilled it.

Then, with the reverence due to all ancient powers, take unto thy lips four drachms of the potion, no more than twice in day. Continue until seven measures in total have passed thy lips.

When the final draught is consumed, and the words, Lord God, please bless me now with the power of the Universe as Protector to fight against evil and with me it shall remain forever more."

Take heed, that whoever shall be blessed as the Protector against evil, shall be fearful that the powers so blessed doth drain every part of thy life and soul. So be wise of wisdom in their use until so restoreth."

Even AI couldn't help deciphering exactly what this ingredient "R" was supposed to be, there were just too many possibilities. It all seemed possible to make but what a shame that word of the potion had been stained so much over the years that it had made it totally illegible, it was destroyed apart from the first letter "R."

No matter how hard Dominic tried he could just not make out the last ingredient which would probably be vital to the potion's success.

Was it redcurrants? Surely not, his head told him *How could you possibly dice those finely.* After ten minutes of toing and froing in his mind, he eventually decided to settle on Rhubarb.

Now he had deciphered the potion, well almost except one ingredient, the exhaustion from his day's excitement started to kick in. He was now totally exhausted and it was all he could do was to collapse onto his bed and fall into a deep sleep.

The next morning arrived and it was a nice surprise to wake up to a dry and more cheerful day. But even if had it been raining cats and dogs it wouldn't have bothered Dominic, he was on a mission to make the potion and school was irrelevant today, indeed more an inconvenience. He had much more important things to do. Where could he get all those ingredients was the only thing on his mind. He would pretend he was meting his friend Will straight after school to discuss how he had got on with his mock exams but instead rush around and find all those ingredients.

Finishing his breakfast in no time at all, Dominic left for school with his mum's approval to be a bit late home. But she made sure that he understood that it was not to be as late as the night before or he would be grounded for a month.

Arriving at school, he was greeted by a very stern, Mr James, his Head of Year. "Well Pepper, what's your excuse for missing yesterday's mocks?" he snapped out.

"Sorry sir, I was taken pretty ill with awful stomach ache," Dominic replying in a half believable fashion.

"Well, you will have to sit your mocks on your own tomorrow" came back the response and with that Mr James turned on his heels and walked off leaving Dominic totally dejected. He knew he would just make an horrendous mess of them, probably not even completing a single question, after all he hadn't done any revision at all.

The rest of the day was the worst ever, not only had he to sit the mocks all on his own in one of the classrooms but one of the teachers was going to be in with him acting as an invigilator. There was no way he could even manage the slightest cheat by taking in some notes, it was impossible and so Dominic resigned himself to his inevitable fate.

The school bell eventually sounded for the end of the day and Dominic snapping out of his misery, remembered the potion and what it may reveal and so with that in mind happily rushed off to collect the ingredients.

Getting the chicken liver was easy enough as was the garlic and olive oil, even the sage and fennel hadn't been too difficult and he now had everything to make the mixture, everything except that last ingredient which had been too soiled to read. *I'll start with rhubarb* he thought; *Mum's always got some in as she loves making rhubarb pie with custard.*

Once again food was of no consequence to him, his normal voracious appetite was totally subdued with all the excitement going on in his mind. His chance of his normal ham sandwich which he always had returning from school was the furthest thing from his mind this time. All he wanted to do was make up the potion.

Almost rushing through the house and with only the briefest of acknowledgements to his mum he made down to the back garden shed. It was easy enough finding a spider's web in there as there were always one or two hiding in the corners. The shed had everything a boy could wish for. Electricity and water had been connected in and together with his own kettle and hob, he could have a coffee and warm up some baked beans whenever he wanted, it was a perfect boy's den.

He had always loved tinkering around experimenting with various things and anything electrical that was broken, he would carefully dismantle and try building something new out of it. This time though it was different, it was for real, it was serious and his heart started to beat stronger with the adrenalin pumping through his veins. He was now after all, dealing with the most precious thing that's ever been in the human race, a gift from God

It didn't take him long to get things underway. Once again, the use of the powerful search engines were put to good use in order to convert the centuries old measure into today's equivalents.

Two pints of water with the olive oil, a locket of his hair and of course the spider's web soon started to boil.

Next was the immensely daunting task of injecting his bicep with the holy silver needle. Dominic, not one for being scared of a needle, after all he had enough vaccinations at school, but this was even beyond the end of anyone's spectrum of injections. It was the ultimate holiest of holy thing he was about to do and for once, had to try as hard as he could to calm his nerves down. After all, someone or something wanted this to be done or they wouldn't have left such detailed instructions.

With that reassuring thought, he inhaled one deep breath and slowly exhaled deciding that he wasn't going to stop now. Finally, convincing himself that it was just one simple jab and that would be it, off came his tee shirt. Being as careful as Dominic has ever been in his life and holding his breath to help control his body, Dominic took hold of the blunt end of the precious silver needle. Placing it against the bicep muscle of his right arm, he pushed the needle in about a centimetre. The five seconds he had to wait seemed like an eternity but it was soon over and the needle extra carefully replaced onto the muslin cloth. At last, he could breathe again and flopped down into his chair to take a few moments rest.

Dominic sat there anxiously for several minutes waiting for a reaction to what he had just done and re-set the time on his mobile for thirty minutes as the instructions stated. As he now had nothing to do for a while all sorts of worrying possibilities started to play in his mind. *What if the needle had a virus on it or some bacteria from the black plague?* His mind was running amok with possibilities now.

"That's it, I've had enough," He suddenly shouted trying to suppress his fears and think positive thoughts. "I'm going to fetch one of mum's needles ready for the next part," and with that, put his tee shirt back on walked back up to the house.

Finding a needle was easy. Mrs Pepper loved needlework as a relaxation and after choosing what looked like the newest one, Dominic returned to the shed to continue making the potion.

The thirty minutes was soon up and now it was time for him to prick the thumb of his other arm and squeeze seven drops of his blood into the simmering mixture. This part was far worse than the other needle's injection as he had to prick his thumb three times to be able to get seven drops but eventually, he succeeded although now with a sore thumb.

Next, he sliced the fennel bulb and brought to the boil again before letting it all gently simmer for another thirty minutes. Next it was ready for the diced chicken's liver, half a clove of garlic both of which he promptly added and now for the "R" he thought. *I'll have to try rhubarb, I have no other good idea.* He knew two things; First was that it had to be some sort of fruit or herb as it had to be sliced and secondly, quite large as it had to fill a quarter gill, which he now knew was one quarter of a pint and off he sneaked back into the house to raid his mum's fruit and vegetable store.

Sure enough, there was lots of rhubarb, Mrs Pepper having recently replenished everything with her weekly shop. *Mum will never miss a stick of that,* flashed through his mind and quickly got hold of a long stem. Now he was fully complete with the final element and rushed back to his awaiting bubbling mixture. "That's it," he excitedly blurted out in some sort of profound Eureka moment after adding about a quarter of a pint of it. "It's all finished" and sat down to wait for the final boil and simmer to finish before turning everything off leaving it to cool and reflected upon the last part of the instructions.

"When the sun no longer cast upon the world, strain the liquor clean, and set aside till the cool of night hath chilled it.

Then, with the reverence due to all ancient powers, take unto thy lips four drachms of the potion, no more than twice in day. Continue until seven measures in total have passed thy lips.

When the final draught is consumed, and the words, Lord God please bless me now with the power of the Universe as Protector to fight against evil and with me it shall remain forever more.

Take heed, that whoever shall be blessed as the Protector against evil, shall be fearful that the powers so blessed doth drain every part of thy life and soul. So be wise of wisdom in their use until so restoreth."

Dominic murmured to himself, "I have no idea what all that means, I guess I'll just have to try it and see what happens" when he realised; *What now?* raced into his mind. He had not given one second's thought of who was going to try it first.

I'm not trying it first, it smells awful, continuing to think loudly He was right, it was just as well he was doing this at the bottom of the garden away from the house. The putrid, obnoxious stench of something like the carcass of a rotting dead animal which would wake the dead, let alone his mum would have given the game away. Searching his mind for who could be his guinea pig, the only solution he could come up with was Randolph. Although the dog could obviously not communicate to him what effects it would have, it had the advantage that Rudolph couldn't obviously talk and could never tell on him if he was sick. So satisfied that this was the best answer he could come up with, he went back into the house to find him.

For the third time, he carefully managed to sneak back in unnoticed still not wanting to being seen by his mum or sister in fear of any questions. By luck, his sister was as usual upstairs in her bedroom talking to her friends and his mum busy in the kitchen. Randolph would probably be, in his favourite place in front of the imitation electric coal fire. Sure enough, there was the dog curled up in the sitting room with his favourite teddy bear. Randolph loved the bear and over the years with all the constant sucking on its nose, the nose had completely disappeared. Not only that, there was now a deep hollow there instead, but it was Randolph's favourite cuddle and not even a new one could replace it.

"Randolph," Dominic whispered softly and the dog's ears pricked up. "Come on boy" and up the dog rose and after stretching his legs out followed him off to the shed.

By the time Dominic returned to the shed with Randolph, the evil smelling concoction of a potion had now cooled sufficiently. Realising that Rudolph would refuse to even attempt to drink it, Dominic lightly coated one of the dog biscuits he kept handy in the shed in the mixture. Eventually, with a lot of gentle persuasion he eventually managed to get Randolph to eat it.

Dominic sat back and waited. "Well, how do you feel?" enquiring of the dog. Of course there was no answer, after all this was a dog. Was this a daft idea? Was it a prank? All these possibilities now flooded into Dominic's mind.

Thirty minutes had now passed and nothing at all. "Well, that's the good news," murmuring to himself "You've not been sick, or gone mad," at least pleased that he must have got something right and he wasn't going to go insane or die from it. He decided it was time to try some for himself.

When, just as he was about to take a spoonful for himself a thunderous fart erupted from Randolph. It was so loud that even the dog barked in fright and literally jumped off the ground from where he had been lying, not believing that he had produced that and looking as if to blame someone else. The odour was worse than even horrific. It was the rarest and deadliest of all to anyone's sense of smell, it was a swamp fart. The whole shed stunk of rotten cabbages mixed with bad eggs and Dominic rushed out gasping for air.

"Blimey Randolph, for such a small dog you can certainly pack a punch" in a berating tone and continuing on; "That's it, before I try it, I'll wait and see what happens with you now for a few hours" pointing at his pet.

Just then, breaking the distant air, he heard his mum's voice calling him in for dinner. "Well, that's that for now," he muttered and at least it gave him enough time for the smell to dissipate and marched up the path into the house with the ever faithful but still slightly dazed and confused Randolph following.

Sitting down for dinner with everyone, Dominic realised just how hungry he was and even his worst hated vegetable, peas he could live with today. They always ate in the kitchen, sitting around the quite large breakfast bar. It just seemed the most convenient place and there was always something going on there. His mum and India quickly got into their normal topic of conversation talking about everyone else, whilst Dominic was totally engrossed in devouring his food.

Just for a minute he'd forgotten all about Randolph who was sprawled exhausted across the floor when without warning, once again another ear deafening eruption of putrid air from Randolph was violently released, shattering Mum's and India's intense gossiping.

This time, the dog had enough and went tearing around the kitchen in a manic craze, barking at everything in sight wondering what was happening to him. India, burst out laughing so much to mum's annoyance whilst Dominic sheepishly tried to ignore it all as if it was quite no big deal.

"Dominic, what have you been feeding the dog?" Mrs Pepper quickly shouted at him becoming increasingly more irritated by the ghastly smell that was now percolating every part of the kitchen.

"Mum, I've not done anything," replying in his most innocent voice as if hurt by her questioning.

It was impossible for them to continue eating dinner in the kitchen now with the pungent grotesque smell from the now exhausted poor Randolph who had collapsed to the floor exhausted and bewildered by it all

"I'm going to finish off my dinner in the shed" and with that Dominic picked up his plate and wandered off down to the garden.

Once back to the shed which at least was now free of that terrible smell Dominic picked up the potion he had made. It was just too tempting not to try it now, after all nothing really unpleasant had happened to Randolph and it was worth a bit of farting to at least try it out. No one would bother him there so he could fart and make all the noises and smells he wanted.

He poured out what he guessed to be the equivalent of half an ounce to swallow in one go and holding his nose to help, quickly gulped it down. It tasted as disgusting as it smelled and was far worse than a mixture of celery and cabbage which he both detested. Thirty minutes passed and nothing. *This is a waste of time*, thinking to himself, *all I'm going to get is an upset stomach and all for nothing* and with that left the shed and made for his bedroom.

Slumping into his favourite chair which he had chosen himself for his birthday, he pulled out the parchment once again. "I wonder what that "R" really stands for," he thought as he stared at the writing. What a shame the letters had faded too much. *Is it radish?*" as he kept searching his mind for the perfect answer.

"I wish India, would shut up talking so loudly" exclaiming to himself, as very audibly he could hear her giggling and chatting to some girlfriend.

"India, can you please talk quieter, it's really annoying" he blurted out. After all, he needed all his grey matter to solve this missing puzzle of what "R" stood for. "India, shut up" once again shouting out, but as before he was ignored, nothing changed. Jumping up out of his chair he stormed out of his bedroom and marched into hers to give her a piece of his mind.

There was no one there. *Funny she must be here, I can hear her so loudly* went through his mind but she just wasn't. He could hear her so clearly chatting away, indeed come to think of it, he could her everything she was saying, absolutely every single word as if she was standing right next to him. Trying to work out where she could be, "India," shouting at the top of voice.

"What do you want?" came back a curt reply in the distance.

"Where are you?"

"I'm in the sitting room, so shut up." Dominic, sat down on her bed in disbelief. How could he hear her? She was the other side of the house and downstairs. Suddenly, the reality of it all sunk in.

His mind now quickly assimilating everything,

Yes, that's it, it's the potion, I can hear everything. It must be a potion for super hearing and sense means one of the five senses we all have. And concentrating for once and on nothing else but listening intently, he realised he could hear everything he put his mind to. The passing cars outside, the Evans's children next door talking outside and even and even music playing from the Johnson's house the other side of the road.

Overcome with excitement, he couldn't wait to tell someone and rushed back into his room and logged on to his Facebook. He would normally go straight to Will first but as he was away for the week now, he quickly decided to seek out Olivia. He knew that she too had hurried away with her parents to visit her ill grandmother in Newcastle but was hoping that by now she might have arrived back.

"Hi Olivia, I hope you're back as I have some incredible news to tell you." Typing in quickly to her WhatsApp number. But no response appeared and so Dominic emailed his other friends. *"Anybody spoken with Olivia tonight?"*

"No, I've not spoken with her for a few days now," replied Delores Parker who Dominic knew she fancied him but her name just put him off. He just couldn't date a Delores, after all, he was Asher Effron and had an image to maintain.

He had to speak only with Miriam as she was outside of Will, the only person he felt he could trust the secret with. So logging off, he thought he would email her as well and hope she would respond.

An hour past and nothing and then her response appeared:

"Hi Asher, sorry I've been out of touch, been up to visit my grandmother in Newcastle for the last two days but I'm just back home in the last five minutes."

Quickly typing in, Dominic replied.

"Olivia, I have something so brilliant to tell you and it can't wait. I just have to meet up with you tomorrow; Can you make it?" Dominic already knew from previous chatting that Olivia only lived twenty miles away in Prestatyn and so he could easily meet her near her there.

"OK" came back the response, *"Where do you suggest? You will have to come here though, as I would probably get lost trying to find you."*

A few more exchanges passed between them and they agreed that Dominic, would meet her at 5.00pm at Prestatyn train station near to her high school. Satisfied that at least he had someone now to tell of his incredulous discovery, he relaxed back into his chair.

"Oh, blimey," he uttered closing his eyes and sighing. He had totally forgotten in all his excitement that she only knew him as a sixteen-year-old, tall and athletic Asher Angello. Not a fourteen-year-old ordinary school kid who suffered from the odd bout of spots. Anyway, it was too late now to do anything about it, and hopefully once she heard of the spell he had discovered she might still like him.

His head was full of ideas and everything needed planning properly. First, was to ask his mum and see if it was all right for him to go and visit another friend straight after school on the pretext again of discussing the mock exams they have to sit. Mrs Pepper, although certainly puzzled by Dominic's new found interest in school work, was more than happy to allow this considering what it was for, and she would keep his dinner in the oven for when he got back.

Rushing back upstairs and shutting down the computer he packed his bag ready for the next day. He decided to at least help his image, he would stuff in a jar of hair gel that he had been given two years earlier as a birthday present. Plus, some trendy Nike Air trainers his mum bought him but was only allowed to wear on special days out.

He couldn't wait for the next day to come now and just hoped that his new super hearing would still be working. Even school now would be enjoyable as he now had super powers.

CHAPTER THREE

DOMINIC MEETS MIRIAM

Waking up in the morning, the noise was immense, it was a cacophony of a mixture of sounds, from; the sounds of birds, traffic, televisions indeed everything. His hearing was still incredible and if anything, even better than before. He soon realised that he had to try and control it, otherwise it was useless. It was just impossible to take in all this information at once. He tried concentrating on just one sound, the television downstairs and after a bit of practice, it was not too long before he could blank everything else out and just hear that. After more practice he found he could do this almost at will and, on any noise, and it even got better than that. This super hearing only activated when he really concentrated. His hearing was just normal otherwise. He was made up with this new development, as it would be too much if it was like that all the time

Arriving at school, Dominic settled in for his first lesson when Mr James, his Head of Year entered.

"Pepper, Mr Griffiths will take you for your mocks in room 25B, the exams will start after lunch at 1,00pm prompt so don't be late." And in the next breath he continued but singling out Danny Pearson this time. "Pearson, Mr Griffiths wants to see you about your results so please stay in this classroom during lunch break," and with that he walked out as swiftly as he had entered.

Dominic in an instant had an idea, was this his chance to gain some answers by using his super hearing? He could just wait outside in the corridor pretending to do some homework and listen in.

Soon enough, lunchtime came and Dominic, sat down in the corridor pretending to work and started to concentrate on his special hearing. After a few anxious moments, his ears suddenly exploded with the immense mixture of noises that was school life. He had to concentrate and block out everything but just voices. Focussing on nothing now but what was being said behind his classroom walls he closed his eyes. Suddenly, all he could hear was Mr Griffiths talking with Danny Pearson. It was so clear, he could hear every word and every other sound was completely blocked out.

It was better than he could ever had hoped, Griffiths was quickly going through all the test papers and what the answers should have been and why. He could hardly keep up jotting everything down in his notebook.

Thirty minutes later they were discussing the very last paper, history and Dominic was delighted with himself. He didn't fear at all the exam tomorrow, just the opposite, he was now looking forward to it.

Just as a wry smile crossed his face, the voices disappeared. "Oh No," he whispered to himself and tried concentrating again, but no matter how hard he tried, his super hearing had vanished and he was left once again with just an ordinary mortal's ability.

Consoling himself with the fact that at least he had every subject except history boxed off and that it all worked perfectly he rose to his feet and went off to room 25B to start his mocks.

He was to sit two this afternoon and three in the morning. 1.00pm came and Dominic opened the first paper which was his most hated subject, English. But this time it was different, it was brilliant, No! It was better than brilliant, it was sensational, it was pure fun and for the first time in his school life he knew all the answers and what he had to write. In no time at all he had settled down to the task and with a nice satisfying smile on his face.

The next exam was science and this too was a breeze. The answers just flowed from his pen and of course all would be correct.

Two down and both perfect, I'll enjoy tomorrow's exams now, Dominic extremely satisfied with his effort.

3.45pm came and the greatest sound in the world came; the school bell. Quickly packing everything away he rushed out of school to catch the train to Prestatyn. Finding a single seat on the train, he produced the hair gel he had stored away and quickly spiked his hair. He threw off his heavy soled school shoes and replaced them with his fashionably coloured Nike trainers. Now he felt much better, at least he looked slightly taller with his air-filled heels and he was sure with his spiked hair, that it all added at least twelve months to his age.

He arrived at Prestatyn Station with ten minutes to spare before Olivia was due to arrive and sat down to wait on a platform-bench. Gazing around to keep himself occupied he noticed sitting a few benches down, was a possible sixteen-year-old, very squat looking slightly plump girl with the most dreadful pink coloured hair he had ever seen. He couldn't see her face too clearly as she had it buried into a magazine but was she Olivia? It must be he thought as no one else was around and the time was exactly 5.00pm now

Totally forgetting that he was not Asher Angello the stunning good looking sixteen-year-old, he approached the girl.

"Excuse me," and the girl looked up from her magazine.

"Yes! What do you want Spikey?" Snapping at him and clearly referring to his newly formed gelled hairstyle and thoroughly annoyed that he had disrupted her reading. He was devastated, how could this person, who was his dream-girlfriend Olivia, be this most unpleasant aggressive person when he was being so polite? Without thinking, and for once ditching good manners he decided to give as good as he got and responded.

"Blimey, God was in a foul mood when he created you."

The infuriated girl throwing her magazine down on the bench jumped up shouting.

"Well, I've never been so insulted in all my life"

To which Dominic couldn't resist saying.

"Well, you should get out more often then," and with that turned and marched off.

He knew he had been extremely rude and unfair but she had been so nasty and rude herself in the first place, let alone he was devasted that his six months dream of his beautiful Olivia had been destroyed. Deciding that there was nothing else to stay for now, Dominic went across to look at the timetable for his next train back. He had just worked out that in twenty minutes time there would be a train back home to Chester, when there was a gentle tap on his shoulder.

"Excuse me, are you by any chance, Asher?" Dominic spun around and standing there was this delightful young girl of about fourteen. She was wearing glasses and wore an orthodontic tooth brace but clearly, she was so beautiful.

Dominic, this time stuck for words and still in shock over just how rude he had been earlier to the other girl, meekly stammered; "Yes." They just looked and stared at each other for a few moments then simultaneously burst out laughing, following which simultaneously they both blurted out,

"But you're not sixteen" both highly amused with the pretence they had been keeping up for six months gave each other a huge hug. They exchanged their real details; She was called Miriam and who was the same age as Dominic. Neither of them was disappointed with the other indeed they were even closer friends now the truth was out.

It didn't take Dominic long to explain all about the parchment, it's like a sense recipe and his adventure of how he got it. Although he showed it Miriam, he could tell from her expressions that she didn't really believe him.

"Look" he said, "Why don't you come over for dinner tomorrow and I'll prove it? I will meet you at our train station and walk you to where I live so you will not get lost." After a few moments for Miriam to gather her thoughts, she agreed to come and they arranged to meet at the same time but at Dominic's train station this time.

The next hour, the time flew by as they chatted non-stop about everything over what they had messaged each other over last six months until his train arrived for him to go back to Chester. After a huge hug to each other, Dominic boarded the train and waved continuously through the carriage-door window to Miriam as the train departed and she was out of sight.

CHAPTER FOUR

EVEN MORE POWERS

Dominic returned home thinking all the way of how to stop that awful embarrassing side effect. *I just have to solve that I'm ever going to make a success of it,*

Reaching home again and not stopping except for a few quick words with his mum, he immediately made straight for his shed faithfully followed by Randolph to see if there was there some way, he could solve the problem. As he played around with his mind exploring all the alternatives and possible solutions, it suddenly occurred to him that if he drank more, it might make his hearing even more acute. Would it be possible for his hearing to become that good that he could hear Miriam even twenty miles away? The possibilities in his mind were endless

"Oh, what the heck," encouraging himself to try it and he poured out another half ounce measure. This time the effect was almost instant. After all it wasn't long ago, just a matter of less than two hours, since he last took some and not long after, he started to feel really ill. His flatulence was worse than ever but this was not funny now, it was seriously unpleasant and painful. "Oh, my poor stomach" moaning out loud and now curled up in a heap on the floor holding both knees tightly to his body.

Randolph this time, thinking it was some sort of game Dominic was playing took delight in jumping upon his back.

"Get off Randolph" Dominic shouted suffering with his bowel problem. The Bulldog immediately obliged but now instead just ran around him in circles thoroughly enjoying this game.

"Go away you daft dog can't you see I'm not well," this time in a strange mixture of both shouting and groaning at him. Randolph totally ignoring his master, just barked believing that this was some sort of new fun game and carried on regardless.

Dominic glared intensely at the dog and just wished him to go away. Then no sooner had he thought it, Randolph began to levitate slightly and slide across to the door. The poor dog was so startled, all he could do was let out a muffled yelp.

"What the devil" Dominic exclaimed loudly suddenly forgetting all about his cramps and of course farts. "Did I just do that? I couldn't have," continuing muttering excitedly to himself and immediately set about trying it on his mountain bike. Once again Dominic stared intensely looking at the bike. With all the concentration and telekinesis power of his mind, the bike started to shudder and rattle but sure enough levitated off the ground.

Dominic let out a huge sigh of exhaustion, it had taken a lot of mental effort, which with school he wasn't really use to. He just couldn't come to terms with what had just happened, it was surreal, his imagination, even a dream possibly, but he knew it was real and it did happen. He was wide awake, far more than any other time in his life. Even more than the time when he was chased by some older lads who were going to take him to the local canal and throw him in. He sat up, even firmly pinching himself to prove he was wide awake. The pain certainly proved that he was very wide awake.

Now he had totally accepted what had just happened, the enormity of it all started to sink in. It was so incredible and was even better than his super hearing powers and that was mind-blowing enough. So that next hour was spent having some momentous fun transporting all sorts of objects across the shed. After a while he was even able to open draws, take things out and even turn the light on and off. By the end of the night, he was reasonably competent with his new found telekinetic skill. It was a pity though he didn't have a potion for tidying up as his shed as by now it was in an appalling state with everything strewn all over the floor.

For the first time in his life, Dominic was quite happy trying to put everything back into some sort of order. His mind was now focused on conjuring up various pranks to play on everyone at school the next day, and mischievous thoughts were running amok in his mind of how they were all going to suffer for the misery they had poured on him. "Yes, tomorrow is going to be a great day," he whispered silently to himself, and now exhausted by the mental effort of the last hour or so.

CHAPTER FIVE

SCHOOL & SWEET REVENGE

Friday morning came around and this time when mum called Dominic, He was up like a shot, happy, smiling and even polite to his sister. Well, as polite as boys can be, he could never refuse just one distasteful remark about her appearance. But this was a totally different Dominic, even Mrs Pepper was astonished. "Are you not feeling well? She asked whist he was devouring his cereals.

"Of course I am," Dominic replied munching away.

"I've never seen you so happy, something is definitely up?"

"Mum, nothing is up, it's just the last school day before the holiday," as he placed his empty bowl in the sink. He was of course looking forward to his day of pranks and revenge and boy was he going to make the most of it.

Grabbing his backpack, he made for the garden shed and carefully measuring out another half ounce, carefully poured into a small container to take to school to help with the mocks and pranks just in case. Everything was now set for him to wreak revenge.

Arriving at school, he had already decided that first, he would wait to see who was being particularly nasty to him today and after his mocks in the morning and the lunch break, he would get his own back. in the afternoon.

First though, he had his mocks to finish. That was no problem at all now for him as he knew the answers, well all except history but four out of five good results would be good enough for anyone, went through his mind

Sure enough Alex Butcher, a large overweight boy with short cropped red hair was as usual the first one to have a dig about his name.

"Hi Dopee," he shouted emphasising the "e," across the school courtyard as they waited to go into school. Alex, although one of the largest boys in his year could say what he wanted and get away. He played hooker for the school rugby team and no one dared take him on. As usual Dominic tried to ignore it but made a mental note of whom he was going to punish first today.

It wasn't long before the lunchtime break arrived and with his mocks now successfully completed behind him, it was his turn for some fun. He headed for the toilets to retrieve the small dose of potion he had brought and without even noticing the foul-tasting concoction, hurriedly gulped it down in one go. *Right*, he thought as he smiled to himself, *just you lot wait till we get back in class,* and with that swaggered his way back ready for class.

The first lesson of the afternoon was German with Frau Brandauer and boy was she strict. She could bring tears to the eyes of even the toughest pupils when she had a mind to. Everyone was scared to death of her and no one would try anything for the fear of what would happen to them. Well, this was the perfect target for Dominic's first step to getting even. He knew the potion was already working as he could hear the teacher next door talking to Aaron Taylor for forgetting to bring in his homework.

Dominic had already practised his kinetic powers by moving one other boys bag some ten metres away when no one was noticing and then watch him punch the nearest boy to him in the belief that they did it. This lesson with Frau Brandauer was the perfect opportunity and Alex Butcher was the perfect victim.

Alex was sitting two rows in front of Dominic and one column to the left so he had him in perfect vision. As usual, after some oral exercises Frau Brandauer set them, followed some grammar to punctuate, which they had thirty minutes to complete. No one was allowed to even breath let alone make any semblance of a noise or she would berate them mercilessly.

At the edge of Butcher's desk, Dominic could see a bag of pens and pencils. This was a perfect start and focusing all his concentration on the bag, he slowly moved it to the edge of Butcher's desk without him noticing anything. "***Crash***," went the bag as it fell off his desk and hitting the floor the floor loudly, spilling all his writing implements all across the classroom.

"Who was that stupid boy?" demanded Frau Brandauer. Butcher very nervously slowly put up his hand trying his best to stop it shaking uncontrollably. "Well pick them up you imbecile and you can write over the holiday a hundred lines; "I must not throw my pens around the classroom" and with that left Butcher to scurry around picking them all up.

Dominic could hardly contain himself. He had to pinch his arm so tightly to stop himself bursting out laughing that it almost cut into the skin. Butcher, looking very puzzled by it all as he was positive that he had not knocked them off returned to his desk, placing his bag further away from the edge so it could never happen again. Ten minutes later when all was quiet and forgotten about, Dominic saw his chance again as Butcher was deeply engrossed in completing the grammar exercise. Dominic once again applied his telekinetic skills to the task and once again focussing his mind, the bag slid to the edge and over it went for the second time.

That was it, Frau Brandauer exploded, her face deep purple which for a moment looked like it would explode. Screamed at the top of her voice; "Butcher, was that you again?" Butcher, managing to feebly stutter a reply.

"Yes Frau Brandauer, but it wasn't me, they just fell off on their own." The whole class now thoroughly enjoying the break away from German fell about laughing and that made matters even worse.

"Are you telling me that they moved themselves boy?" she whipped back.

"Well, I know it sounds daft but yes Miss." Well, the whole class now was in hysterics and calling Butcher all sorts of rude names. Now incensed at his cheek of such a lame excuse she increased his lines to five hundred. Oh, this was such sweet revenge and music to Dominic's ears. He would be happy going to school every day from now on now. It was even a shame that it was now half-term.

Well, the afternoon just went better and better as Dominic wreaked his revenge on everyone who had made fun of him. Adam Stone was next to be messed with when in the science lesson, Dominic kept spilling his beaker of distilled water all over his notes again and again. Last but not least and perhaps the best of all, it was Kieron Bishop's turn. He had made his life at school a complete misery hiding his books and sports clothes dozens of times. Whilst waiting outside room 3G for their geography lesson to start, Bishop was leaning on the wall of the corridor idly chatting with some of his friends and within touching distance of one of the school's fire alarm.

It was a perfect target for Dominic and so sitting down in corridor some forty metres away, holding one of his text books he feigned to be deep in reading it. He managed to concentrate such psychic energy on the protective alarm glass that it shattered and triggered the alarm. Well, all hell broke loose. Teachers were dashing everywhere mustering all the boys in the school outside into the safety area on the school fields. Even the fire brigade turned up with four appliances.

It didn't take them long to work out what had caused the false alarm and Bishop's friends, not happy to take the blame quickly pointed the finger at Bishop. Using all that mental energy with all the tricks he had played had by now exhausted Dominic's powers but he didn't mind at all they had served him well today.

Dominic didn't know what happened to Bishop after that but he was marched off to the headmaster's study with his parents being called so something unpleasant happened.

That was the best day in my life, thought Dominic packing his bag as the final school bell rang for the end of that term and smiling to himself that nobody would ever bully him again and get away with it. School would now never be a problem again for him.

Dominic was the first out, rushing home to get ready to meet Miriam at 5.00pm. He'd already asked his mum the night before about Miriam coming for dinner and she was delighted to see a fresh face, especially that he was friends with a girl who might make him more conscientious in school.

Needless to say, Dominic arrived back at the station in time and just as Miriam's train pulled in surprisingly two minutes early and there, jumping off onto the platform and waving excitedly to him she was. She looked so special, even in her school uniform. They hugged briefly and whilst they set off for Dominic's home, he excitedly told her of how he beaten the mock exams which brought out the giggles from them both.

Mrs Pepper was the perfect hostess, and when he introduced Miriam to her and they instantly took a liking to each other, chatting away together over dinner about Dominic for what seemed like ages. Dominic just sat there through it all, highly embarrassed that his mum was recounting some of the silliest things he had done when he was younger. Miriam thought it was wonderful though and could have listened to stories of his younger years all night.

At last, it was time for Dominic to interrupt, after all they were there to show Miriam his potion.

"Miriam, I need to show you something I made in the shed the other day," and after thanking his mum for the dinner, off they disappeared down to the garden shed. "Here's the potion I made," holding up the pan of a vile looking dirty green coloured liquid, which although very cold now still smelled terrible.

"It looks revolting" said Miriam with a disapproving look on her face.

"If you think that that is bad, just smell it," as he handed her the pan of it. She hastily refused, quickly working out that if it looked that bad then the smell must be worse than even awful.

"Well, are you going to try it and show me what happens?" She demanded. Dominic couldn't back out now, after all that is why he had invited her

"Look," he said, "Because I can't make out one of the words properly, I've assumed that "R" must mean rhubarb. I don't know for sure but it seems a good guess to me. Anyway, it does work but there is a bit of a side effect."

"What do you mean, side effect?" queried Miriam, and with an embarrassing look on his face, Dominic explained that it might bring on a farting episode and revealed what happened to Randolph. Miriam burst out laughing uncontrollably and eventually pausing for breath told Dominic,

"Well fart away as much as you like then, I can always stand in the garden," still slightly giggling away.

Dominic waited a few moments whilst building up some courage again and poured out another measure of the mixture as he didn't want to fail. Another gulp and a large burp and it was gone. It was far worse than yesterday and he ran around frantically looking for something nice to chew on, much to Miriam's amusement and laughter.

Fifteen minutes went by since his drink of it and then just as before Dominic's hearing burst into a crescendo of noise.

"It's working," he shouted to her, "I can hear everything."

"Well prove something to me then" questioned Miriam.

"All right," you go into the kitchen close the door and say four different words. I'll stay here and when you come back, you'll see if I'm right."

Miriam hurried off, now becoming excited herself about this possible magic formula. Into the kitchen she burst, closing the door behind her and without a moment to waste, softly whispered the words; "Purple; Bus; Sprouts; Netball." No one could possibly hear that, not even someone who was in the kitchen with her. It was impossible for Dominic to hear what she said, and as they were so varied it would be even inconceivable to even guess them. Satisfied that she had not given him any chance at all of hearing her, should rushed back down to the shed.

Dominic was sat down with a smug smile on his face. "You surely didn't hear anything?" she quickly burst out desperate to hear his answer. He smiled delightedly and nodded.

"Let's say, it was: "Purple; Bus; Sprouts and Netball" by now full of pride and sticking his chest out like a prize peacock. Miriam was speechless, it was impossible. Could he have cheated? Did he have a hidden microphone somewhere? No, he just couldn't have she deduced, it must be a genuine magic potion.

"Dominic, what now?" she quickly asked enquiringly; "What are you going to do with it, you could sell it for a fortune, you will be famous?" Her mind, just like Dominics was also now full of suggestions and questions. Dominic was just about to at least try to answer some when once again an all-mighty fart erupted from him and surprising Miriam so much that she jumped back almost knocking the table over. This time they both burst out laughing as they quickly dashed to get out into the fresh air.

"Well for a start, I think we have to sort out all this blowing off" Dominic replied. "Who will want to buy it if all they do all day is fart everywhere?" They both saw the funny side to this and giggled hysterically.

Dominic continued, "Secondly, what does it mean by, *When the final draught is consumed, and the words, Lord God please bless me now with the power of the Universe as Protector to fight against evil and with me it shall remain forever more. Take heed, that whoever shall be blessed as the Protector against evil, shall be fearful that the powers so blessed doth drain every part of thy life and soul. So be wise of wisdom in their use until so restoreth.*

"I didn't feel anything at all like that, ok. the hearing is good, even incredible but power of the universe, I don't think so."

Miriam chipped in, "Well, it's probably something to do with the missing ingredient beginning with "R" which we don't know yet."

The time just flew by as they chatted about all sorts of things they could use the potion for and by now even Dominic's constant farting had become at least slightly tolerable.

Forgetting the time, Dominic glanced down at his watch. "Gosh, look at the time, we've only got quarter of an hour before your 8.00pm train arrives, and I've not even shown you the telekinesis power it can do It will have to wait for now," and with that they rushed off to the station. Ever punctual, the train arrived on time and after a brief hug the two friends departed after promising to keep daily contact.

CHAPTER SIX

The DEVIL'S SERVANTS

With the start of the school's half term week, the Pepper family were all going away to Colwyn Bay on the Monday. They went there every year and always stayed in one of mum's friends caravan. It wasn't too bad there and if the weather was half decent even the sea could be tolerable even in February.

Dominic until now had forgotten all about it. *Oh blimey*, he thought, *I won't be able to show Miriam what else I can do now*, referring to his telekinetic powers. He pondered around for a few moments trying to come up with a solution. He had an idea, he would ask his mum if she could come with them, even just for a few days. There were four bedrooms in the caravan so privacy would be maintained and Mum and India would love another female companion to discover some gossip from.

With that, off he went to locate his mum who was nicely settled in the sitting room watching television with ever-faithful Randolph, still slightly agitated by all his bowel problems. It didn't take long to convince his mother, that it was fine to ask Miriam if she would like to come as she would be good company for everyone. Although he had to first agree, that he would take the dog for a walk every day whilst on holiday and make his own bed.

With a huge beaming grin which stretched from ear-to-ear, Dominic, two steps at a time dashed back upstairs to his computer to tell Miriam the great news and ask if her parents would allow her to come. He couldn't wait to show her his new powers but wanted to keep it a surprise until he saw her.

Thirty minutes later back came the reply he had been hoping for; They had given their permission to go for a few days as long as they could chat things through with Mrs Pepper and get the full details. Dominic gave his mum their number and within minutes both sets of parents were getting along famously. It was agreed that Mrs Pepper would pick up Miriam from their home at 11.00am on Monday and it was all systems go from there on.

All the effort of his concentration throughout the day was immensely tiring and all he wanted to do was chill out and off upstairs he went to his room. He didn't even have the energy to make a ham and cherry tomato sandwich, which was something that had never happened before together taking a quick nap.

Two hours went by and the sound of Mrs Pepper shouting him for dinner finally brought him out of his far deeper sleep than he ever intended. Getting up from his bed, the aftertaste in his mouth from drinking his mixture was worse than normal. Indeed, thinking back, it was getting more unpleasant the more often he took it. The good news was that the highly embarrassing bowel problem had dissipated substantially but the taste in his mouth was shear purgatory.

"I can't go on like this" muttering to himself whilst at the same time forcing his feet into his unfastened trainers as usual. He quickly understood that the only way was to solve what that "R" was in the formula as it was unlikely to be rhubarb. He decided that after dinner he would search the internet to see if he could find anything.

The whole house was now in holiday mode and Mrs Pepper was making Dominic's favourite dinner, pepperoni with ham, cheese and pineapple pizza. "Mum, can you put loads of pepperoni on it please?" asking his mum hoping that the sharp-tasting meat would help get rid of the awful taste still left in his palate. Mrs Pepper duly obliged and in no time at all the pizza was devoured. At least this spicy tangy flavour gave him some temporary respite from the taste the horrible potion had left.

It didn't take Dominic long after that to be back in his room with his computer switched on. He sat there for a few minutes staring blankly at the screen trying to work out where he should search on Google for his missing ingredient. Eventually he decided that given the place where he found the parchment was renowned for witchcraft that would be the right place to make a start. Typing in "witchcraft" into Google's powerful search engine, he was amazed to see just how many sites there were and just how vast and diverse the topics covered. There were sites like; Learning witchcraft; witchcraft shop; witchcraft spells and even how to become a witch. After trying a few of the avenues, Dominic decided that witchcraft spells may give him the best chance. There were spells for everything imaginable; protection; revenge, even getting rid of spots and pimples which he made a note of promising himself to try it later! Once again Dominic found one that he thought most suited his current pressing need; "Charmed Spells" and typed it in.

The first page flashed onto screen. Dominic let out a gasp of despair; "Oh no! There were so many web sites, even the differing topics alone looked like being in the hundreds and then in each of these there were hundreds more. "This is going to take ages," grumpily muttering to himself. But after a few moments to take stock, he at least consoled himself in the knowledge that this was far too important to be upset over such trivial things and so he started his laborious search for an answer.

Now Dominic had already thought carefully about how he was going to approach this. After all he couldn't scan the parchment in and ask for help, that would give away the secret. He decided that on any site that he thought might supply the answer he would alter some of the ingredients of the potion.

Ten o'clock came and no one had been able to help, he was becoming weary and progressively more annoyed with each passing web site. Eventually one site suggested that the "Devil's Servants" web site might be able to help, and so Dominic thought he would give this one last try before shutting down for the night

Typing in the name, he was quickly directed to their web page. The front page was grotesque with animated sacrificial animals being slaughtered and their crimson-red blood cascading down the page through the text that it displayed. A little shiver went through Dominic and the sight of this snapped him out of his tiredness.

At first, he thought that this was a site for weirdos as surely nothing like that could possibly happen today and just as he was about to close down, he noticed in the bottom left corner of the page a link which read;

"Try us for unusual and rare spells." Thinking that this was as good as anywhere to try for an answer he quickly clicked on to the hyperlink. Almost instantly he was on a new page where all sorts of spells and mixtures were being advertised. There was one for wealth, another for beauty even one for revenge. *This was worth a try Dominic* thought and with that clicked the "contact us with your question" button.

Dominic, first typed in his email address which was the initials of his name followed by a lucky number he always used; Dp3017@gmail.com   Next, he was asked to put in his contact name; He hesitated for a few moments as he realised that he shouldn't reveal too much about himself or as a fourteen-year-old, he wouldn't be taken seriously. After all, who would believe that a fourteen-year-old schoolboy had anything of importance. Frantically searching his mind for ideas of a name, he somehow came up with the name, Dr Pepper. This was a brilliant name he thought, as it kept his initials on his email address and it sounded as if it was someone in authority and after all, doctors were always respected. Then came the question he needed to ask and typing in the newly altered ingredients he had come up with to disguise the real ones he entered:

"Dr. Pepper here: I've discovered a parchment in an old castle ruin and it gives the details of an ancient potion/spell of some sorts. The trouble is, one of the

ingredients, beginning with "R" is destroyed. I cannot make out what it should be: can you advise please."

Continuing on he typed in the spell in exactly the same font as it was written but changing a few of the ingredients as he had previously decided. He changed the chicken liver to lamb's liver, changed the fennel for basil, which he quickly gleaned from a herbal web site and substituted, finger nail clippings instead of a locket of hair. Most importantly though, he totally omitted anything about the silver needle blessed by God.

His amended potion now read,

""Last. Blessed by God the divine gift of sense and Protector from evil.

Potion of Eternal Accordance

Take ye eight gills of clear water and set within a stout vessel. Place it o'er a lighted flame and bring to a fearsome boil. When the vapour riseth as spirits from the deep, add thereto eight drachms of olive oil. With solemn hand lay in 2 drachms of fresh cut nails and one whole spider's web, gathered with care. Let this stand and gentle to the boil till the space of twenty minutes pass, as the sundial be told, and stir it not.

Bring again to angry boil until count of ten and next to gentle boil until the sundial hath marked another half hour. Whilst the fire endureth, place within the vessel:

- *One lamb's liver, cut by four,*
- *Half a clove of garlic, well bruised,*
- *And at the last, one finely diced r******, the measure of a quarter gill.*

Raise the flame once more until the broth doth bubble full strong for five minutes, then abate the fire and suffer it to still yet another half hour.

When the sun no longer cast upon the world, strain the liquor clean, and set aside till the cool of night hath chilled it.

Then, with the reverence due to all ancient powers, take unto thy lips four drachms of the potion, no more than twice in day. Continue until seven measures in total have passed thy lips.

When the final draught is consumed, and the words, Lord God, please bless me now with the power of the Universe as Protector to fight against evil and with me it shall remain forever more."

Take heed, that whoever shall be blessed as the Protector against evil, shall be fearful that the powers so blessed doth drain every part of thy life and soul. So be wise of wisdom in their use until so restoreth.

When he had finished entering the amended recipe, he clicked the send button and sat back to see whether anyone would respond. His mind conjured up the picture of what it would do and taste like if they actually made the recipe as he had done and started to snigger away at the thought of the nail clippings being in it.

An hour past and nothing had come through on his emails, it was now 11.30pm and he had to get some sleep ready for a hectic weekend and meeting Miriam. Not shutting down his computer for once, Dominic collapsed into bed. Even the excitement and fun of the school day couldn't keep him awake and within minutes he was sound asleep.

He must have been so tired that he never moved a muscle all night and exactly where he had first lain down, he awoke in the same position. Opening his eyes, it didn't take long for all the previous day's pranks and excitement to come flooding back to him. His brain was coming up to speed now and then he remembered about last night's search for the missing ingredient and his email question. Quickly jumping out of bed he rushed across to his monitor to see if he had received any email response to his question.

There was something in his in-box and his heart started to beat quicker. An email from, Devil's Servants sent at 3.30am earlier in the morning. Dominic nervously opened the message.

"Dear Dr. Pepper, we were most interested to hear about your discovery of the Extreme Sense Potion and we believe that we may possibly know what the missing ingredient is.

We should be most interested in meeting up and discover exactly where you found it in the castle. Our passion is historic churches and castles and any knowledge you have would be most valuable to our understanding of them better.

Incidentally, did your uncle find anything else with it?

We are not too far from Conwy in North Wales, but we would be willing to travel to a destination of your choice if this is not convenient.

When we meet, we can tell you our thoughts about what we think the ingredient is.

We look forward to hearing back from you.

Regards,

Devil's Servants"

Dominic quickly realised that these Devil's Servants were certainly clued up on spells and witchcraft as they mentioned, was anything else found. Obviously referring to the silver needle so he needed to be absolutely careful about what he should disclose to them. Bringing up a road map on his monitor of North Wales and studying his options, he carefully formulated his reply. Somewhere near Conwy seemed ideal. It was only five miles away from their caravan site and was linked by both local rail stations and road and not far at all for him to travel. This seemed an ideal place to meet.

It was a stroke of luck that Conwy was not too far away from where they were going on holiday but he felt uneasy about asking them to come to the caravan. It was definitely too scary to invite strangers who were obviously into the occult and that he had never met to the caravan. Let alone his mum would go mad that he was bringing such people back and she would find out about him wagging the day off school. On top of all that, they would see he was a fourteen-year-old schoolboy. Racking his brain for a few moments for a solution, a plan came into his mind. "I know, what I'll do," he murmured to himself and quickly typed out a reply.

"Dear Devil's Servants,

Many thanks for your response but rather than involve you in travelling, which is really nice of you to offer, I am on holiday from Monday near where you are, Colwyn Bay and it's no problem for me to visit you.

It's actually my uncle's discovery who is Dr. Pepper but he is not well at the moment and unable to travel, so I'm just helping him out but he told me exactly where he found it, so I could come instead, even tomorrow if that suited"

As far as I know, my uncle never mentioned finding anything else, I'm sorry.

I await your reply

Kind regards,

Dominic Pepper"

Dominic, clearly stretching the truth as far as he could as it would now make sense of the fact of a fourteen-year-old being there and waited eagerly for their response. He didn't have to wait long before a reply pinged into his mail box.

"Dear Dominic,

Many thanks for offering to come to us, that's most kind of you and we are most sorry to hear of your uncle's illness and we hope he recovers very soon.

As our premises are down a long narrow winding lane which can be a bit awkward, we suggest meeting, in the visitors car park of the Dutch Pancake House at Conwy Water Gardens if that's acceptable. It has an excellent bus service and is only a few short miles south of Conwy. Shall we at say 6.00 pm Monday?"

We look forward to chatting about your uncle's discovery and please bring the original parchment he found.

Kind regards,

Devil's Servants"

That was it, it was all go and very soon Dominic would know what the missing ingredient was and quickly followed their message up with.

"Dear Devil's Servants,

Many thanks and see you tomorrow. I will be with my pet dog bull dog, Randolph so it will help you to recognise me.

I hope this is acceptable and see you then

Kind regards,

Dominic"

Just three minutes later, their reply came back happily agreeing to the arrangements and a cold shiver ran through Dominic's body. He was deeply unsure about meeting up with such people and why the heck did he suggest meeting at 6.00pm when it was virtually dark. But when he remembered the missing ingredient and wondered just what other powers could be harnessed when he had the complete potion, he managed to shrug it off and decided that it was definitely worth the risk to meet them.

CHAPTER SEVEN

THE CARAVAN PARK

Monday morning arrived and the Peppers were like a whirlwind passing through the house. Mum and India were rushing around shouting at each other for losing missing bits of clothing, hairdryers and all sorts of things they had to pack for the holiday. Dominic wasn't normally flustered at all, he had two speeds, slow and stop but this time it was different. He was going to pick up Miriam for one, and he had this awesome potion to sort out, he couldn't wait to get to the caravan and even he was tearing around looking for things.

Eventually they were all ready and packed and just as they were getting in mum's car, Dominic suddenly thought that he better take some of the potion with him, just in case he might need it and the original parchment.

"Mum, I've forgotten a book I need to take," shouting as he ran back inside the house and down to the garden shed. He quickly found a decent container and poured most of what remained of the potion into it and grabbing the parchment and nearest book he could find to fool his mum he rushed back to the car and they were off. Dominic sat back with his mind darting around with both excitement and worry thinking about everything that lay ahead.

Forty minutes later they arrived at Miriam's house. It was a pretty, red brick semi-detached house with a carefully manicured lawn and well tendered rose bushes. The narrow grey flagged path zig-zagged up to timber framed porch.

Mrs Pepper thought it best that all three of them would go up to the house and introduce themselves. Needless to say, Randolph was left in the car just in case he had another farting episode which wouldn't be the best way of introducing themselves.

Dominic rang the bell and Miriam together with her mum and dad answered the door. They were invited inside into the sitting room and it almost immediately seemed that the two families had been good friends for years. The parents chatted away with India listening intently for any juicy gossip whilst Dominic excitedly explained quietly to Miriam in the far corner of the room what had happened in the last twenty-four hours. Especially the arrangements to meet with the Devil's Servants later that day. Miriam gasped in astonishment at how much had happened since they last parted. Eventually the talking finished and they were all back in the car together with Miriam this time and underway.

It didn't take long at all to travel the short distance to reach the caravan park at Llanddulas, Colwyn Bay and they quickly unpacked the car and made ready the caravan for their stay.

The caravan was in a magnificent position overlooking the Irish Sea and Dominic and Miriam were becoming more excited by the minute with their meeting later that evening and studiously studying the bus routes to Conway Water Park. They soon discovered that unfortunately, the bus took quite a long winding route and it would take them over an hour to get there, therefore, they would have to leave at 4.30pm to allow a bit of time for safety.

Turning their thoughts more now to the logistics of it all. If their meeting was at 6.00pm and allowing thirty minutes for the meeting and one and a half hours to get back, then that would mean they would not get back to the caravan until after 8pm and too late for dinner so they needed an excuse to tell Mrs Pepper why they were going to miss dinner. Dominic always had an answer when he really needed one.

"Mum is it all right if Miriam and I go into Colwyn Bay later and have a good look around. Don't worry about dinner for us, we can get a McDonalds or something. We can also take Randolph with us so he can have good walk, it will do him good?" Clearly remembering that he had told the Devil's Servants people he was meeting that he would have Randolph with him.

Mrs Pepper was fine with that suggestion and after all her and India would enjoy a walk without the constant giggling in the background. Dominic glanced across to Miriam and discreetly gave her the thumbs up. All they had to do now was plan for the meeting and off they went for a walk along the beach.

Although slightly chilly, the sea breeze was so invigorating and was an ideal tonic to refresh them after the last few manic days. They needed their wits about them and be totally focused when they meet with the people from Devil's Servants later on.

"What about the potion?" asked Dominic looking at Miriam.

"What do you mean?"

"Do you think I should take some before the meeting just in case?"

"In case of what?" and Dominic continued on.

"Well, I'm not too sure about these people, they are certainly into the Devil and the occult and such stuff, so it could be dangerous."

"You're frightening me now," Miriam clearly becoming nervous about the whole thing. "Do you really need to know what the missing ingredient is after all, what it does now is astonishing and we can do lots of fantastic things with it?"

"Yes, I was thinking the same but it has two problems. One the farting, which is so embarrassing and unpleasant for anyone around. Secondly. the correct ingredient is definitely needed if we want to find out what the spell means by the power of the universe will remain yours forever. It could mean that it would give us the power to fly." Dominic's head now full of ideas of what it could mean.

Miriam now quickly becoming excited as well and totally forgetting that just a few moments ago she was all for not going.

"I agree we must go and I think it's a good idea to drink some potion beforehand just to be on the safe side."

The two walked on, continuing their walk along the beach thinking of all sorts of other powers it might hold. Possibly even time-travel Dominic suggested, so they could return back in time to see the dinosaurs and photograph them and watch everyone's faces when they returned back to today and showed everyone. They were having brilliant fun imagining all sorts of things that it could be and now couldn't even wait for the meeting.

The next few hours flew back so quickly as they were so engrossed in what it all could mean and returned to the caravan where Mrs Pepper made them sandwiches, ham and tomato of course, so they had full stomachs before they had to leave.

It was soon time to leave for the meeting and Dominic picked up his imitation potion draft that he had sent them. Then leaving behind the authentic parchment, went into the bathroom where he poured out one more potion to drink, and as usual now in one swallow downed it. He didn't even think about the awful taste as his mind was completely occupied with the meeting that lay ahead and collecting Randolph, off they set.

Dominic by now had some control; over the powers the potion gave him, not the farting though, most unfortunately for Miriam. Unless he concentrated hard, his powers remained unresponsive. This was ideal as the last thing he wanted was the deafening sound of the traffic and everyone around him incessantly chattering.

CHAPTER EIGHT

THE MEETING

It was real now, it was actually happening. Their fear and anxiety were again coming back into their minds as they waited at the bus stop. The thoughts and excitement of seeing dinosaurs had totally evaporated away, now it was all about trying to calm and control their fears.

"Do you think we will be all right?" Miriam becoming more nervous with every passing minute.

"Of course we will," Dominic trying to put a brave voice on for her benefit but inside his stomach, he too was starting to feel slightly churned with fear. "Besides, we have Randolph who although is as soft as a cuddly bear, I'm sure would bite anyone who tried to harm us," continuing to reassure himself as well.

A few minutes later the bus arrived and they were on their way in trepidation of what was to lay ahead.

It was soon 5.30pm and dusk was falling quite quickly now.

"I should have arranged the meeting for 5pm," whispering to Miriam. "Everything looks far worse in the dark" and their hearts started to beat louder now. "Take deep breaths, it will help a bit and focus on that we will be back in the caravan in two hours." At least that brought out a small gentle smile from Miriam and even a little squeeze of Dominic's hand.

Twenty minutes later, the bus driver's voice rang out; "This is the stop for Conway Water Park" as they had asked him when they boarded to let them know and off they got. It was only a short distance for them to walk to the water park and they quickly found the car park. It was completely dark now and the car park was completely empty.

"That's good, we can hide over there until they come," Dominic pointing out some bushes at the side of a path leading from the Dutch Pancake House down to the lake. "Then if we are not happy, with what we see when they arrive, we call the whole thing off and go back."

"That's a good idea" and silently whispered to herself, "Oh, please don't come." and with that they bent down behind the bush to wait.

The seconds seemed like minutes, and with each passing one, their fear grew worse. They wanted it all to be over and be on their way back when just as they were going to stand up, a car's headlights came into view and turned off the lane into the access for the water park. Their hearts started to race now and their mouths started to become parched, Dominic wanted to swallow, but it was impossible and also too late. The car pulled into the parking area and drove across to the far side, turning around as if to face them and pulled up.

Dominic immediately started to focus his concentration on the occupants of the car and although they were almost eighty metres away, he could hear them talking,

"There are two of them," he lent over quietly whispering to Miriam. "I can hear them talking,"

"Can you hear what they are saying?"

"They are talking about me and the potion, well about my made-up uncle anyway," referring to the uncle Dominic had concocted so it didn't seem stupid that a fourteen-year-old was turning up.

Suddenly, Dominic froze with fear and Miriam could feel him become agitated.

"What is it, what's wrong?" digging her elbow so sharply into Dominic's ribs that he let go of Randolph's lead. Randolph instantly realising that he was free, immediately seized his moment and wandered off into the dark surrounds before he could grab the lead again.

"What's wrong?" repeated Miriam in a far more pressing manner now.

"I heard them say that no matter what they had to get hold of the original parchment the potion was written on, and to kidnap me so my pretend uncle would hand it over."

"Let's go," Miriam immediately snapped. "I want to go" with a more determined voice now.

"We can't, we don't have Randolph now," quickly reminding her.

"Where could he be?" Miriam pondering quickly regaining her senses. Even Dominic with his extraordinary hearing couldn't tell, nothing was moving, it was deadly silent.

Then all of a sudden, the car's interior light came on as if the occupants of the car could sense Dominic was hiding and the driver's door opened. For the first time both Domnic and Miriam could now faintly make out the driver and another person sitting in the rear passenger seat of the car.

The driver was a man and Miriam guessed at about fifty. He was quite tall and wearing a long dark what looked like waterproof waxed coat. The rear passenger was too hard to make out but they assumed he was probably a male too.

"Dominic, Dominic Pepper," the deep throaty sound of the driver's voice shouted out suddenly shattering the eerie silence. The driver continued; "Don't be scared, why are you hiding?" Clearly not aware of Dominic's special hearing and that he knew what they were planning to do.

"Dominic," the voice echoed out again as if commanding him to come to them. "We have something that belongs to you" and with that leaned back into the car and pulled out what appeared to be a lead followed by Randolph, hesitantly being dragged out of the car.

"I think this animal belongs to you," and at the same time yanking hard on Randolph's lead. Miriam squeezed tightly on Dominic's hand feeling the dog's pain.

The driver continued, "If you don't come out now and talk, we are going to leave and take the dog with us."

Miriam almost panicking now,

"You're surely not going to go," whispering in Dominic's ear "You know what they said, they are going to kidnap you and then I'll be all my own." Dominic gave Miriam's hand a gentle reassuring squeeze.

"Don't worry, I'll be fine. I know what they are going to try and do and I'll keep at least a two metre distance from them and I am a quicker runner than they are. I might be able to distract them enough to snatch Randolph so I have to try," and with that Dominic stood out from the bushes shouting

"OK, I'm here, I'm coming, please don't hurt Randolph" and started the short walk across to the car.

With each step his breathing was becoming deeper and more pronounced, he was planning that in the event he had to run away as fast as he could, he should take deep gulps of air in readiness for the sudden exertion.

Approaching the car, he could now make out the driver quite clearly now, holding Randolph's lead who was now lying subserviently at his feet, when a flicker of light illuminated the rear of the car. The rear occupant had lit up a cigarette and Dominic got a glimpse of the shadowy outline of a thin scrawny long jagged face of a man, in his sixties with a sharply pointed nose and grotesque bushy eyebrows

"Why, were you hiding?" The driver brusquely addressing Dominic.

"I was just being careful as I have no idea of who is who around here, and I wanted to make sure it was you," was the best excuse he could come up with on the spur of the moment. It seemed to suffice as the driver's stance became slightly more relaxed.

Dominic had now reached the two-metre distance safety mark from the driver and was racking his brain about how he was going to snatch Randolph from him. Even if he could, would Randolph be able to keep up with his speed? Which was very doubtful but he felt he just had to try something.

"Can I have Randolph back now please? "Asking the driver nicely.

"Yes of course," holding out Randolph's lead for Dominic to take and as he stepped forward to immediately take it, the driver made a lunge to grab Dominic's wrist.

Dominic, jerked back in a reflexed action, he was in shock at being taken by total surprise, it all had happened so quickly. He had only for a few moments taken his mind away from being prepared for such an eventuality, but it was enough and too late as the driver's hand gripped his tightly in a cold vice-like grip.

"Where's the parchment, where's the potion?" the driver's commands immediately barked out.

"It's in my pocket," Dominic now stammering with fear.

"Then hand it to us"

Dominic trying his best to control the shaking of his free hand reached into his pocket and produced his imitation potion, handing it to the driver.

The driver instantly snatched it out of his hands and turning to the rear passenger handed it to him. The rear occupant now back in the shadows flicked on his lighter once more and glanced at the document.

"Rubbish, it's utter rubbish," he angrily shouted, screwing it up and throwing it at the driver bouncing it off his shoulder.

The startled driver glanced down to find it and Dominic saw his chance. Biting the driver's hand as hard as he could, he relaxed his grip enough to pull his hand free. In the same instance Dominic turned and ran as fast as he's ever run in his life back into the darkness towards where Miriam was hiding.

It didn't take long before Dominic realised that no one was chasing him as his concentration was still completely focused on any sounds. He could clearly hear that the two men were talking to each other and wondered what was going to happen next. Surely, they were not just going to go and leave in peace. He didn't have long to wait for his answer.

"Dominic," the driver's voice once again cut through the night's silence. "If you want to see your dog ever again, be back tomorrow with the original parchment or else. We will leave a note at the foot of the Dutch Pancake's entrance door with instructions," and with that the driver got back in the car and they left.

Dominic, still breathing heavily from his quick escape called out Miriam's name in an almost loud whisper, in fear that they car's occupants might have sneaked back. But they had not returned and for the time being they were safe for now.

Miriam, rose from her hiding spot from behind the bushes and immediately rushed to him throwing her arms around him in the tightest squeeze ever and bursting out crying uncontrollably.

"I saw everything and when he grabbed you, I thought that was the end. Oh Dominic, what are we going to do, they have Randolph?"

Dominic, trying to relax Miriam's squeeze even just a bit so he could breathe, softly tried to comfort her. He knew it had been a terribly frightening ordeal for him let alone a girl left on her own in the middle of nowhere in the dark and with some extremely scary nasty characters.

"Don't worry, we have several options if we want. We can call the police and be immediately safe but that will be end of our adventure, the potion and we will get into huge trouble when we get back. Or we can try and sort it all out on our own, well for a little longer anyway."

Miriam, her crying now had diminished to a gentler sobbing with the occasional sniff. "What do you suggest is best?" wiping the tears from her eyes

Dominic, pausing for a moment to carefully think about everything,

"Well, the first thing is, we may as well find the note they left at the door of the Dutch Pancake House. There is no harm in reading it and then we can decide further." Miriam nodded her head in approval and off they strolled to retrieve the note.

A minute later they had reached the Pancake House and found the note exactly as they had been told next to the entrance door. Dominic, quickly picked it up and is it was too dark for them to read properly, decided they would take it with them to read on the bus back to the caravan. Let alone, that last thing they both wanted to do was stay around there for one second longer than they had to, and so off they went to make their way to the bus stop.

Ten minutes later their bus appeared and not a moment was wasted in boarding it and finding he two nearest empty seats they wearily dropped heavily into them, the relief in them both was palpable. The stress of the last hour soon over-whelmed them and suddenly they became extremely exhausted and closed their eyes recollecting the trauma of it all.

A good five minutes passed before Dominic opened his eyes and whispering to Miriam.

"We better read the message just in case we have to do something immediately." And with that, took out the message from his pocket and opened it, half displaying it to Miriam who still had her eyes closed and quietly read the contents of it to her.

"Hello Dominic, we are sorry about what happened tonight but that document is so important to our research into spells and such like we got overly excited. We do apologise and hope we didn't frighten you. We promise that we will take good care of Randolph, I think you said the dog was called, until you come and collect him tomorrow.

Given that it will dark again as the weather forecast is not good when you come, we think it best to meet at our old farm which is only twenty minutes' walk from the Dutch Pancake House and at least all the lights will be on.

Our address and directions are.

Leave the bus 400 metres before the Water Park and head towards Rowen Scout Camp, it is well signed and only a fifteen-minute walk.

At the Scout Camp, continuing in the same direction, follow the signed footpath alongside the wood, and across the field for 15 minutes more and you will arrive at Llangelynin Old Church.

This is where we are.

We will see you at the slightly earlier time of 5.30pm."

Miriam now wide awake; "So what do you think, are we going or do we tell everyone the truth?"

"I'm not sure what to do yet," Dominic rubbing his forehead. "We need to have a good think about it all, because if we tell everyone, it's gone forever, it won't be ours anymore. We might get a small bit of recognition about it but I don't think much more than that. Plus, there will be a huge telling off from everyone for what we've done and I might even have my mock results cancelled."

"I see what you mean," Miriam in a state of despondency now. "It's all a bit of a mess"

CHAPTER NINE

PLANNING THE NEXT MOVE

Luckily, the hour bus ride was well needed to at least give them time to decide what best to do, and if they were going to keep it secret, they needed to hatch some sort of plan.

The bus ride back to the caravan park was a bit like a question and answer time, with each in turn raising a question and the other posing an answer. Eventually, the decision was made. It was the hardest thing that they both had ever to decide upon. One way meant entering into possible hugely dangerous situation, a bit of which they had just experienced when the two men from the Devil's Servants tried to kidnap Dominic. The other way was, they not only lost everything, what they had done would have severe repercussions from both sets of parents and possibly Dominic's school.

Eventually at almost at the caravan park, Dominic had decided what he thought would be best and turned to Miriam.

"I have no choice and I have to go back, I've lost Randolph. I'll be grounded forever, my mock results will be cancelled and I'll probably have to resit them but this time with no magical help so I know I'll fail. But you can stay, you're in the clear. You have no exams to worry about, it was me that took Randolph and the whole thing was my idea."

Incensed by Dominic's suggestion that he would go on his own, Miriam pushed herself away from him in complete annoyance.

"Well, if you think you're going on your own, your very mistaken, I'm coming too and you can't stop me, so that is that."

Dominic, burst out in a huge grin, and immediately grabbed Miriam's arm and pulled her back again.

"Of course we will go together, we are a team and we have to stick together," and continuing on in a more serious and pensive tone. "But we have to really plan this well this time, we know about them and what they are capable of, so that will help, but planning is key. Also, what excuse are we going to give to my mum, we better come up with something good before we see her," and with that the bus reached their stop and off they got.

Walking back to the caravan was although not far, was so slow as they would stop every twenty metres or so to discuss some plausible reason or another. But then reject it as not good enough as Mrs Pepper would see straight through it.

"I have it!" Dominic excitingly shouted out, making Miriam jump. "It's brilliant," he boastingly continued. "When I was here last year, there was a pitch and put course just near the Great Orme at Llandudno and next to it was a large area of field, full of holes that all the rabbits had dug for their burrows. There were dozens of them, and mum was talking to some local woman who told her to keep Randolph on a lead at all times near there."

"Visitors to the area who don't know about the burrows, always lose their dogs down them. They never find them until the next day when someone sees a dog wandering around on its own and takes it to the police station. Luckily no dog has been permanently lost yet but lots go missing for the night and have to be collected the next day when someone hands them in."

"That's brilliant," chirped in Miriam in full of praise for Dominic's excuse. "That's definitely believable."

"Yes," Dominic in full flow now and his brain going into overdrive.

"And that's our excuse as to why we have to go back again tomorrow. We went for a walk around there and forgetting all about the burrows, as it was a year ago. I let Randolph off the lead and he caught sight of a rabbit and ran off after it. We looked for ages until someone reminded me about lots of dogs going missing chasing rabbits for the night but turn up the next day, so we went down to the police station to give them our details."

With Miriam's full agreement with everything, a few minutes later they reached the caravan and now the moment of truth arrived to see whether Mrs Pepper would believe the excuse.

Mrs Pepper was furious about it all. How could Dominic have lost Randolph? She told him last year about lots of dogs going missing chasing rabbits. "You never listen Dominic," shouting at him but in a more controlled way than she would normally have done because of Miriam's presence.

"That's why you don't do well in school, because you never listen."

Eventually, Mrs Pepper started to slowly calm down realising that it all might turn out fine if as everyone says, the dogs always turn up the next day. Until then, she would defer further judgement.

"I suppose with all what's happened you have probably not had time to eat anything, would you like me to make you something?" Her mood returning to some normality again, and they both eagerly nodded their heads and went off to clean themselves up.

Dinner didn't take too long at all and even in less time it was quickly devoured by the famished pair wanting to rush to Dominic's bedroom to plan for tomorrow's encounter with the Devil's Servants.

The next two hours they were in deep thought and conversation over how they should tackle their next encounter with these obviously dangerous people.

"Whatever you do please don't leave me on my own again, I couldn't stand it," pleaded Miriam.

"I promise I won't," reassuring her but also knowing that he would never let her get too close to them. The risk was far too much, plus she would be needed to call for help if something did happen to him.

But then Dominic reflected further on the idea now feeling that it was too high a risk. Last time they were there, well close by at the Dutch Pancake House, there was no reception for their phones and there was a risk it may be the same again there. She would have to walk back all that way on her own in the dark not knowing the area at all and terrified. No, Dominic concluded that idea was no good, he needed another solution.

Then, as quick as he dismissed the idea a solution to it sprang into his mind.

"I know, I'll ask Will my best friend from my last school to see if he will come. There's enough time for him to make it if I ask him now. You will love Will, he's really funny and nice and gentle, and then you will have his company if I have to go off on my own."

Miriam, pausing for a moment could see the sense in it all and besides, she would feel safer now there would now be three of them.

"Ok, ask if he can come," now excitingly agreeing.

Dominic was already texting, his mind was already made up and a few moments later Will replied asking why all the rush. Dominic did his best to outline what had been going on but it was just too much detail and would take ages for Will to understand properly. Eventually, Dominic sent a final text.

"Will, I just can't explain properly, it's just too much detail and you wouldn't believe me either. You need to be here so I can show you. Please Will, I/we need you."

Will, now quick to reply, "Dominic, this all sounds far fetched so you better not be playing a prank. O.K, I'll go and ask my mum if it's ok to go for a few days."

And a few moments later, Will's answer arrived saying that he could come.

Dominic and Miriam, in unison shouted in joy at the news and so much so that it brought Mrs Pepper in to find out why they were so pleased. Dominic explained that Will was back home from holiday now and has asked could he come and join them. Mrs Pepper's only concern was enough room but if the lads could bunk together then she was happy for him to come and so that part of the plan was set.

Dominic checked the train timetable and Will could catch one from Chester arriving in Colwyn Bay at 12.30pm. It was perfect, as it was only a short walk to their caravan and so he text Will back with the details. All was agreed and they would meet in the station's waiting area.

The next morning came with the sun trying to penetrate the caravan's curtains, quickly bringing a degree of warmth. Dominic and Miriam were up first and the place felt empty without Randolph mooching around.

"I hope they are taking good care of Randolph," Miriam pensively reflecting.

"Me too," Dominic in agreement, but he knew in his heart that they would probably not even feed him, perhaps some water but that would be all. All this reinforcing Dominic's resolve to rescue him.

Whispering to Miriam so no one could hear. "I think when we go to meet Will, I will take some of the potion first so I can show him what I can do. Otherwise, he might think it's all a big joke and won't come with us later."

"Yes, I think so too and, in any event, you will need it for later on anyway."

It wasn't long before everyone was up and tucking in to one of Mrs Pepper's delicious English Breakfasts. It was always the best start to the day when they were on holiday. Mrs Pepper and the two girls were having a thoroughly enjoyable time talking about make up and fashion whilst Dominic's thoughts were firmly focused on the day ahead.

With breakfast finished and Miriam helping Mrs Pepper and India to wash up, Dominic set about making their beds as it was now fast approaching time for them to leave to meet Will.

With all the jobs finished, Dominic retrieved the potion from its hiding place and took a small sip before collecting the original parchment to show Will. With a quick goodbye to his mum and a promise to let her know immediately if they get any news on Randolph, off he and Miriam set to collect Will.

It was a beautiful sunny morning and the sea air with the gentle breeze was exhilarating. The seagulls were as usual fluttering all over trying to dig out any discarded morsel of food from the trash bins and hopping away when anyone passed close by. Half an hour later they had reached Colwyn Bay Train Station and sat down in the waiting area for Will's arrival.

Dominic's now gentle but still unpleasant farts reminded him that he better quickly test whether the potion had worked sufficiently. He was now becoming quite proficient with doing this and focussed all his mind on trying to hear what some other travellers sitting fifty metres away were talking about. In just a few moments, his ears burst alive with the crescendo of sound once again. They were talking about what to buy their daughter for her birthday. That was enough, Dominic had heard enough to show it was working perfectly well and once again reverted to normality.

No sooner had he done this, the station's Tannoy system burst into life.

"The 11.25 train from Chester for Conwy and Caernarfon will be arriving on platform two, please stand clear."

They both jumped up in excitement, especially Dominic as he couldn't wait to show Will what he could do.

Four minutes later, this mass of red hair appeared sticking it's head out from the last window of the train's door.

"Is that him?" Shouting Miriam pointing to the wind-swept locks of red hair

"Of course it is, who else would have hair like that," both laughing away as this slender young fourteen year old schoolboy jumped off the train, shouting madly and waving his outstretched arms.

The introduction of Miriam to Will didn't take long at all and instantly it was clear that they were going to get along famously.

"So, what's all this joke about, super-powers, you're not being real about it surely?" was the very first question out of Will's lips.

"I am totally serious, look sit down and I'll explain everything that's happened over the last few days." And so Dominic, and with of course Miriam's help, relayed everything that had happened.

"Incredible, really incredible, indeed it's too incredible," responded Will to what they had just told him.

"Ok, if you want me to believe it all, prove it," daring Dominic to take up the challenge.

Dominic, knew that Will would end up asking this, after all who wouldn't?

"Alright I will. Walk to the end of the platform," which was about seventy metres away, "and looking away from us, quietly whisper four different words and one number and I'll tell you what you said."

With that, Will marched off to the end of the platform and in his quietest whisper said; "Dominic, mad, utterly, mad, two." And smiling to himself that it was impossible for Dominic to even in the remotest chance guess that, walked back.

"Ok, magic man what did I say?"

"I'm not repeating that you think I'm mad."

Will was stuck for words, totally dumbfounded. It was impossible but clearly Dominic must have heard him.

"Ok then, what was the number?"

"It was two," Dominic answered with a huge grin across his face.

That did it, Will collapsed onto the seat totally stuck for what to say.

"See, we told you," chirped in Miriam "and he can do even more things."

"What do you mean more?" Will quickly interested in hearing more.

"He can move things."

"Now, that is impossible, good hearing, ok I can live with that, but move things, impossible."

"No, it isn't," Dominic now joining in quite firmly, hurt somewhat by Will's lingering doubts. "I can honestly move things, I'll show you," and Dominic scouring the area looking for the right opportunity.

Eventually, he spotted an opportunity which would show his new found talent.

"See that young woman sitting on that bench over there with the sunglasses on top of her head?" Will looked across and nodded, "and see the two men standing quite close behind her," Will again acknowledged. "Well, keep a close eye on her glasses."

Dominic, not too sure that his telekinetic skills would work after only taking a sip of the potion but it was too late now to back out and have Will doubt him. With extreme concentration even screwing his eyes tightly up to help, he focused all his energy on them. A few moments passed and then the glasses first started to shake and then slowly rose from her head before sliding off onto the floor behind her.

The young woman immediately jumped up and seeing the two men standing quite close behind her, stared at them as if blaming them for that. One of the men protesting their innocence, immediately picked the glasses up and handed them back to her. Although not entirely believing them, she accepted their innocence and replacing her sunglasses once again, sat back down.

Will and Miriam, were doing everything possible to stop themselves bursting out laughing, even digging their nails as hard as they could into the palms of their hands. Dominic letting the moment pass for a couple of minutes, once again told Will to watch and then repeated what he had done with her glasses.

This time, no matter what the two men said, she was in full swing telling them off for doing such childish tricks and picking up her glasses stormed off to find another seat elsewhere.

This was all too much for both Will and Miriam and it had become impossible to contain their laughter with even Dominic joining in this time. And with that, the three left the station to walk back to the caravan with Will now a firm believer in Dominic's new found powers.

On the walk back, Dominic and Miriam detailed to Will all about what had happened with their meeting of the men from the Devil's Servants and how frightening it had all been. Especially as they had taken Randolph after being infuriated with Dominic for handing them a false potion recipe.

"Can I see the original parchment?" Will excitedly asked wanting to see the part about blessed by God. Dominic pulled the parchment from his pocket and handed it Will.

Although difficult to understand, as the measures were in Olde English which Dominic had originally to Google to see today's equivalent, with Dominic's help Will gasped in amazement at what it read.

"I wonder what that means?" Will pointing to the paragraph about the power of the universe.

"*When the final draught is consumed, and the words, Lord God please bless me now with the power of the Universe as Protector to fight against evil and with me it shall remain forever more. Take heed, that whoever shall be blessed as the Protector against evil, shall be fearful that the powers so blessed doth drain every part of thy life and soul. So be wise of wisdom in their use until so restoreth.*"

"I'm not sure, but I certainly didn't feel any other power just the hearing and the telekinesis powers. Anyway, that's more than enough for me."

"What are you going to do? You won't get Randolph back if you don't hand it over to them but you just can't to give it to them."

"I don't know, but I definitely will not give them it, these people are capable of doing all sorts of awful things if they get it. We have to just to play it by ear as we go along and hope we can get a chance to get Randolph and get away. We all have to agree on this as we are all at risk if anything goes wrong, so if you're not ok with that we need to sort it out now."

Will looked at Miriam and they both nodded their approval to the plan.

"One other thing," Dominic still explaining, "If we fail to get Randolph, it's all over and we have no choice but to tell the police and my mum. She will not accept any excuse this time as to where he is. So, if we are going to do this, we just have to make it a success no matter what risks we have to take."

Once again, Will and Miriam nodded their agreement.

Will now fully understood the dilemma of keeping it quiet from Dominic's mum and the consequences if it all came out or went wrong. But although somewhat daunted by the danger it presented, he was certainly up for the chance of a brilliant adventure. After all, this was once in a lifetime opportunity of something to remember and talk about forever. Well, as long as they came out of it alright.

They were soon back at the caravan and with Will fully in the picture of the excuse that Dominic was going to tell his mum. The police had rung and they had Randolph, so they were going to collect him from them.

Mrs Pepper was delighted to see Will again and have him stay with them and inundated him with questions asking him all about school and their holiday. The next two hours flew by and then it became time for them to put their plan into action as it would take about an hour and a half to get to where they were to meet the people from the Devil's Servants. They would leave slightly earlier though to find a good hiding place first so they could study the layout and plan what best to do.

Dominic made his excuse to go to the bathroom and upon his return announced that the police had rang him to tell him they had Randolph and could they come and collect him. Mrs Pepper was delighted to hear the good news and told them do go immediately and with that they quickly prepared for the daunting evening that lay ahead.

Dominic realising that they wouldn't be back until late again, asked his mum that now that Will was here could the three of them have a walk around the pier at Llandudno. Adding, that they could be a bit later this time as they had a fun fair there and would also get a McDonalds. After all, they missed out on that the night before. After mulling it over for a minute or two and following which a severe warning that they better behave, she agreed in light of Will being with them and he is always sensible.

A few minutes later, after replacing the original parchment in its hiding place and collecting, a torch, Randolph's lead and of course Dominic taking one more dose, they had everything ready and just about to leave when …

CHAPTER TEN

THREE BECOMES FOUR

…. when India interrupts everything.

"Dominic, do you mind if I come too, I can't wait to see Randolph again and I would like to go to the fun fair and have a McDonalds as well please?"

To say Dominic was in shock was a complete understatement, not only that, he was totally lost for an excuse as to why she couldn't.

Luckily Miriam was quick to react.

"Well, Dominic and Will wanted to challenge each other in a knock out competition on the air football machine on the pier and I'm the referee so you would only find it boring."

"Yes, you'd only ruin things standing there," chirped in Dominic now picking up on Miriam's lead.

"No, I wouldn't" India responding indignantly, "I'm good at playing that and I can beat you at it Dominic," gesturing towards him

Hearing all the commotion, it was Mrs Peppers turn to now add her weight to the discussion.

"Yes Dominic, it's a good idea for you to take your sister along. She's missed Randolph too and she is also better than you at that game, so you can now play a foursome which is surely better."

That was it, there was no way out. How was Dominic ever going to explain the truth to India before they reached the Devil's Servants place. Even if they managed that, would she agree to come and even if she agreed to, could she keep everything secret. The possibilities and difficulties were endless but they were stuck now with the decision that had been forced upon them and that was that. There was no point discussing the matter anymore as when Mrs Pepper put her foot down, no one could move her and so reluctantly, they agreed to take India with them and off they all set.

One thing that was good with India coming along, it had taken their minds completely off worrying about what lay ahead of them. They were now far too concerned how to explain everything to her and what her reaction would be.

Over the years that Dominic and Will had become good friends, Will had visited Dominic's home many times for dinners, weekend stays, birthday parties and all other sorts of things. And during that time, he had got to know India extremely well and they'd become good friends so, whilst India might not believe what Dominic was about to tell her, at least she might believe Will.

It didn't take too long for them to reach the bus stop and Dominic knew that it would be far easier explaining everything to India before they got on the bus, instead trying to explain it all with the other passengers listening in.

Dominic had thought long and hard whilst they'd been walking on how to even start things so he decided that it would be best to show her a demonstration of his powers and turning to his sister.

"India, I'm going to show you something and I'll explain everything afterwards. But you have to promise, in front of us all that you will never tell anyone, including mum about what you are going to see and what we are about to tell you. You must promise"

"What! Dominic, what are you going on about? Don't be stupid, I'm not promising to do anything."

Will, hearing India's total refusal to promise anything at all, thought he would add his weight to see if he could persuade her.

"India, we've been good friends for a long time now and you've always trusted me, so please believe in what Dominic's about to show and tell you, it's immensely important and getting Randolph back depends on it."

"What do you mean, getting Randolph back depends on me promising something?" becoming more puzzled by the second.

Now even Miriam joined in.

"India, I know we've only known each other for a few days but we do get on well. I'm sure as time goes on, we will be the best of friends, but you have to believe that what we have to tell you is so vital for Randolph's sake. So please, please promise us you will not tell a soul about what you are about to see and hear."

Eventually conceding to the pressure and the fact that they could all not be up to something stupid and if getting Randolph back depended upon it, India made the promise.

Dominic, first started with his hearing super-powers and asking Miriam to walk down the road they had just come from, and whilst keeping facing away from him to choose four random words and whisper them. Miriam would walk with her to confirm the four words and then they could come back.

It only took three minutes before they returned and without wasting a moment Dominic said.

"Your words were, green, Randolph, shoe and cabbage." India, like both Will and Miriam before, was completely in shock, it was an impossibility to have heard her but yet he did.

"How did you do that, is it a trick?" were the first words that rushed out of her mouth.

"No, it's an old potion he found," Miriam now joining in. "He drinks a little bit and these super powers start. He can move objects and break things as well, just by his thoughts."

"What you mean, he has some sort of telekinetic power as well?"

At last Dominic managed to squeeze back into the conversation and explained all about finding the parchment, making the potion and then realising the powers that it brings.

India was bewildered with it all and still really couldn't take it all in but having witnessed it, and hearing the others say it was all true, then it must be true.

"So, what's all this got to do with getting Randolph back?"

And Dominic, with Miriam's help of course, explained what had happened and all about the Devil's Servants and that's where they were going now.

"What, you're going there now?" India exclaimed in astonishment. "After what they did and you're going back? You must all be mad, I'm certainly not going there and I don't think any of you should too. Just tell the police and they will sort it."

Once again, they all took turns trying to convince her that it was the safest way to get Randolph back. The potion was too valuable and important just to let it go as that is exactly what would happen if they told the police.

Although it proved extremely difficult, India finally agreed. She would go along but on the strict understanding that her and Miriam would not be parted, and that the boys would not do anything dangerous. With really no other choice, everyone nodded their agreement to her terms.

So at last, everything was in the clear and with no more secrets between them they could now start focusing on how they were going to tackle the meeting.

CHAPTER ELEVEN

LLANGELYNIN OLD CHURCH

With the worry of telling India now all sorted, and once again focusing on what lay ahead, everyone was starting to become nervous. Dominic, to make sure his telekinetic powers were functioning, decided to try it out on the bus. It was on a woman's bag, which was lying on the seat next to her a few rows in front of him.

He was sat with Will whilst the two girls were sitting on the two seats immediately in front of them. Tapping India on the shoulder, he whispered for her to watch the woman's bag and a few moments later, he made the bag slide off the seat and onto the floor. India immediately turned around, mouth open in amazement at what she had just witnessed and now totally convinced that everything they had said was completely all true.

An hour later they were off the bus and starting the walk down the lane towards the scout camp, discussing more in depth what ideas they had for when they arrived there. When Dominic turned to them all.

"Look, just to remind everyone that we are here for one reason and one reason only, to rescue Randolph. Does everyone agree?" All three instantly agreed, after all, they just wanted to get out of there as quickly as possible.

"OK, if we are all agreed, then I suggest that when we get there, we first find a good hiding place for Miriam and India where they also have a decent position to see what's going on. Will and I will see about finding some way of sneaking in and rescuing Randolph. Hopefully if my hearing is performing well, the girls can whisper to me if anything untoward happens outside." Once again, the others nodded their heads in approval.

They soon reached the scout camp and paused for a moment to check their mobile signals which were just acceptable but would do. Ahead of them was the narrow path that had been mentioned in the directions, leading away passed the woods. Dusk was falling quickly now and what would probably have been a nice stroll in the afternoon sun was now looking decidedly ominous.

The wood had now been transformed into a most frightening place. The trees were now not something to be admired and photographed but were now, multi limbed tall monsters daring them to walk past them. The slight creaking and rubbing of the branches and the intimidating noise of the windswept decaying leaves on the floor played havoc on their nerves.

"Do you think they're watching us?" Miriam whispered, clutching India's arm.

"No, not at all, they're probably like all sensible people at this time, sitting down for dinner in front of a nice warm fire," trying to reassure both of them.

Dominic and Will led on using the torch now they brought with them and just four minutes later, especially to the relief of the girls, the path through the wood ended opening up into a wide expanse of grazing land.

"I'm not sorry to see the end of that," Miriam exclaimed now feeling somewhat better about the situation.

"Look, look over there in the distance," Dominic's voice abruptly bursting out and pointing in the direction they were going. "Look, you can see lights, that must be where they are, that must be Llangelynin Old Church."

Suddenly, the reality and danger of it all fell on them as if in partnership with the almost pitch-black night sky which had now fallen. The walk past the woods which they thought was so frightening, was nothing now compared to the next ten-minute walk across the fields to the lights in the distance.

Pausing for just a moment, Dominic quietly repeated their plan again adding,

"From now on you must all keep silent as I will be concentrating trying to pick up on any voices or sounds" and with that they continued on but without the benefit of the light from the torch which they now had turned off.

It didn't take long for them to reach the old, heavily weathered crumbling stone boundary wall of the church. It had taken a heavy toll over the years from the bitter winters and gales and staying out of anyone's view they knelt down beside it and peered over.

Dominic now relaxing his concentration, spotted that there were various out buildings and a large abbey of some sort which seemed to be leading off from behind the church. Whispering quietly to the others

"Look, if we can work our way around the wall to the rear of the church, we can get a better look at what's happening." With that, stooping as low as they could they made their way around to the rear of the church.

Dominic was right. A dark grey, coloured stone-built corridor with two long leaded windows led off from the rear of the church connecting to a large dominating, what looked like a former abbey. Single storey in design, yet towering in authority, its sheer walls dominating the far end of a courtyard.

The cobbles beneath were the same grey granite as the abbey itself, peppered with black flecks that seemed to glisten like wet coal in the dim light. The courtyard formed a tight square, hemmed in by three squat outbuildings. To the far right, the dark mouth of an abandoned stable gaped open, the wood of its doors warped and swollen with age. Beside it, with a narrow gap and next to them quite close, was a hay storage barn crouched in shadow, its interior claimed by the low, flickering glow of an oil-filled lantern. The flame danced, casting restless shapes across the walls over a pair of stray hay bales that looked as though they had been left in a hurry.

As quietly as they could and keeping as low a profile as possible, they carefully slid over the boundary wall, passed the barn and took refuge inside the dishevelled stable. It was littered with farming implements and loose hay scattered around but there in the corner they could make out what appeared to be a goat tied up kneeling down

Dominic, gathering everyone into a tight huddle around him whispered.

"Shhh, keep quiet and don't disturb him or he might start bleating and give us away," then turning to the matter in-hand.

"This is where you girls can stay. You can get a good view from here without being noticed and it shouldn't be too far for me to hear your voices if a problem arises. So please only speak if it's absolutely necessary and if we're not back in forty-five minutes then go for the police and leave us."

"What! You think there's going to be a problem?" Miriam immediately becoming deeply concerned.

"No, not at all, it's just that we all need to know what to do, that's all," trying to be reassuring now before turning to Will and pointing to a specific door of the abbey.

CHAPTER TWELVE

THE SEARCH FOR RANDOLPH

"We may as well try that door first and if that's locked, we can move down to the one after."

Will nodded his head acknowledging that he understood

"Ok, wish us luck," Dominic whispered to the two girls and out he stepped from the stables when suddenly he jumped back in.

"What's up?" exclaimed Will in shock.

"I can hear people chanting something coming from inside the church." No sooner had he finished his sentence, two ghostly shadows silently appeared walking from the church through the connecting corridor into the abbey.

As they passed the large leaded windows, they could clearly make out the two figures wearing hooded black cloaks, gently swinging a candlelit lantern from side to side. Its flickering light casting eerie shifting shadows across the walls and ceiling as if daring them to enter a place of pure evil.

Soon they had disappeared into the building and a few moments later the door to what Dominic had intended to enter by, opened and he could hear them talking

"Quickly, take the cloaks off and hide them in the cupboard, that kid will be here soon and we best wait at the front of the church as he will be coming from that direction."

A few moments later without robes, the two figures walked out across the courtyard heading to the front of the church. Dominic with a sense of urgency now turned and whispered to Will

"This is our chance to get in, they've not locked door and they can't see us from where they are going." Immediately the two of them darted out from the shadows and ran to the unlocked door and entered.

It was a large rectangular kitchen and although old and untidy, it had a strange, unsettling blend of ancient and modern with a what appeared to be a now well used heavily faded black double Aga. Placed in the middle of the room was the most gigantic well worn, dark oak dining table, showing its age with twelve identical chairs surrounding it. At the head of the table stood a formidable high backed carver chair decorated with ornate carvings and symbols of the occult and was clearly intended for someone of importance. But the two boys had little interest in all this and needed to move quickly before the others came back after realising that Dominic wasn't coming. Off they moved to leave by the huge arched heavy wooden door opposite leading further in the house.

Grasping the large iron ringed handle ready to open it, Dominic's hearing suddenly picked up a distant faint sound and whispering to Will in his quietest voice ever despite his excitement.

"I can hear some people chanting and a dog barking and it sounds like Randolph." With that he turned the handle for the door to pull open the tiniest fraction, so he could put his ear to the imperceptible gap that was now created. Now he could hear the chanting and barking clearer and it was definitely Randolph.

With no other sounds he could detect, he pulled the door open enough for them to enter into a long dimly lit ominous looking stone hallway with the lower half panelled in a grim dark oak. Above the panelling several disturbing paintings hung depicting the Devil in various grotesque forms together with numerous satanic symbolic signs. Dominic looked at Will and blew out a large puff of air to steady himself for what evil lay ahead of them.

As they took their first step, the barking suddenly stopped as if the dog had paused to listen as well and for once, Dominic wished Randolph would start again so he could try and pinpoint where the sound was coming from. He could see four large doors leading off from the hallway. Two from the same side as the kitchen, one the opposite side and the last at the far end of the hall facing them. Not wanting to chance their luck and enter each one of them, if Randolph could bark just once again, he would know which room to look in. But there was no more barking, apart from the chanting. It was deadly silent and the total silence just made the whole thing even more intimidating than it already was for them. They had no choice now but to enter each room.

The first door was some five metres along on the opposite side and as stealthily as possible, they made their way along the hallway until they reached it. Both their hearts were pulsating ferociously thinking of what may lie in wait for them behind the over-bearing large door. It was made even worse by the horrifically frightening satanic painting hanging from it, depicting the image of the Devil bending over to take the life of a sacrificial lamb laid out on an altar.

Dominic turned to Will and put his finger up to his mouth to signal to keep totally silent as he placed his ear to the door to listen. Apart from the faint background chanting, there was no other sound at all. Half relieved that no one was there but also disappointed that he could not hear Randolph, he slowly opened the door a few centimetres. Still there was nothing to be heard and once again he opened the door but enough this time so that he could poke his head around and take a look.

It appeared to be some sort of a gruesome satanic meeting room, with a stage at the far end and twenty or so chairs lined out in military precision in front. The pungent smell of incense was everywhere and making it almost unbearable to breathe. Everything was draped in black with numerous terrifying satanic pictures everywhere but most importantly there was nothing else there and definitely no Randolph.

The two boys breathed a sigh of relief that at least they could get out of there. and quietly closed the door stepping back out into the hallway.

Time was not on their side and they were becoming very conscious of how long the men had been gone, Will glanced at the time on his phone and already they had used up nearly fifteen precious minutes. Every second was critical if they were not to be caught and realising that there was no telling what these people might do if they were found. Tapping Dominic on the shoulder, he held out his phone for him to realise that time was moving quickly on and that they better hurry. It would be unlikely that these men would wait too much longer before giving up and returning.

Dominic nodded to acknowledge the time and exhaled an even larger puff of breath to steady himself for what lay ahead. He looked down the long spine-tingling dark hallway, that stretched some forty meters into the distant shadows, as if daring them to proceed further along. He knew that they had to go down the passageway, there was no other way, they dare not go back without Randolph, no matter what dangers lay in store. He tried consoling himself with a scrap of comfort as his mind strayed for a moment with the thought that in two hours, they would all be back at the caravan laughing about it all.

How he wished it could have been light outside. The narrow mullioned leaded ceiling windows that appeared occasionally running along the passage would have at least offered a break in the cloak of shadows that hid along the passage.

Refocussing once again, they continued cautiously tiptoeing their way along the grey granite flagged floor, stopping every other stride to turn and check behind them in fear that some satanic demon would suddenly pounce on them. With each step they were becoming even more scared, as they both knew that with each step along the passage, they were becoming more entrapped. But still they silently continued on and after ten metres reached the next of the large arched doorways.

Pausing at the side of the doorway for a few moments to steady their already exhausted and frayed nerves, they glanced at each other and with a gentle nod of encouragement to each other readied themselves for what lay behind the door.

First turning yet again to check that nothing sinister was stalking up behind them, Dominic once again slowly moved his body inch by inch closer to the archway, closing his eyes once more to concentrate listening. He could still hear the sound of distant chanting coming from the opposite side of the abbey and took some comfort from knowing that they were still occupants were busy elsewhere. Nothing else could be heard but the overbearing silence. His heart once again increasing with intensity knowing that each room could be fraught with danger. Closing his eyes he prayed for no one to be inside and with the hope that his prayer had been heard, gazed inside.

His prayer had reached its destination, no one was there, it was empty. The room was a disused old dining room. Against the far wall stood the remains of what once was a proud fireplace. The heavy over mantle and the stone hearth displaying the scars of years of wear. He was growing to hate those flagged floors that spread their coldness and chill everywhere like a sea of grey mist and stepped inside. "Randolph" but nothing. Even the sound of his bark would now be music to his ears. "Randolph," in slightly louder whisper but once again nothing but the lonely echo of his returning whisper.

Carefully looking around, they quickly checked for any means of escape in case they couldn't go back the way they came. The large old doorway which once led out to the courtyard had long been boarded up and even if they had some tools, it would take far too long to even attempt to get it open. The old stone mullioned window which gazed over the outside cobbled courtyard was completely impenetrable too.

Dominic walked over closer to it and carefully peered out over the courtyard to the out-buildings beyond. He could clearly see the stable where the girls were hiding and the adjacent hay barn with the lantern still flickering, casting its grimly dancing shadows everywhere. Every moment though was precious and almost immediately turned his attention back to the stable door, hoping the girl's heads would appear even for the merest glimpse. But, just like Randolph, nothing happened.

However, knowing the girls were so close by and would go for the police if they were not back in about another twenty-five minutes was incredibly reassuring. This gave him more confidence than ever to continue on but for an instant though, he let his mind wander back to Miriam.

He could picture her anxiously waiting for him with India and the warming smile that would greet him. How they would hug each other and when back home talk excitedly about their adventure. This momentary dream disappeared as quickly as it came as he realized that he had to be brave for her as how could he let down anyone who supported him like that.

Gathering himself together, and whispering to Will that they should move on, they made their way back into the hallway.

He was now used to stopping at every opening and listening before peering out and this time proved no exception. Save for the constant irritating and totally frightening vibrating background chant, he could hear nothing and carefully looked out into the passage. It was still all clear and once again they slowly stepped out. It was the same deliberate routine as before, stopping every other stride to double check that any evil spirits were still at bay.

They were fast becoming exhausted from the extreme tension of it all. They had totally forgotten about how long they had been gone as they continued further into the waiting abyss. Another few steps, and now just ahead the next doorway, and stopping once more, straining his gifted hearing powers for any sounds coming from the other side.

The chanting was more audible now and had taken on a more frenzied pitch. "Please don't let it open into a temple" turning and whispering quietly to Will in an almost pleading way.

Pausing to focus listening again once more before opening the door, he picked up the faintest sound barking. It was in the distance but definitely the sound came from somewhere the other side of the door. He knew it was definitely Randolph and for a brief moment his fears dissipated and a feeling of hope warmed his body.

"I can hear something."

"What can you hear?" Will too, struggling to talk with his throat becoming parched from fear.

"I can hear chanting but at last, I can also hear Randolph now barking again as well and it's all coming from inside this room." Their fear was palpable and even tiny beads of perspiration started to show on their brows.

"Yes, I can hear them clearly now, there's a few of them and it sounds like they're in some sort of a ceremony."

"You're not going to open the door?" Will becoming extremely concerned now.

"We have to, we have to get Randolph, that's why we came, at least have to try our best and besides if anything goes wrong the girls know what to do and get the police."

But little did the boys realise that the phones had no signal now. The girls found this out a few minutes earlier after the boys had left them. They were Googling for the location of the nearest police station just to be ready in case it was needed, when they discovered that there was no signal, nothing at all. They were devastated, the only piece of comfort they had was contact with the outside world and now without this they were totally isolated on their own.

They had no choice and had decided that when the forty-five minutes was up, as Dominic had told them, if they weren't back then, they would make their way back and hope that along the way, near the scout camp, they pick up a signal. In the meantime, they just had to tightly hold each other's hands and hope that the boys would return with Randolph sooner than the forty-five minutes.

Slowly turning the door handle, Dominic carefully opened the large arched oak door. The sound of the incessant chanting instantly grew more audible and the faint choking smell of incense once again filled the cold air. He knew that the next few moments could betray them to the horrific occupants of the building, but his overwhelming desire was to find Randolph.

Pushing the door further open and without moving his legs, Dominic slowly protruded his head level with the edge of the door. Then holding his breath, his eyes drew clear and in just one quick instance that it takes to blink, he whipped his head back to assimilate the picture his eyes had seen.

He exhaled with a deep sigh of relief as no one was inside and scrutinised the pictures of the room flashing through his mind. It was a short rectangular shaped room enclosed by four bare sandstone walls. The furthest one had an archway with a black curtain acting as a screen hanging across it, and behind which seemed to be another larger room. He could only guess what it could be but the only way to find out was to look, but first this room needed to be checked.

With no one in it, at least he felt it safe enough to risk stepping inside. Slowly pushing the door further open, still not completely convinced that the cloak of blackness wouldn't suddenly rush out and devour him. He braced himself and clenched his fists as a meagre gesture of defiance that he knew would be useless against what lay within and entered.

CHAPTER THIRTEEN

THE SATANIC TEMPLE

Instinctively Dominic ducked, as the demonic shadows of light from a distance candle danced all around him as if replicating the grotesque ceremony that was going on nearby. Once again "Randolph," his voice croaking with the dryness from his fear, he tried to swallow but it was impossible, any moisture that his mouth once had, had deserted him long ago.

"Randolph," again repeating as quietly as humanly possible but nothing was returned and his heart sank. They had entered into some sort of vestibule. There were places to hang clothing together with a tall free-standing cupboard, presumable for holding the grim looking cloaks they wore and a half height smaller one.

"I know you're in here somewhere, please don't make me come looking further inside for you," now becoming slightly annoyed. Again, nothing came back but the faint ritual chanting sounds. They crossed the room to examine a tall old oak cupboard which stood covered in a thin layer of sandstone impregnated dust. The flagged floors at least offering them some degree of comfort as they totally deadened any noise from their ever-careful footsteps.

Gripping the pear-shaped handles Dominic gently pulled open the cupboard doors fully expecting his Randolph to be there with his tail wagging furiously to greet him, but Dominic's posture said it all as his head bowed in disappointment.

It was bare save for the delicate silver threads of cobwebs which hung from the corners together with their sleeping occupants. Quickly managing to cast off his despondency, he realised even though he wasn't there and although he had a particular adversity to its spidery occupants, at least they could use it to hide in if they quickly had to. This at least, cheered him up enough to muster his flagging will power and continue on.

Stealthily he approached the black curtain across the stone archway of the vestibule and noticed several sets of men's clothing hanging up along the far wall. Surprisingly, he felt the better for seeing this, as it at least showed the tiniest bit of normality and took his mind off the occult and its frightening scenarios.

The smell of the Hazel incense had become more intense now irritating their eyes and which had now started to moisten. It seemed to be a prelude for the penetrative chanting which had now changed into a different shorter verse that vibrated and resonated with even more threatening under tones.

"Oriens splendor lucis aeternae
 Et Lucifer justitae: veni
 Et illumine sedentes in tenebris
 Et umbra mortis"

Stopping slightly back from the curtain, Dominic angled himself to one side so he could see a reasonable view without giving himself away. In front of him, expanding into the distance was a large imposing room with lofted vaulted ceilings and flecked grey stone flagged floors that were laid completely bare.

The massive imposing sandstone walls were devoid of their natural beauty having been completely covered in what appeared to be in a matt black coating, ensuring their complete silence. The multi vaulted ceilings that once stood with pride had suffered the same fate and now capped the dark grisly casket of the room. Lights and shadows cast from the black candles that lit the room flickered and danced everywhere as if portraying the deathly dance of demons at a satanic ritual.

Was this the temple, flashed through Dominic's mind. *It certainly looked terrifying and was there another room behind them and one to the side.*

Like the vestibule at the bottom of the temple, at the head was another stone archway behind where the chanting occupants stood. This time though no simple curtain hung but instead two enormous robust ancient black oak doors protected by a deep bold claret colour inverted pentagram. They were daring anyone to enter, and which stood in sober silence guarding whatever evil monstrosity lay behind.

To the side near the head of the temple, opposite a large circular black table made from the blackest of oak, stood another smaller simple rectangular doorway. Again, sealed by a pitch-black oak door, leading to some sort of ante room.

Dominic felt a shiver go through his body, warning him that this was a place of pure evil. The blackness of the room extended lengthways and at the far end he caught a glimpse of a group of tall figures, massively enhanced in size by their ghostly silhouettes projected against the walls. Dressed only in hooded black robes they were standing bare foot around the table. Dominic couldn't move he eyes, he was spellbound, there was an uncontrollable fascination about it all. He was seeing into the depths of evil itself and for a second the consequences didn't matter. The trance was suddenly broken as the sound of chanting continued echoing and bouncing along every façade of the room.

"Dies irae, dies illa
Solvet Saeclum in favilla
Teste Satan cum sibylla.
Quantos tremor est futurus
Quando Vindex est venturus
Cuncta stricte discussurus.
Dies irae, dies illa"

The eeriness of the chanting was even more accentuated by the constant monotone key of their voices that only varied in pitch on the last sentence of the verse.

"Dies irae, dies illa
Solvet Saeclum in favilla
Teste Satan cum sibylla.
Quantos tremor est futurus
Quando Vindex est venturus
Cuncta stricte discussurus.
Dies irae, dies illa"

They kept chanting the verse over and over again but with each repetition, the monotonous pitch of their voices was becoming louder and more passionate. Realising that they had stumbled upon a secret satanic temple, and that some sort of ceremony or blessing to the Devil was taking place, fear now took over the two boys.

The little they knew about these satanic sects terrified them. They believed in and worshipped Lucifer, the Prince of Darkness and they lived for evil. If they were caught what horrible fate would await them? Their minds exploded with ritual sacrifices, and they knew that they had to get out of there as quickly as they could or the consequences would be…

Dispelling the grisly pictures their minds were beginning to imagine, they had seen enough and stepped back focussing back on what they came for.

Without warning, the chanting stopped and the silence was deafening. This was worse than the chanting, their whole bodies were on edge, tingling with the thought of anticipating what evil was about to befall them. Dominic immediately took position again at the curtain and with an immense sigh of relief, the men were leaving the room and walking across into the ante room at the side of it. Then they had gone and the heavy deep thud of the solid door as it slammed shut echoed eerily throughout the whole room.

"Will, this is our chance, I know Randolph is in here somewhere, I can sense him," and bravely the two boys cautiously stepped out from behind the curtain and quickly walked towards the round table where the hooded men had been standing.

Laying in front of them as if waiting for the ceremony to continue was an old large biblical looking black book, with tattered frayed gold bindings and edgings as if the worshippers had been reading from it. In the corner as if standing guard. were two tall full-length cupboards, dressed in a shroud of black fabric.

Keeping their eyes half pinned on the oak door of the room they men had passed through, Dominic quietly and as gently as he could pulled open one of the cupboard doors. But yet again Randolph refused to be there. The cupboard lay empty except for more empty silver chalices that had been placed inside two large silver vessels that nestled for space with the cobwebs in the corner. A large sacrificial wooden handled knife which had grotesque ornate figures sculptured out of its handle pointed menacingly outwards, and several broken pieces of white chalk were scattered in the bottom.

Making a mental note of the pieces of chalk, thinking they might come in handy if he has to leave messages of help or S.O.S. he closed the door leaving it exactly as he found it. As he stepped back away to open the other cupboard, his eyes were drawn to the large black book that lay open on the table.

A thin bead of sweat slid down his forehead. The woven material seemed the same as that of the rough, ancient parchment he had. His stomach now beginning to tighten with the fear of it all and he bent over closer.

The curling old-English letters danced in the candlelight, and the strange, jagged hieroglyphics along the page edge seemed to twist and shuffle when he wasn't looking. They matched perfectly, the same chilling symbols, the same sinister order as his parchment.

A shadow rippled across the black casket-shaped ceiling above him, making it feel as if the whole room might collapse. He froze, the silence pressing against his ears.

It had *to be connected,* quickly flashed into Dominic's mind.

Hands trembling, he looked back at the book and is heart gave a sickening lurch. In all his excitement, he hadn't realised the title at the top of the page:

The Black Mass.

The words seemed to pulsate on the page, as though alive. His eyes began to trace the curling lines of text. Without meaning to, his lips moved—whispering the strange script into the still air.

"Prince of Darkness, hear us!
I believe in one Prince, Satan, who reigns over this Earth,
And in one Law which triumphs over all. I believe in one temple
Our temple to Satan, and in one word which triumphs over all:
The word of ecstasy. And I believe in the Law of the Aeon,
Which is sacrifice, and in the letting of blood
For which I shed no tears since I give praise to my Prince
The fire-giver and look forward to his reign
And the pleasures that are to come"

He stopped and shuddered, feeling almost physically sick with fear, he couldn't bring himself to read any further, but he had to find out whether his page belonged there. Turning over the page and quickly skimming down it, he was looking for the give-away jagged missing section. It wasn't that one it was intact, the next page was the same and also the next, each turn of a page becoming quicker with more urgency. On and on, page after page of satanic rites and ceremonies, he flicked past.

Soon he had reached at the last but one penultimate page of the book with still no missing page, when turning that page, there in front of him lay a page which had a portion that had been hurriedly torn out. Studying the jagged contours and the sentences that had been abruptly interfered with. He knew that his segment of the page would fit exactly here. A gratifying sense of achievement, that Sherlock Holmes must have often felt enveloped him as he pictured in his mind the jigsaw fitting exactly together. Stepping back to walk away Dominic suddenly realised that in his engulfment with his self-praise for his investigative skills, he hadn't noticed what evil ritual his script was part of. With a sense of urgency now, he rushed back and flicked over to the previous page and whispered the title......

CHAPTER FOURTEEN

THE INCANTATION OF LUCIFER

...... **"The Incantation of Lucifer"**

"The rite must begin on the night of a new moon and when at least five planets are in alignment

The High Priest, and servants should gather in an isolated room devoid of all light, excepting only black candles

He continued further on and then realised in horror what it was he had been reading and which he had part of it in his possession; it was the rite to invoke Satan himself and bring him to life on Earth.

He quickly gestured to Will to come over and see what he had discovered. As soon as Will saw the terrified fear in Dominic's eyes he knew instantly it was something awful and rushed across.

Dominic immediately brought his attention to the shape of the missing page and whispered into his ear,

"Look, it matches the one we have perfectly," Will immediately confirming with a gesturing of his head and Domnic continued quietly whispering the whole of the preceding passage for both of them.

"Nythra Kthunae Atazoth," it went on, with explicit instructions of how to summon Satan. He suddenly he felt a chill and froze as he felt the hairs on the back of his neck prickle as if touched by an invisible presence; an eeriness filled the room. The full impact of how much desperate trouble they were in began to dawn on him. The colour totally drained from his face as if already offering itself up for sacrifice and fear exuded from every pore in his body.

"You realise what we have?" Turning to Will.

"No, not really"

"Our parchment and needle must be the only thing on earth which can stop Satan. I just wished we knew how to use it. It can't just be for special hearing and moving objects around," now becoming cynical of how little real power he had.

He knew now there was no way they would stop until they had the page and especially the needle and even if they had it, they would not stop at that. He was now never going to be safe now. He reflected upon the previous week and wished he could turn the clock back to then and had gone to school instead of that stupid castle. For the first time in many years, he wished for the safety of his mum, as she always knew how to protect him. He always had the comfort of a warm safe haven, but this time he was totally alone and in a place of death and up against inhuman goings on.

Casting aside his retrospective wishful thinking and returning to his nightmare reality, he gathered his wits. They had to get out of there now. They couldn't risk any more time looking for the Randolph, they would have to leave that for the police.

Anxiously, he returned the book back to the page it was originally opened at and started to quickly walk away when a thought occurred to him and for a moment his fear turned to anger and blurted out in his mind.

Well, I'm in trouble now and it can't get any worse so blow it and rushed back to the sombre black Book lying on the table.

Quickly turning over a couple of pages and then randomly selecting another one he tore it out, again he flicked over several pages, and ripped out another page and one more until he had three pages.

"This will teach them to mess up or lives," quietly, but aggressively mouthing to Will.

Suddenly, they became acutely aware of the absolute silence that had engulfed the room without them realising. The chanting had stopped, their minds raced ahead with the possibilities of what was going to happen next and whether they had they finished and were they coming back.

The extreme danger they were in came flooding back as Dominic whispered, "Please start chanting again, please." Hurriedly folding the pages that he had roughly extracted from the book and pushing to hide them into the only place he could think of so quickly, his trainers.

Making a frantic dash back across the temple, they were desperate to get out of there by any means possible irrespective now of making any noise. Through the curtain into the vestibule they ran, to reach the door back into the hallway. Not even pausing to think who might be the other side. Dominic was just about to grab the handle when in the corner of his eye, he caught a glimpse another low-level cupboard. It had been pushed tightly to the adjacent wall and somehow their attention had not been drawn to it when they first entered the room so it had never been checked.

Without thinking, he darted across the few metres to the cupboard and purposefully pulled on the pear-shaped oak handles. The twin doors shot open and in front of him deep asleep in the bottom of the cupboard lay Randolph. He had now automatically come to accept that each time he opened anything his pet was never there, and for an instance of a second his brain hadn't appreciated what his eyes had seen. It had already triggered a command to close the doors again. The briefest of moments passed before Dominic's brain realised the signals that the eyes had sent were wrong and instantly corrected the command. Dominic threw open the doors again and was overcome with relief that at last, they had found Randolph.

In the few seconds that had already elapsed since he had opened the doors and noticed him, he knew there was something wrong. He appeared to be in a very deep sleep and there was no sign of any acknowledgement at all from him towards Dominic, not even opening his eyes and that was normally impossible. Randolph had always, ever since they first met when he was a tiny puppy, been unable to contain his excitement whenever he saw Dominic. But this not the Randolph he knew, there was no sign at all from him.

Suddenly the still dank air was abruptly broken by the sounds of muffled voices approaching; they were coming from the temple. His heart, forgetting the relief of seeing his pet once again, burst into life. Forcefully pushing his arms underneath his slumbering pet and gathering him up, almost turning at the same time towards the door leading out to the hallway, sprinted across to the door. Will was just about to place his right hand onto the handle when they heard more voices approaching from the hallway side. They were trapped in the middle with no way out and turned back again into the vestibule.

Silently screaming at himself at what they should do, Dominic's eyes flashed around the room looking for an answer. There against the wall was the cupboard, the one they found Randolph in. It was their only chance and rushing across to the half height oak cupboard, swung open the doors, once again shaking its spidery occupants from their newly resumed sleep.

In one movement Randolph was unceremoniously almost thrown into one corner while he and Will darted in onto their knees into the other corner. They instantly stretched out for the open doors and pulled them speedily closed, praying that no one would hear the solid thump of their closure.

They were exhausted and needed to catch their breath. The reality of their terrifying ordeal was extracting its toll upon their bodies and made even worse knowing that they were trapped. They wanted so much to take in large gulps of air but all they would allow themselves to do was to take small sips of it otherwise they would surely be heard.

Dominic closed his eyes and concentrated on trying to slow his heart rate and breathing down. It was so painful, he wanted to cough but he knew he couldn't allow that. *Damn you concentrate*, instructing himself. *Breath in through your nose and slowly out through your mouth; keep doing it… concentrate*, he kept repeating in his mind and slowly but surely it started to work. He could physically feel his heart and breathing rates slowing quickly down and praised himself for persevering with the agony of not being able to inhale as much air as he first desperately wished.

Abruptly, the sound of a door slamming solidly closed could be heard close by. It had to be the one into the vestibule, into the room in which they were in. Now he had to reduce his breathing to just a fraction of the level he had been so pleased to get it down to a few moments ago.

The tiny shaft of dim light from the candles drew his attention that the key to the cupboard's keyhole was not in place which at least offered the opportunity of some outside vision. Leaning forward to peer out, he could hear two voices and the sounds of scuffling feet as two ghostly figures, dressed in long black robes, their faces swallowed by the large black hoods swept into the room. Dominic immediately sensed them stopping in front of where they were hiding and could just make out their voices and a sinister laugh.

He was desperate to know why had they stopped and were they going to open the cupboard? Were they playing with him, knowing that he was in there, deliberately allowing him more time to contemplate his impending fate. He had realized for some time that his powers had been slowly diminishing but now they were totally exhausted otherwise he would be able to clearly hear every word that was spoken.

The extreme effort and exhaustion of his efforts was now quickly taking its toll and he was far too tired to offer any resistance and closed his eyes bracing himself for the inevitable end.

The seconds seemed like hours as he waited for the doors to be flung open. And when even more precious time had further elapsed, he realised that they would have surely opened the doors by now had they suspected something.

Feeling it safe enough to open one eye and then the other Dominic carefully strained to listen to anything that might give him any clue as to what was happening outside. Once again, and now with basic "human" hearing he could make out the same two voices talking close-by and through the cupboard's keyhole he could now male out the cloaked two figures. For a moment he felt safe once again and his body slightly relaxed again from the tension it had been stressed under. He realised that they had for some reason they just stopped to talk and were taking no notice of where he may be laying.

How he wished they would move away as they might change their minds and notice the cupboard at any moment flinging it open.

Please go away into another room, trying to sub consciously will them away. He gazed at Randolph lying prone next to him and reflected upon the little good fortune that had so far fallen their way. It was a blessing in disguise that they had drugged him. They would have had no chance of keeping his ever exuberant and playful playmate quiet, but how long will it be before they would notice that he was missing?

The answer to his question was abruptly answered.

"Noctulius, Ranulf," a loud deep grating voice lashed out from the other side of the curtain startling Dominic so much that he jerked his head backwards with such force that it struck the back of the cupboard.

"Noctulius… Ranulf," the voice again impatiently commanded growing louder and more aggressive.

"Where's the boy?" Dominic froze, whoever it was, was now approaching the vestibule from the temple that he and the two hooded figures were in. Sweeping the curtain aside in a fit of temper, into the room stormed a furious, tall lean faceless figure dressed in the blackest of all hooded robes, His face totally hidden far away at the back of the hood, as if challenging anyone's imagination to guess the grotesqueness of what lay within. The merest of colour breaking the blackness, was emblazoned into the robe, the scarlet sign of the inverted pentagram. Dominic realised, that whoever had joined was the figure of pure evil and a shiver vibrated through his body.

"He didn't turn up Master," the two Apostates hurriedly and subserviently replied. "We waited for over an hour but he never came." The tall, hooded figure went into a rage hurling obscenity after obscenity at them.

"I want that missing page before he understands what he has in his possession," screaming loudly as he walked back through the curtain. A deathly silence fell on the room, then his voice barked out again,

"Where's the dog?"

"We've not touched him Master," returned a frightened reply.

"He's gone, and I need him now for the sacrifice," venomously shouting back and following it immediately with a menacing threat, in a more controlled sinister voice.

"I want him found now or YOU will have to take his place."

"Yes Master, Yes Master," timidly responding. Dominic could hear them retreating and the oak door to the hallway slamming closed once again. He breathed a sigh of relief, knowing that they had they had left the room and felt sure that their hiding place was safe now.

Tapping Will's leg, Dominic whispered that he thought they were safe there for a while and that at least, they could move their bodies to a more comfortable position. Slightly relaxing, they both agonised as they gently tried uncrossing their aching, cramped legs.

"How long do you think we need to stay in here for" Will asked.

"I think we should wait at least a good five minutes until everything settles back down again. We have Randolph now so all we to do is wait for our chance and go back the way we came. I imagine the girls will have rang for the police now as we have been gone far longer than forty-five minutes," little realising that they hadn't. He knew that there's no way now that he could take the chance of moving from there for a while, they had to wait for their chance when they gathered again inside the temple.

Relaxing as best and as comfortable as possible and for once in his life not caring about the previous occupants, as his fear of spiders paled into total insignificance compared to what danger he was now facing. He half-stretched his legs out trying to push Randolph further away in an effort to make himself more comfortable for the dark lonely wait. After several more minor adjustments, he finally settled for the best position possible.

Given that they were stuck inside a dark, filthy cramped cupboard with an unconscious bulldog, he put his head back against the cupboard and slowly let his eyes fall closed. He desperately wanted to fall asleep but he knew he could not afford the luxury or else it may cost them their lives. Instead, he let his thoughts escape their solitary confinement and they wandered invisibly, totally immune to their captors through the cupboard and out along the passageways back to Miriam.

CHAPTER FIFTEEN

CAPTURED

The forty-five minutes had well passed now and the two girls were becoming more anxious with every passing second. They just wouldn't accept that the boys had run into problems but now had to accept that they must be in serious danger.

"What do you think we should do, they're miles past the time Dominic said to wait?" Voiced an extremely nervous Miriam to India doing her very best not to burst out crying.

"I know, I've been thinking the same. We have to do something, their lives could be at risk and waiting doing nothing at all is the worst thing. They're probably depending on us now and expecting the police to arrive any moment had we acted when the time was up. But now anything could be happening to them."

"Do you think we should go then?"

"No, What I think is best is that I'll go, at least that way we are keeping both options open. If they come running out, you can tell them about what we've done and if they don't" ...., India pausing for a second. "Then at least I'm on my way to the police. What do you think?"

"Yes, I like that idea, are you sure you'll be alright on your own going back along that horrible path by the woods?"

"I'm fine, it's nothing compared to this, you're the one being brave," which brought out a gentle smile from Miriam.

"Anyway, I'm hoping that I can pick up as signal before too far and I can ring them instead and be back quite quickly."

A big hug goodbye and off India went.

Miriam settled back into her shadowy hiding spot even more terrified now that she was on her own and softly whispered to herself for comfort.

"Look, I have to be brave, everyone is now depending on me. I need to act like an adult and not a cry-baby. Dominic and Will must be going through something terrible and India is so brave going past that wood on her own, so the least I can do is act brave and wait."

And she leaned back against the cold, damp, mottled grey limestone wall that had almost all but collapsed into heaps from the dereliction to await the passing minutes. For many years, it had never seen the sight or had the company of the horses it once used to shelter under its rusting tin corrugated roof from those many bleak and barren winters. The decaying hay and rotten vegetation now gave the only clue to its previous history of occupants.

She started to imagine of how India would explain the whole story to the police fearing that they may never believe such an unbelievable tale. But even if they did, India first had to find her way back unnoticed across the fields and down that petrifying narrow footpath by the woods which would now be even more frightening.

She shivered with the cold from the night air and from the chilling cloak of fear that had kept her company for almost two hours. She tried comforting herself with the thought of her sitting in the glowing warmth of the caravan. Sitting on the green and yellow paisley settee eating some of Mrs Pepper's delicious homemade cakes whilst cosying up tightly to Dominic. How she desperately wished to be there now, when a single droplet of water from a hole in the overhanging corrugated roof fell on her forehead, rudely awakening her from the few precious moments of daydreaming.

Wrapping her arms around herself and pushing her freezing icy blue fingers under her arms pits that now remained the only place of warmth. She reflected upon the numerous opportunities that she had missed from stopping them from being there. Why didn't she stop Dominic from wanting more, surely the powers he had were more than enough for anyone. We should now be having a nice holiday together, instead of all this. Angrily stamping her foot in annoyance at herself, making matters even worse, when the circulation in her foot immediately responded causing an agonising bout of pins and needles.

"That's it, five minutes more," she mumbled as she jumped about trying to restore the circulation in her foot.

"Then I'm going to go and try and find them."

She was so fixed upon the discomfort in her foot and with her total frustration of everything that she missed the dark silhouetted hooded figure silently creeping up behind her. Suddenly, she grimaced with pain as a cold hand firmly gripped her shoulder.

"Gotcha," a man's menacing voice barked out, "What yer doing ere? Who are yer watching? What are yer waiting for?" The sharp awkward questions following in rapid succession giving her no time to answer. She hadn't yet recovered from the shock of that vice like grip let alone face an interrogation.

"I…. I was lost," cleverly slightly stuttering to give her time to dream up a plausible reply.

Gaining her composure a little now she continued.

"I was lost and hungry and thought I may be able to get something to eat from that abbey or whatever it is."

"Don' talk rubbish," angrily replying and asserting his dominance by grabbing her arm. "We'll give you something to bloody eat alright" and dragged her into the courtyard.

Miriam, starting to panic was frantically searching for a means to escape, but her arm was held so tightly she knew she could never wrench it free quickly enough. She stumbled across the cobbled courtyard trying to keep her balance as her captor dragged her towards the same doorway of the abbey that Dominic and Will had entered through.

As they approached closer, the dim light from the gently fluttering candle hanging outside the door of the chapel unveiled her dishevelled captor. Miriam had not until now realised the real horror of her situation but when she turned and saw the tall, robed cult figure who had her in his grasp, her whole body went instantaneously limp. She was on the verge of collapsing onto those foreboding dak cobbles when she was viciously yanked back into a state of awareness. They had almost reached the chapel entrance when suddenly her grim escort shouted out,

"Noctulius," a brief unanswered moment passed, "Noctulius," then through the damp bleak cold night air an unsavoury voice echoed back,

"What is it?"

"Look what I've found," gripping Miriam's arm even tighter.

Miriam strained her eyes to see who it was that he had beckoned when slowly appearing out of the pitch-dark night was the grim almost lifeless specimen of another of the Devil's evil disciples slowly strolling into view.

"Where's she from?" Enquiring in a threatening tone of voice.

"I found her spying from the back of the stable."

"Do you think she was with the boy?."

Ranulf now replying with a sense of anger in his voice.

"Well, she says she got lost and was looking for food, but that's a pack of lies," and pulling her arm with even more urgency towards the Abbey's door way.

"At least the Master will be pleased to see what we have found for him, even if we can't find the bloody dog."

Miriam had totally missed the threatening undertone when the word, Master was mentioned. As when she heard him say that they hadn't found Randolph and was she with Dominic, meaning that they hadn't after all caught the boys. Her mind had ignored everything else that followed. For the first time in a while she felt a touch of hope as she thought to herself, that possibly Dominic did find Randolph and escape or at least may have hidden somewhere safe.

They had now reached the doorway and she was roughly pushed inside by the increasingly more aggressive Ranulf, as he became more eager to show the bedraggled little trophy that he had captured. They quickly crossed the kitchen that only offered the merest warmth to the dour surrounds and entered the long same foreboding grisly hallway that Dominic and Will had so torturously travelled.

Miriam kept analysing and dissecting every word of that one sentence that Ranulf had said, about not being able to find the dog and furthermore, was she with Dominic?

She was thinking that if Dominic had found him, then surely, he would not have left without her. He would have definitely have first gone to where she had been hiding and if he's not come for her and he's got Randolph, then he must be in hiding for some reason.

Along the hallway she was led and bundled into the room in which Dominic and Will were. Little did she realise that at that exact same time as the thoughts of Dominic were flashing through her mind, she was within two metres of where he lay, crouched with Will and Randolph hiding inside the cupboard.

"Master…Master," Ranulf excitedly shouted out, through the curtain into the temple which abruptly woke Dominic from his much needed nap into a fully conscious state.

"We have something even better for you." Dominic strained to hear what the excitement was all about. The tall, hooded venomous figure who angrily burst in before once again made an unwelcome entrance into their room and immediately upon noticing Miriam, snapped.

"Who is this, and what is she doing here?"

"We found her spying on us from behind the stable in the courtyard," blurted back Ranulf. "I think she has something to do with the boy."

Dominic's heart missed a beat as the reality of whom they had dragged in dawned on him, *not Miriam*, he thought, *it just can't be.*

He pressed his ear tightly to the cupboard door so not to miss even the minutest fragment of the conversation.

"So, you're a friend of this ridiculous brat, this so-called nephew of a Doctor Pepper?" Sneering but with a threatening edge in his voice. He walked around to the back of her and stood silently for a few moments. Suddenly, he lashed out with his voice making them all jerk almost to attention.

"Where is he?"

Miriam wallowing hard, "I…. I don't know who you mean" managing to answer back with tears now starting to trickle their way down her cheeks.

"You're lying."

She was terrified, it was impossible to fight back the tears, she intuitively felt that this person was evil and he would stop at nothing. Her only chance lay in not telling him about Dominic for if she did then they were both doomed. She steadied herself and then gaining her composure replied in a firmer but softer voice,

"I'm not lying. I am on holiday and I got lost in the dark lanes and took the wrong path. I just wanted to find somewhere warm for a few minutes and get something to eat," and waited, praying that this evil thing would believe it.

The tall black foreboding figure walked around to the front of her and stood motionless with his back to her. Then slowly turning around, stopped and faced her, staring intensely into her face. A cold chill went through her whole body and she started to slightly tremble again. She couldn't make out his face as it was too far back inside the hood of the cloak and the shadows had encased it totally in black.

Terrifying pictures jumped into her mind of what this person or thing looked like. She instantly conjured up the picture of the frightening monster from the film, Alien and tensed herself ready for the rows of teeth and dripping saliva to be savagely unleashed upon her. She could feel that he could tell that she was lying, the moments seemed like hours as he stood there motionless in front of her.

He started to move again and her body went limp with relief. He believes me, she thought as he again moved around to stand behind her. Without warning, she felt a hand grip her right shoulder and then it moved across her back firmly caressing it as it reached her slender youthful neck. She shivered, repulsed at the thought of this alien-like creature caressing her. A scrawny disfigured hand emerged from within the cloak and took hold of her long, bedraggled auburn hair that the hours of waiting in the damp stable had taken its toll upon and started to stroke it.

Sensing the presence of this black featureless face drawing close to the side of her face, she could feel his slightly warm breathing on her neck. Still getting slowly closer, she tensed herself ready for the inevitable pain that was about to happen and tightly squeezed eyes and waited.

It seemed like an eternity had passed, as the warm breathing stayed close to her ear. This monster was inhaling all the aroma of pheromones that were flowing profusely from her trembling body, when a deep voice whispered in her ear,

"I think our Prince may be well pleased with you" and then the stench of the toxic breath disappeared as he pulled away from her. She relaxed her exhausted body and slouched slightly forward with relief of not being bitten by those endless rows of teeth, as the picture of the alien monster slowly evaporated from her mind.

"Take her to the altar and prepare for The Invocation of Bestia Terrae," firmly commanding to his two Apostates. Obediently, they both lowered their heads in compliance and then he turned and left shouting,

"And send someone to look for that Pepper boy. Follow the route he would walk to get here, in case she is telling the truth."

"Where are you taking me? What's going to happen? My parents will call the police if I'm not back soon so you better let me go or you will be sorry." But nothing Miriam could say had any effect, her captors remained totally silent.

Even as they passed through the curtain into the temple, Miriam was still vainly trying to persuade them to let her go.

"You'll be sorry...." were the last words Dominic heard her say as she was forcibly led off with each arm being tightly held by a captor.

Dominic, sat back away from the cupboard doors relieved that she was still all right and puzzled over what was meant by prepare her for the *"Invocation of Bestia Terrae."*

Will was also wide awake now and had heard almost as much as Dominic and in the quietest whisper,

"They've taken her into the temple then?" to which Dominic nodded his head in a despondent way.

Dominic was ur<u>gent</u>ly trying to assess the situation and his brain racing for solutions and answers to the barrage of questions that were flooding into his mind. *Would they leave her alone? What does prepare mean? Should he try running for help now or wait to see if he could get her out?* Putting his hands to his head he continued with his analysis and assessed their options, all of which he didn't fancy in the slightest.

Where was India? Had she been captured or had she managed to escape? She might be lying hurt somewhere and if he went for help, then what about her?

First though was the problem of getting out of the building unnoticed and that so far had proved impossible. He would then have to find his way back in the dark across the fields, down past the woods and then the scout camp. That would take at least thirty minutes, even without Randolph and then he had to get help and return with it. So perhaps getting on for as long as two hours.

No, that would be useless he concluded, by then anything could have happened to Miriam. He had to stay and wait for his chance to rescue her but what did they mean by prepare her, searching his mind for answers.

Were they going to tie her down to be sacrificed? Were they going to use that ceremonial knife and drain off her blood into those chalices to drink in some sadistic ceremony? The possibilities were endless and all of them were too horrific for him to even think about. He had to know what was going to happen.

Come on think, think, you're her only chance and it's all your fault she's in there, scolding himself vigorously.

He lowered his head once more and lifting his hands he pressed his thumbs into his temples and concentrated. His mind went through all the passageways and rooms he had entered scrutinising every bit of detail he had seen in his search for an answer and then he remembered the large black book lying on the stone table in the room next door. The answer had to be in that book, he must find out what was in it if he was to save her.

Gathering his resolve for the task that lay ahead of them, he knew it would take every last drop of courage that they had left and every last grain luck as well. They had to face revisiting the sickening horrors they had endured in the previous half an hour and just hope they would get away with it once more.

Gently nudging Will,

"Will, we just have to do something, we just can't leave Miriam with those animals like that. She's so brave and stuck up for us by not telling them anything. She must be terrified all alone except for these evil monsters. Let's hope that wherever India is, she's getting help so we might not have to be on our own for much longer."

Will instantly agreed, that no matter what the danger they must rescue her.

"What do you suggest then?"

"I wish I had my powers back and could hear where they are and what they're saying but there gone so we just have to be extra careful. First, we have to leave Randolph here, he's too drugged to move anyway and we will probably have to come back this way and we can collect him then. We need to get out of here now and get to the curtain for a peek to see if anything is going on the other side," after that we just have to play it by ear."

"Ok, let's go then," Agreeing with him

Dominic pressed his ear, once more against the door and listened. Nothing could be heard, not even chanting, the silence was overbearing and conspicuous by the total absence of any noise. It was if it was laying down the gauntlet for him to pick up and enter into the evil arena that awaited him. How he now wished to hear the chant of voices that before he found to be so hideous, because it would mean that at least they were occupied and it would reveal where they were. But no such luck was forth coming, perhaps he had used it all up.

Steeling himself ready for what he knew they had to face ahead, he slowly pressed against the doors but they refused to move, he pressed again, firmer this time but still they refused to open. They didn't need this now, he angrily thought and pushed again. Suddenly, to his horror the doors flew wide open and instinctively he threw his arms over his head and curled up in a ball as tightly as he could, hoping that it was all a bad dream and waited and waited. The moments ticked slowly past relishing upon the drama that was unfolding on this macabre stage but nothing happened, and he slowly prised open his eyes and glimpsed out.

All around him the familiar dancing figures of the demons from the candles were performing their black magic with even more fervour now, beckoning them to the fate that awaited

His face had now completely drained of the small touch of colour that the ordeal had savaged upon him, and at least he took comfort from knowing that his luck had decided not to desert him yet. Slowly he uncurled himself and along with Will, stumbled out of their hiding place. Immediately they grimaced with the pain from their limbs that had been so cramped for so long and tried stretching as best they could in the fractions of time they could spare.

He looked fondly down at Randolph oblivious to what was been going on all around him,

"So long fella, I'll be back but at least you're safer here" and they closed the doors carefully behind them.

Once again, they slowly stepped across the familiar grey stone flags that epitomised the sinister characteristics of its inhabitants to the ominous black curtain screen covering the open archway that led from the vestibule room to the temple.

He knew the procedure now. Standing back slightly back to give himself that slight angle without betraying him and glanced into the temple. It was clear, there was no one there and the two boys once again entered the temple.

"They must have gone into that side ante room again, that doorway at the far end almost opposite that round table," whispered Dominic and wasted no time in crossing the room to the table again.

"We have to find that black book, without that, whatever they are going to do to Miriam they won't be able to, I'm sure of it.!

At first, he could see that nothing had altered, the clothing was still hanging up against the wall, the table was still there, as were the silver chalices. He paused to listen, the building was still totally quiet just waiting for him to give himself away when it would erupt into a deafening crescendo. He reached the table and felt its cold chill and turned his head to find the Black Book.

It wasn't there, he began to panic, his heart rate, as if in unison with his state of panic rapidly increased. *"It has to be here… it just has to,"* he prayed. He turned around and bent down to look under the table. The dark shadows that the candles formed deliberately making it difficult for him to see clearly, he stretched out his arms to search into the black corners; but nothing but emptiness greeted him. He stood up and gazed around the room, the only two places left that it could possibly be, were in the tall cupboards.

Forgetting the extreme danger, he was in for most fleeting of moments, he rushed across and reached the nearer one and without any thought of minimising any possible noise pulled it open. The cupboard lay empty but this time even the silver chalices, bowl and the sacrificial knife were missing; had any colour still remained in his colourless complexion it would surely now disappear.

The realisation of what lay ahead for Miriam came flooding back into his thoughts and he closed the door again.

What do I do now? pausing to think, there was only one option left for him; he had to take a look into the room behind the two large doors which carried the demonic sign of the inverted pentagram and see if Miriam was in there.

Of all the rooms before, this without doubt was the most daunting. He knew that there would be something so terrifying in there, that's why it had the most robust doors of all.

"Will, we have no choice, she must be here behind these huge doors."

"I know, I was thinking the same but praying she wasn't"

"Ok, lets both go in together at the same time."

And Dominic turned and faced towards the imposing oak doors that led into the room from Hell. He knew what he had to do but if this went wrong then that would be the end of all three of them.

Purposefully he stepped towards the door and wiped the droplets of sweat from his forehead that were glistening in the candlelight and reached the door taking a deep breath before opening it.

Once again he heard nothing,

Was it because there was no noise coming from inside? Or was it because the door was too solid to hear through? Went through his mind and how he wished he had brought some potion to restore his hearing powers.

There was no way of knowing and Dominic knew that there was only one way of finding out.

He studied the flickering light from the candles trying to work out if there was a possible sequence when they went a touch dimmer. He felt that the darker his side was the less noticeable it would be when they opened the door. After a few moments he realised he was clutching at straws and wishful thinking was not going to help in this of all places. Again, he inhaled deeply and exhaled as slowly as he could collecting his mind and body to be ready for the challenge that awaited them and tightly gripped the cast iron ring handle of one of the doors and slowly turned it.

Suddenly, a tiny crack appeared running the full length of the door between the jamb and the oak door, brighter light flooded in. He paused for a few seconds and waited for any response from the other side. Nothing happened, had they not noticed or was nobody there? He continued to open the door further, slowly but deliberately he pulled it further open and took his first peek inside.

Their thoughts were right and Dominic glanced at Will as if to confirm the same. They had entered into the most sinister and evil room they could ever imagine. It was a continuation of the temple but the most evil and secret part kept only for the most special of rituals. It was the most gruesome and petrifying place there ever could be.

It was the Altar Room and long black candles adorned the black painted walls, offering the only source of light into the room. The high vaulted ceiling was similarly meticulously blackened out as if the slightest resemblance of any colour was the gravest of all the satanic sins. The ever present large grey bare stone flagged floors once again seem to embrace the setting that they were in. There appeared to be the remnants of a window that had been skilfully covered over and once again the sea of black had again done its evil task and engulfed it.

Keeping a close eye on the door which they had entered through, in the middle of the stone floor and painstakingly carved into it was a four-metre sized occult sign of the inverted pentagram painted in the same deep claret red as the one on the doors. Dominic, carefully skirted around the symbol believing that to tread upon it or walk across would meet with certain fate.

He looked up towards the full-length stone altar, which by the various compass markings was set in the east of the temple. And was immediately taken aback by a huge image of half-dressed woman, hung from the wall and which the candles had suddenly brought to life, daring him to approach this satanic place of worship. She was seated and bare from the waist up. In her left hand she was holding two broken halves of a silver needle and in her other hand a burning torch touching the bottom of a book of what looked like a religious book of some sort as if to set it on fire. Dominic immediately noted the relationship of the image of the broken needle to the one he possessed. Perhaps that's what they really wanted, the needle!

Without knowing it, Dominic had discovered the image of the Bride of Lucifer, The Baphomet, a violent Goddess.

One silver candleholder adorned the altar at each end, each encapsulating a black candle which flickered, lighting up the black altar cloth that covered it. At the head of the altar resting open on a black oak lectern lay the Black Book he had been searching for. Two large silver chalices lay on the floor in front together with the sacrificial knife that had disappeared from the cupboard in the main temple.

Dominic, tried to swallow but his throat was too dry and parched. He steadied himself and then climbed the two steps leading up to the altar. In the middle of the black altar cloth was emblazoned another satanic inverted pentagram. He paused, there was the contoured shape of a person underneath the cloth. The cloth was covering someone. His heart yet again jump started into action.

Was it Miriam? Was she dead?

His head once again flooded with grotesque permutations. He braced himself for the worst and with Will, they each took hold of a corner edge of the black covering that were the nearest to the topographical features of a person's face.

Dreading this moment, as they could not see the cloth rising and falling, as it would naturally be if someone was breathing, they slowly lifted it up until it was sufficiently high enough for them to bend down and look underneath.

Fearing it was Miriam and they would find her dead, Dominic's almost natural instinct now of taking a deep breath before embarking on any such traumatic actions once again came into play. He held his breath and bent down to see.

"Miriam" he gasped in total relief, letting out the breath he had been holding in, "Your alive."

The terrified look of total and absolute fear in her eyes greeted him, as if she had been expecting that with the pulling back of the black veil, it signified the start of the final scene of her fatal hideous end. The penetrating look of terror in her eyes changed to one of complete and utter relief as her eyes welled up with tears. The raised red blotched swellings under them from where she had been previously crying revealed the full trauma of her ordeal.

Her wrists were tightly bound together underneath her by plastic cord bindings and a white silk scarf was tightly tied around her mouth ensuring her complete silence. Her clothing had been totally removed and she had been re- dressed in a plain white simple nightdress.

Dominic, glanced up at the repulsive picture of Lucifer's bride, hanging above the altar and shuddered at what they had in mind for her. He put his fingers underneath the white silk gag and forcefully prised it slightly away from the tight grip it had held across her mouth. She gulped in a huge mouthful of the so precious air she had been deprived of.

"Dominic….," she could utter no more, as tears continued to stream profusely down her face. Dominic, gently holding her shoulders pulled her upright into a sitting position and held her closely in his arms placing her head against his shoulder. He held the embrace that they both desperately sought for only a few precious moments until the flow of tears abated and then carefully moved her slightly away. He wanted to hold her forever, he had never before experienced the warmth and helplessness of a girl and it felt so overwhelming, but he knew that to do so any longer would be perilous. He started to frantically work on trying to undo the nylon cord that was viciously biting into her wrists.

"Just listen," he whispered. "If they come back, we have to dash away."

Miriam threw her head violently shaking from side to side in complete panic, the few brief moments of respite, when she thought she was being saved completely vanished only to be replaced with the overwhelming fear of what lay ahead.

"Miriam, listen to me," pleading with her. "We won't be far, but if we don't, we've had it."

Miriam was almost hysterical and shaking her whole body as if she knew what fate awaited her. Dominic, let go of the binding and firmly but as kindly as he possibly could, held her soft face in his hands and looked into her innocent and frightened tearful jade eyes.

"Miriam…. Miriam," he repeated again in a firm but friendly whisper," I am not going to leave you; do you understand?"

Miriam slowly started to calm down and Dominic, loosened the firmness of his grip on her face, now gently holding it once more. Again he repeated, as if to re-assure her, now she understood.

"I am not going to leave you, but if they come back, we've got to hide somewhere until I get my chance."

The torrential flood of tears had now subsided into a gentle trickle and she nodded her head as if to accept complete surrender. Dominic smiled at her and slowly whispered,

"I've missed you" and Miriam as if to say the same to him nodded her head.

It was now a race against time, Dominic, furiously trying to undue the steel like grip the vicious nylon binding had her wrists in. He knew that there was no hiding place big enough for the two of them, it was essential that she was totally freed from all her bindings for them to stand any chance of making a successful escape. At least by doing it this way, if they suddenly re-appeared they could quickly cover her back up and dash off to hide and they hopefully would not notice that anything had happened.

The sweat rolled down the side of his face as both he and Will continued to try to force open the cord enough for her to slide her hands out. But the redness of her wrists showed that the battle was extracting a painful toll. Dominic knew he couldn't see her suffer any more this way and somehow, he would have to find something sharp and cut through the heavy plastic. He turned to glance around the room looking for any sharp implement.

"The candles" he hastily but excitedly whispered, "Of course, when didn't I think of that before," reprimanding himself. The candles that had once been the malignant source of those villainous dancing shadows could ironically now, help save them. He reached across for the silver candle holder that grimly adorned the top of the altar and placing it next to him reached inside for the candle. Without warning the very faint sound of a distant drumming abruptly broke the silence. He stopped and put his finger against Miriam's mouth.

"Shh," he whispered, Miriam focused on him. Dominic tilted his head to one side to pin point the sound. The distinct sound of a single repetitive drum beat could now be clearly heard. He quickly, turned around and looked at Miriam,

"I have to go now," he gently whispered, "but I won't be far."

She nodded back to him, too emotionally exhausted now to disagree. He quickly replaced the candle holder onto the altar and carefully holding her in an embrace, he wished would last for ever, gently laid her back down onto the waiting cold altar table. Gently, pulling back over her the suffocating black altar cloth, he gave her one last reassuring smile. Her heavy sad eyes looked forlornly at him, overwhelming him with a sense of loss that he had never experienced. He desperately didn't want to leave her there.

For the first time someone so precious and innocent was totally dependent upon him and all he could do was run away. He felt disgusted with himself but deep down he knew he had little choice.

Quickly standing up and straightening out any creases in that terrible veil that covered her, Dominic turned to make his way back through the temple to their hiding place with Randolph. Jumping silently down from the two altar steps they quickly returned back through the huge door that led back into the temple, closing the door on Miriam.

It didn't take them long at all to cross the temple and had just crossed back through the curtain into the vestibule, when the sound of the drumming became sharply and audibly louder but now, it was joined with the distinctive mono tone chanting. It was coming from the hallway and about to enter their room. It was far too late now to jump back into the cupboard where they hid before and where Randolph lay.

"What now?" In the loudest whisper Will could manage and in a highly agitated state of desperation

"We have no choice but to go back," and both started to sprint back across the temple to where the round table stood. Almost simultaneously, they heard same malevolent sound of another procession, and with the same unison chanting and drumming but it was approaching from the side door to the ante room opposite.

They were trapped inside the temple, there was no way out and they both reeled around, frantically thinking and looking for a hiding place.

Both processions were closing in on the temple, the sound of the single repetitive drum beat from both directions on the taught dear hide of the wooden tabor together with the chant was numbing their minds.

Dominic shook his head as if to clear it when his eyes fell upon the tall slender wardrobes in the corner. One, of which they had never looked in and there but he had no time to worry about that and they made a dash across to it, immediately noticing the brass key hole in the door.

"Please don't be locked," his mind begged and gave the handle a stern pull. The door flew open and almost without caring they both jumped inside simultaneously pulling the door closed behind them.

They were in shear panic and made ten times worse by trying to control their breathing to almost no existent state. There could not be a more dangerous and frightening place to be in the world. Their hearts had never before beaten as fast and all they could do was hold their nerve and hope.

The drumming and chanting had now reached directly outside where they hid. Both processions had now joined together in the temple.

A few moments later Dominic could hear the sounds of the two enormous arched doors to the alter room being opened.

The temple had now become fully, just one grotesque place of evil.

CHAPTER SIXTEEN

BESTIA TERRAE IS SUMMONED

Although Dominic had heard the chanting verses for almost half the time they had been trapped inside the chapel, he knew that this time that they carried a most deadly and sinister threat in them. He thought of Miriam lying there and how petrified she must be. The reciting was penetrating right through to the very soul of him let alone her as she lay so unprotected and helpless there.

"Dies irae, dies illa
Solvet Saeclum in favilla
Teste Satan cum sibylla.
Quantos tremor est futurus
Quando Vindex est venturus
Cuncta stricte discussurus.
Dies irae, dies illa"

The drumming stopped, Dominic wished he could see what was going on, he had to, he was Miriam's only chance. Painstakingly slowly he started to twist his body away from the corner he had squashed himself into when he jumped inside the wardrobe. Inch by inch he slowly turned, stiffening his body each time to conceal even the most diminutive of noises. As he twisted, he noticed a tiny shaft of speckled dusty light hitting his shoulder, which immediately focused his thoughts.

The key hole," of course it's not covered up, "if only I can somehow just turn enough to see through. Cheered by his discovery he agonisingly, carefully wriggled and manoeuvred himself into a position where at least he could glimpse outside and see what macabre spectacle they were performing. Ignoring the discomfort that his twisted body was now in, he pressed his eye to the key hole.

"Dies irae, dies illa
Solvet Saeclum in favilla
Teste Satan cum sibylla.
Quantos tremor est futurus
Quando Vindex est venturus
Cuncta stricte discussurus.
Dies irae, dies illa"

The familiar awesome words greeted him as did the spectral beat of the tabor as it once again took up its rightful place in the Theatre of the Devil.

Against the backdrop of ghostly un-earthly shadows that papered the whole room, as if setting the stage for this final dramatic drama, he could see that both altar doors were now wide open. Seamlessly the altar room formed the headstone to the whole temple

A group of twelve tall slender faceless figures, robed completely from head to foot in black, were walking bare footed in slow procession around the engraved pentagram on the temple floor. All but one were carrying a silver lantern enclosing a single, fluttering black candle. They were slowly swinging from side to side in perfect rhythm with the beating tabor, which was being carried by the twelfth apostate. Each rotation they paced around the altar's encircled pentagram was perfectly timed to accomplish the complete single verse of the chant and then the ritual was repeated. The setting was awe-inspiring and Dominic was becoming hypnotised by the sinister performance of it all.

Abruptly, a loud handclap echoed through the darkness shattering the drone of the ritual performers who ceased immediately. Freezing in mid step as if totally controlled by an external mystique force. Dominic pulled back from the keyhole in shock, a thin film of perspiration on his forehead started shimmering as it was caught in the beam of light. He paused, waiting to gain some composure from the trembling that was vibrating through his entire body.

"Hail Satan, Prince of Life," a deep voice that Dominic, instantly recognised the evilness in it and knowing it to be of their Master, boomed out splitting the silence of the temple.

"Prince of Darkness hear us."

Dominic, summoning up his courage once more, peered out again through the keyhole.

"May Satan the all-powerful Prince of Darkness
And Lord of Earth
Grant us our desires."

Dominic, looked across to the Pentagram where he had witnessed the sinister circular procession only moments before. One by one they were now silently making their way up the altar room towards the altar itself and where Miriam lay. He turned and looked towards the altar and standing there, in front of it with his arms raised as if in honour to the grotesque picture of Lucifer's bride was the most fearsome figure of all.

Standing with his back to the approaching congregation and robed completely in black, with the scarlet sign of the inverted pentagram displayed across his shoulders was the High Priest. Dominic realised, that it was their Master who was this figure of the darkest evil, as he turned and faced his grim followers,

"Hear me, all of you gathered in my temple! Hear me, all you bound by the magic of our Lord the Prince of Darkness! Hear me, you dark gods gathering to witness this rite."

And then he signalled with his hands that they should form a motionless circle around the altar. One by one they took up their static positions, and when they fully encircled the altar, he again turned to the symbolic picture on the wall.

Dominic was powerless to do anything. He had never felt so hopeless in his life before, he could see the forlorn, limpness shape of Miriam lying under the black veil and could only imagine the terror that she must be going through. He knew that all he could do was watch in silence as the hideous ritual unfolded and pray for just one chance to rescue her but he all he could do until then was watch and wait. He turned his concentration back to the High Priest who was continuing with the deadly rite.

"I believe in one Prince, Satan, who reigns over this Earth, and in one law which triumphs over all. I believe in one temple, our Temple to Satan, and in one world which triumphs over all:" The High Priest then turning to his assembled brethren signalled them to re-commence their procession but this time around the symbolic altar.

One by one, in an anticlockwise direction, with the tabor leading, they started their deathly walk. The sound of the single beating of the drum resonating through every sinew in Dominic's body. Around and around the altar the cortege proceeded but with each turn the drum beat becoming louder. Around and around they went and louder and louder became the sound of the tabor, when on the seventh cycle the priest signalled for them to stop. Immediately, an ominous and ghastly silence fell across the temple. Dominic's instincts instantly told him that the ceremony was now moving on to a more ghastly phase.

The High Priest turning to face the altar, picked up one of the silver chalices from the front of it and raised it in the air towards the picture. And gestured a toast to their gruesome idol of what was about to happen to their pagan captive.

"I, Oger, the High Priest and Master of this temple, I am here to begin my sinister quest! Prince of Darkness, hear my oath! Baphomet, Mistress of Earth, hear me! Hear me, you Dark Gods waiting beyond the Abyss!" Then slowly reaching across to the open Black Book on the stand, tore out a section of one of the pages. Then blessing it, placed it into the chalice.

Dominic, his eyes transfixed on Miriam's profile knew that the moment had come, all he could hear was the intolerable overwhelming pounding of his heart. The High Priest lowering the chalice looked down upon Miriam's prostrate outlined form and with his right hand made the sign of the inverted pentagram over her.

"I believe in one temple
Our temple to Satan,
And I believe in the law of the Aeon,
Which is sacrifice, and in the letting of blood
For which I shed no tears since I give praise to my Prince
The fire-giver and look forward to his reign"

With those words he flung back the black veil exposing her to the horrific pageant that she was the centrepiece of. Miriam was sobbing uncontrollably; her whole body was trembling with cold and fear. She had lay there, totally defenceless and vulnerable and had been subjected to hearing the whole hideous ceremony waiting for that dreaded moment. Oger, the High Priest looked down on her bloodshot eyes and from deep within his hood a hint of a sardonic smile emerged. With the chalice still in his left hand he stooped down and picked up the sacrificial knife by the other hand and held them both aloft in a symbolic gesture to the picture.

"To you, Satan, Prince of Darkness and Lord of the Earth,
I dedicate this offering,
A sacrifice for your power and an expression of your glory"

Dominic froze, all the feeling in his body left him, he wanted desperately to throw open the doors and rush out but he was totally paralysed. He tried shouting but not a sound uttered from his parched lips, all he could do was watch helplessly. Miriam screamed but the dryness of her throat and the muzzle around her mouth thwarted all her attempts. She closed her eyes and waited for the inevitable end.

Oger slowly lowered the knife and chalice to just over Miriam's forehead and without emotion or feeling, swiftly cut his protruding left thumb. Dominic, still spell bound watched in utter relief as he let the drops of blood sprinkle on to the waiting parchment lying in the chalice.

"With my blood I dedicate this humble offering
Prince of Darkness, hear me, Baphomet, Mistress of Earth, hear me! Hear me, Satan, please send forth your messenger Bestia Terrae to carry to you our humble offering."

With that plea, the priest reached for one of the altar candles and lit the contents of the chalice.

"Satan, may your power mingle with mine as my blood now mingles with fire"

The parchment fluttered into a ruby flame glimmering faintly against the silver goblet. Moments passed as the flame died and then the priest, placing his forefinger into the liquefied embers, inscribed on Miriam's forehead their evil inverted pentagram sign. Then placing the cup to his mouth, tasted the potion.

"With this drink I seal my offering. I am yours and shall do works to the glory of your name. Agios o Satanas, Agios o Bestia Terrae, Agios o Bestia Terrae, my offering awaits."

"Satanas - venire! Satanas venire! Agios 0 Baphomet"

With that, the Priest removed the veil completely from Miriam and signalled to his expressionless congregation for them to depart. Slowly, he followed them out of the temple, through into the vestibule, once again to the drumming of the tabor abandoning Miriam to await the fate of the Bestia Terrae.

Dominic, his exhausted body starting to free themselves from their paralysis collapsed in nervous exhaustion. She had got through it, somehow Miriam had survived, it didn't matter what ritual had just taken place, she was still alive. He could hear the diminishing sound of the cortege as they left the temple. He knew that he had to desperately restrain the uncontrollable urge to rush out to Miriam, for he realised that they had probably gone out through the vestibule. He had to wait and be patient and make sure that they had gone but at least now he felt slightly easier. He put his head onto his folded arms, closed his eyes and breathing a huge sigh of relief, whispered to Will.

"Will, that was terrifying, thank God, nothing happened to her, I couldn't watch anything like that again. I think they may be gone now for a while as something called Bestia Terrae is coming, whatever that is but it doesn't sound good that's for sure. We'll give them two three minutes and then try and rescue her and get out of this place as fast as possible."

The three minutes seemed like an hour but at last they pushed open their cupboard doors ready to step out. He could see Miriam still lying there motionless and the candles gently flickering around her but nothing else moved it was totally silent. Stepping out and closing the doors behind them Dominic quickly rushed over to the door to the ante room opposite where one the nearest procession had entered from.

Putting his ear to it was totally soundless but he had to know whether anyone was in there or not as to risk untying her without knowing that was just too great. He gradually turned the handle of the door until the slightest of gaps appeared and then paused. Nothing happened, it was totally quiet, seemingly everyone must have left via the vestibule. They were completely all alone in the temple.

"Will, you double check on Miriam and try and undo those bonds, I need to check the vestibule to make sure they've all left and we're safe."

His heart lit up and the adrenalin started to race through his body. Hurrying across to the vestibule curtain, Dominic paused to listen. There was just silence, no noise at all. Convinced that they had definitely left, he slowly peaked around the curtain, the room stood empty. The sense of relief was so powerful that for the first time in ages he allowed himself to take a deep breath.

Randolph, suddenly sprang into his mind. *I better check on him now I'm here.* A sense of hope started to flood through his body, his limbs felt lighter, his movements now had purpose to them all the tiredness and exhaustion he had previously felt had totally evaporated. He hastily pulled open the doors to where his lifelong pet lay and to his relief, still lying there fast asleep oblivious to all the dramatic events that had taken place was his still prostrate friend.

"Sorry Pal, I'll pick you up on the way out," and closed the doors. This was his chance, he could feel that they had all left, he could taste and touch the feeling of freedom. He knew that within minutes he could have them all outside in the safety of the open countryside. He raced back across the room and into the temple to where Miriam lay.

"They've gone, quickly shouting to the two of them," as he eagerly bounded up the two altar steps sending a draught of air into the dimly glowing candles, exploding them into life. He reached the side of her and gently shook her shoulder, "Miriam, I think they've gone," excitingly repeating it. She didn't stir, her body was totally numb and frozen from the coldness and emptiness of the massive stone altar upon which she had lain on for so long. He gazed down upon her face, it was lifeless and totally devoid of any emotion. Her eyes were closed and the constant streams of tears that had previously profusely flowed down her cheeks, were now replaced by caked stained channels of white salt.

The immense trauma that she had unbearably had to endure had taken its toll, it was if she had already accepted a horrible fatal ending was inevitable and she had given up all hope of escape. Dominic put his arms around her and sat her up, talking softly to her as Will reached for the candle and quickly burnt through the vicious nylon cords that had bound her hands and feet for so long. Her wrists showed the brave signs of the struggle she had been through.

He gently massaged them trying to bring a faint sign of life back into her ashen hands.

"Miriam, it's all right now we're safe, I promise that no matter what, I'll never leave you alone again." A faint colour started to slowly seep back into them and he let them gently rest on her lap. He turned his efforts to the silk scarf around her mouth that had forced her silence and fumbled with the knots that it was tied with, in his impatience to get her warm and free. At last, it fell away and for the first time a sign of life fluttered in her eyes. Dominic embraced her tightly trying to share the warmth of his body with hers; "We'll be out of her soon," he whispered in her ear and he felt her head move gently against his cheek in acknowledgement that she now understood.

"I've found your clothes" as he rushed over to the wardrobe where he had hidden in silent witness to the ordeal.

"Look, hear they are," and dashed back to her, placing her clothes on her lap. Miriam smiled as if now believing that her familiar, friendly clothes did really mean that it was all over.

"Dominic, Oh Dominic, is it really over? Have they gone?" At last, Miriam spurted back into life.

"Yes, I'm sure of it, I've not checked outside, but they must have. Quickly, get dressed and let's get out of here," trying now to instill a sense of urgency in her. He still felt highly uneasy about the possibility of them returning, and he so wanted desperately to escape from the foreboding darkness of the temple.

"Dominic, you'll have to turn around whilst a get changed," now gaining more composure as each second passed. Dominic turned around and faced the doors and started to reflect on the past events.

"You know, what I can't understand, is why they went to all that trouble and then just left you, why did they do it?"

"You don't suppose that they've not finished yet?" becoming slightly agitated once again.

"No, I'm sure they've gone, I'm certain of it," trying to be positive and re-assure both of them. "Are you nearly dressed now?"

"Almost, you can turn around now,"

"Look, you just finish putting on your trainers and I'll just go down and double check the hallway.

"Don't leave me," instantly becoming more nervous and the thought of ever being left alone again.

"Will, is here and will stay at your side whilst I'll try the far door… it's the other side of the curtain to the vestibule," pointing to the curtain at the end of the temple. "You can see me all the time, I promise."

"All right, but please be quick."

Dominic hurried down the steps towards the curtain screen and pulling it back a small amount so Miriam could see, went to open the door to the hallway.

"It's locked!" shouting back in a raised voice and immediately becoming suspicious.

"What do you mean, it's locked?" Came back the unison concerned response from both of them.

"I mean they must have a key and locked it. It won't open," as he had one last tug at the door.

Quickly finishing tying the last bow on her trainers, Will and Miriam raced cross the temple to join Dominic. Panic was now beginning to set in. All three tried again to open the door but it was firmly locked, there was no way out that way.

"Quickly, see if the door to that ante room is open, the one near the altar room where we've just come from," and now all three were rushing to try it, becoming more nervous by the second.

Will reached it first.

"I can't open it…. this is locked as well," his voice now displaying a note of fear in it.

"Let me try," Dominic almost pushing Will aside. He was quickly losing patience and starting to sense that something was very seriously wrong. A sense of panic and urgency had now overtaken his previously controlled and calming actions. He turned the big rolled iron ring handle and yanked it with all his might, but it was no use. This door too was securely locked.

"Stand Back," as he tried desperately to kick and shoulder the door open, but the solid oak door that had withstood the test of time was not going to concede to such punitive, feeble attempts. Exhausted, he stopped.

"What are we going to do, I'm sacred…. I couldn't live if they came back and did something else to me, I'd rather kill myself…Dom.." Dominic interrupted her flow of almost hysteria.

"Calm down, let's think…" but it was useless, they were trapped, there was no possible way out. Dominic, knew now that there was more danger to come but what was it?

CHAPTER SEVENTEEN

INDIA CAUGHT AS WELL

It didn't take too long for India to reach the footpath alongside the formidable, intimidating wood again. She paused for just a moment to control her fears, trying to reassure herself that it was all in her imagination and stop being so stupid. In the daylight it would be a beautiful place with people walking their dogs and children playing hide and seek behind the trees.

Tightly squeezing her stomach muscles and taking a deep breath she was ready to continue. As before, when they first came this way some two hours earlier, the sounds of the branches rustling did their very best to unsettle her, but India was made of stronger stuff.

With a steely determination that could not be waived, on she kept going not even diverting her eyes for just the merest fraction of a second to take just a glimpse of the wood. Nothing could distract her from completely focusing on what small bit of the footpath she could see ahead and nothing else.

Five minutes later she was through the ordeal and the stressful emotion of it all evaporated away in almost an instant. She felt even happy that she had passed the most fearsome of challenges. The others would be so proud of her if only they knew. Ahead of her now was easy, the scout camp was not too far and surely anytime soon there would be a signal on her phone.

Her mind cast back to what dangers the others must be facing now and she should stop praising herself and focus on trying to save them instead. On she walked gathering pace in the hope that a phone signal would show soon.

No sooner had she checked her phone, a car's headlights swung into view. Her heart picked up its pace with shear relief that her part of the ordeal was over. It was a brilliant piece of luck as now she could ask for help even without a signal. She stopped and waited as it approached her, the car's headlight beams now picking her out.

Almost simultaneously a phone signal came alive and everything was in her favour now. Phone in hand she started to frantically wave to the approaching car just to make absolutely sure that she was seen, and a few moments later the car had pulled up next to her.

Immediately, India shouted out.

"Please can you help, I need your help urgently. My friends are up there," pointing in the direction of the church, "in a church being held prisoners and need rescuing. Can you call the police?"

The passenger's car window wound down and a voice sounded.

"What's happened to your friends? Someone's kidnapped them in a church you say?"

"Yes, it's up there," once again pointing in the same direction. "Beyond that footpath and across a field, there's a church and they're in there."

"Ahh, I think I know the church, you mean, Llangelynin Old Church?"

"I don't know what it's called but if it's the other side of that path then that must be it. Please can you hurry, I'm really scared for them."

"Jump in the back then and we'll take you to the police station, it's not far," and with that India opened the rear passenger door to get in. She had one foot inside when the interior lighting of the car came on and she could make out that the two men in the front were dressed in black hooded robes.

In that instance, India instinctively realised that they had something to do with the abbey and let out the loudest scream ever as she jumped back out of the car and started to run back towards the woods.

Almost as quick, the two front doors of the car opened and the two robed men jumped out and gave chase after her.

This time the woods presented no fear whatsoever for India, indeed just the opposite. It was her protector and she immediately ran deep inside, stopping behind a particularly large tree and stopped.

In the distance, she could hear the sounds of the two men looking for her. Her breathing was rapid and she had to control it otherwise they would hear it and give her away. Taking deep breaths, she slowly manged to lower her rate to an almost inaudible level.

The men had now separated and she could hear them heading in her direction from different sides. She was doing everything to stop panting so loudly but it was becoming too difficult. She knew she couldn't hide there any longer as they would soon be upon her, and started to run further into the woods when a pair of vice-like arms suddenly grasped around her chest, pinning her arms.

India shrieked and screamed as loud as ever she could but it was futile, there was no one around to hear her.

A rough hand quickly and firmly held her mouth closed and a deep threatening voice whispered in her ear.

"Shut up now, there's good girl or I'll have to hurt you. No one can hear her you. Do you understand?" Emphasising the last sentence. India nodded that she did.

"I'm going to take my hand away now and you better not make a noise or else it will be very painful for you, **Understood!**"

Once again India nodded and he removed his hand from her mouth.

But she had not given up yet, far from it. She had a very good idea in her mind of what would happen to her once he got her back to the abbey. *These were extremely nasty and evil people, otherwise why would they chase me and drag me back? What has happened to Dominic and Will and why did they kidnap Randolph? They were terrifyingly dangerous people and no matter what, I have to be prepared to get away before we get back otherwise it would be too late then. For the moment I'll act compliant with all their instructions and hope that they become less attentive and complacent, then I will make a move.*

It wasn't long before the other robed pursuer reached them.

"Are you ok with her or do you want me to help?" He snapped out breathing quite hard from his exertion.

"No, I can handle her alright."

"Well, the abbey is only ten to fifteen minutes from the path. Rather than take her back to the car and waste time, if you can manage her on your own, you take her straight there and I go and fetch the car."

"That's no problem, she's behaving herself now," giving India a bit of a push and the three of them started to make their way out of the wood and onto the footpath.

Immediately, India's mind jumped into action. *Brilliant, I'm down to just one of them now. I'll try and strike up a conversation with him as that's what they tell you to do if someone ever kidnaps you. I'll walk along talking rubbish but not too far, as I have to race back to the wood again to disappear and catch him by surprise.*

They were soon back on the footpath and after a very brief few words between the two captors, India and her guardian were on their way heading back up to the abbey and almost immediately, she started to strike up a conversation.

"So, what do you do up there? Did you give up with God or something? Are you part of a huge community throughout the country? Almost never stopping with questions. Eventually, she could feel his grip on her start to loosen and he even seemed to be enjoying enlightening her all about their beliefs and up they continued to walk.

They had left the footpath behind a couple of minutes back and were continuing across the fields when, in the merest of an instance she felt his grip loosen. Immediately she forcibly broke his grip from her arm and as quick as a flash, she was away and running as fast as she's ever done towards the wood

"Hey, come back here," screamed her kidnapper after her starting to give chase. It was only some four hundred metres to the wood but the running was made so much harder by the hollows and mounds which were haphazardly littered across the field, caused by the cattle that grazed there.

There was no way on this Earth that India was going to stop. She had a lead of a hundred metres on him and she would be entering the wood in just a few seconds where he would not find her this time.

Her adrenal kicked in, her blood was pumping through her body, she was even pulling away from her chasing captor, she was going to be safe and free.

Too late! She had no chance of seeing that deep nasty hollow and over she fell hitting the hard ground hard. She lay prone on the cold field, bruised and sore and before she could even get to her knees he was on her.

She was devastated, she was there she was safe, five seconds more that's all she needed but fate had cruelly decided otherwise. Her captor thoroughly annoyed that she had played him and almost got away, took no chances this time. Forcing her arm up behind her back, extremely roughly forcibly marched her up towards the awaiting abbey. This time without a single spoken word.

Ten minutes later, they had arrived at the church entrance and a despondent and terrified India was thrust through doors into the startled gathering.

"Who's this?" The High Prest's voiced shouted out, disturbing the sombre ritual that they had been chanting. "Where's she come?" Again demanding to know and expressing urgency.

"We went back as you ordered to look for that Dominic and we found her. She's with them and Dominic is here."

"What!" Now grabbing India himself and vigorously shaking her.

"Are you with this Dominic and you say he's in here somewhere?" India was overcome with fear and finding it impossible to virtually even mutter a sound.

"Speak up girl, is he in here somewhere?" and the best she could manage was to look down at her feet and slowly nod her head. But still the punishing questioning continued.

"How many of you are there? Speak up girl,"

"Four." Meekly responding in a quite whisper.

"Four, you're sure? You better be telling us the truth or it will be the worse for you." Once again, India nodded in total acceptance of her defeat and inescapable situation.

"And where are you staying in Wales. Master Pepper mentioned Colwyn Bay, hurry up, where?" Aggressively shouting at her.

"I think it's something like, Bron-y something Holiday Park."

"I know it, the Bron-y-Wendon Holiday Park, that will do."

The High Priest then turning to his sect.

"As we can't get into the temple or disturb our Prince until dawn, take her to the kitchen and tie her up there, we can then deal with her in the morning. And you," pointing to one of his followers, "can stand outside and keep a lookout in case this Master Dominic appears. Right, off you go."

And with that India was marched out of the church and across to the kitchen and securely bound and gagged to await her fate at dawn

CHAPTER EIGHTEEN

THE BATLLE OF GOOD V EVIL

Back in the temple, Dominic sat down on that dreaded altar and began to take stock of the situation and reflect upon what to do next. The feeling of despondency had once again returned as did his tired muscles.

"We're trapped, aren't we, we're not going to get out of her?" Miriam asking him at the same time as collapsing down next to him. Dominic now trying to work it all out and speaking his thoughts to them both.

"It doesn't make sense, why have they gone. Because they definitely have, they'd have heard all the noise we've been making. Why did they leave you? What was it all about? I mean the ceremony. If they wanted to harm you, they would have already done so. What does it mean?" Dominic asking himself rhetorically. "What was the ceremony about?"

"I don't know, I was far too scared to listen, I just kept my eyes and ears closed to everything and just prayed." Mirriam trying her best to control her sniffing.

"I'm sure it was about an offering or something. I remember the High Priest, or whatever he was saying, he dedicated this offering, a sacrifice for power and something else about, sending forth a messenger, Bestia Terrae to carry their humble offering. It sounds like they expect someone or something else to come. I wonder who or what is this Bestia Terrae?" Dominic pondering his own questions.

"What time is it Will?" Suddenly jumping up and realising the importance of the time.

"It's nearly nine o'clock."

Dominic, still frantically searching his mind for answers to his questions, he knew that whatever was going to happen now all hinged around the Bestia Terrae.

"I know, I know where I might find the answer to what's going to happen next."

"What do you mean?"

"I know where they keep the book that's full of the worship's and rites they use," as he jumped down from the altar and dashed off into the temple.

It was in here," rushing into the room, but the table was empty. He hurried over to the adjacent cupboard and threw open the doors. It was full of the ceremonial implements he had seen before, even the ceremonial knife, but not the book. He then realised that it was too important for them to leave behind. Depressed and with head down, he walked back towards Will and Miriam.

"Did you get it?"

Dominic shook his head in dejection." No, they must have taken it with them." Sitting back down next to Miriam again he recalled his moment of temper with the book, smiling slightly to Miriam.

"Well, they're going to be really upset, because I tore several pages out of it. Of course, the pages," shouting out excitedly and he shot up pulling the folded pages out of his trainers. "It just might be in here," quickly, unfolding and scrutinising each page.

" Yes! I've found something, look it talks about Bestia Terrae...look," unable to contain his new found excitement.

Miriam, forgetting her fears for a moment jumped up to look.

"Look, what it says here, to invoke the messenger of Satan, Bestia Terrae. You must first have a maiden young of youth and virtue, that was you, she must be clothed in white and laid upon the altar, this is it" Dominic, eagerly continued to read the instructions that proceeded the rite.

"Here it is…Here, at the stroke of nine. Satan's messenger will enter forth and collect the offering. What time is it now?" urgently asking Will.

"Five to nine… What does it all mean?"

"I'm not sure yet, let me finish reading." Dominic continued down the page with his forefinger frantically searching for a few words of hope.

"Got it," shouting in triumph and now reading aloud, "Take full heed that the full fury of the Master's messenger will be unleashed for if once summoned, the blessed sacrifice is found to be enclosed within the sacred symbol with blood……." and stopped reading, looking up.

"That's the answer, that's what we have to do."

"Do what?" exclaimed Miriam.

"I'm not dead sure but, I think" …. pointing to the pentagram on the floor. "If we can somehow encircle it with something and drip some of our blood onto it then it sounds like whatever is supposed to come at 9pm won't like it. It seems that it forms some sort of a barrier. I don't know but we just have to do it and hope."

"Let's keep trying to escape first," pleaded Miriam.

"We will, but just in case something starts to happen let's get this circle sorted first and then we'll try again."

They started to search around for something to form the circle, but there was nothing.

"I know, can't you scratch it with something?" Urged Miriam.

"Even better, I remember there was some chalk in the cupboard as well," and Dominic dashed into the next room. Throwing out the Chalices and vessels, still scattered about in the bottom lay several pieces of chalk. Quickly gathering them up, together with the knife he hurried back to the pentagram. Throwing a piece to Will.

"Hurry, you join up the points on that side and I'll do this side" and together they enclosed the five points of the pentagram.

"What now?"

"Well, it said we have to drip some blood along the line, referring back to the page….and…well, I suppose it has got to be me as I've caused all this mess," said Dominic flinching as he exposed the knife.

"You are brave" replied Miriam trying to help his confidence. Dominic smiled and quickly cut a small incision into his forefinger.

"Ouch!"

"That's hardly anything," Miriam shaking her head.

"It'll have to do, I'm not doing another one," squeezing his finger and forcing tiny droplets of his blood to spill down onto the chalk line. Carefully proceeding around the perimeter line until he had completed the circle with one drop at every pace length.

"There, that's it," managing to force one last precious droplet onto the chalk from his now anaemic looking finger end.

"Do you think that's enough?"

"I don't know, it just says…. anointed with blood," once again referring to the document. "I hope it is."

The three of them stood back and looked down in silence onto the fragile line that they had just formed. "It doesn't look much Dominic, do you think that's it?" Will becoming deeply concerned.

"It doesn't say anymore, I only tore out odd pages, maybe there was more on the next page of the book, I can't tell" shaking his head.

"What do we do now then?"

"I guess we stay inside it and wait for 9pm"

"Dominic, I'm terrified," Miriam vividly remembering her last ordeal.

"What time is it again?" Dominic deeply concerned to know every minute

"Almost 9pm."

"God, we have to get into the circle, hurry. Step over the chalk, make sure you don't break the line, I think it will only protect us if it remains intact."

Carefully, they all stepped inside the circle and sitting down onto the freezing stone floor, they huddled together and waited.

"Whatever happens you won't let go of me, will you?" pleaded Miriam softly and Dominic pulled her closer to him and hugged her gently.

"I promise," he whispered. He'd forgotten how beautiful it felt to hold her again and for a moment his mind forgot about the impending fate that awaited them as the warmth of their bodies flowed between each other embracing them together. For the first time, even the flames from the candles had stopped their dancing and were now gently swaying in the gentlest of breezes that was entering through the new opening. It was a moment of peace to savour, the trauma of the rest of the night had all but disappeared.

For an instance they had escaped their captors, their imaginations had joined together and taken them far away to a place full of warmth and light, they were joking and playing together luxuriating in every minute moment.

All of a sudden, Dominic's eye caught the rapid movement of life that had abruptly sprung into the two candles that were burning on the altar. "Did you notice that?" Whispering to Miriam.

"Yes, what do you think caused it?" Miriam, sounding quite nervous.

"I don't know, I can't see anything, but is it going a bit colder in here or is it me?"

"No, you're right, I'm feeling colder too, look you can see my breath now and you couldn't before."

"I think your right," Dominic and Will both shivering with goose pimples. "There's something happening, even the air is starting to have a blue tint to it now...... what's the time Will?"

"A minute after you last asked, it's now 9pm."

"Whatever happens Miriam, hang on tightly to me, don't let go," now holding each other even closer.

The blackness that had enveloped the room for so long had now started to disappear and was being replaced by an eerie icy blueness that almost imperceptibly started to slowly descend across the room. Steadily the temperature continued to fall, the flames from the ever present candles started crackling with the tension that was engulfing the room. As if on cue, all the wall mounted candles fluttered and died leaving only the two altar ones sinisterly displaying the gruesome altar in a myriad of shadows as if setting the stage for what was to happen. Sharply, the door into the Ante Room strangely opened and slammed closed making them sit bolt upright, and a definite cooling draught had now entered the room, swirling its way through the cloak of blue.

"Dominic, I'm scared," Miriam gripping him tightly to her.

Trying to cover his own fear, Dominic whispered back in the most assuring voice he could muster up, "we'll be all right I'm sure, as long as we stay inside here, just hold on."

The air continued to encircle the room, imperceptibly it seemed to be gaining in strength and speed, there was a definite path to it now. Flowing around the altar and then the pentagram in an anticlockwise direction. The flame from the altar candles were now distinctly being bent over in the direction of the beckoning wind.

It was continuing to gain in strength as each second passed and a discerning whistling sound was beginning to develop as it rushed around the island that it had enveloped. Strands of Miriam's hair were beginning to ripple outwardly into in the swirling current of air, she gripped Dominic even firmer, huddling themselves even tighter into the centre of the circle. The flow of air had now developed into a chilling breeze as it continued to quicken its pace.

With each speeding revolution of the rushing wind, the whistling was becoming more acutely audible. Louder and louder, it was growing, the breeze now developing into a biting gale. Miriam's hair now totally out of control was outwardly billowing towards the impending storm.

"Hold on," shouted Dominic through the shrill of the wind, "Hold on, whatever you do, don't let go." The gale growing with even more ferocity, the whistling had now developed into a grotesque howling that was all around them now, totally engulfing the whole room.

Suddenly the room was plunged into total darkness as the altar candles were sucked into the howling squall and hurtled smashing against the walls annihilating their flames. They clinched each other even tighter as they started to feel the full might of the raging winds as it hurtled around them as if trying to drag them out of the circle. Unbelievably it was still accelerating, screaming its way around the altar and where they sat tightly knitted together as if outraged at what they had done. Never abating, not even for even the merest of moments to allow them any respite.

The shrieking storm as if even more incensed, had now developed into a roaring tempest all around them that seethed with the fury of a frenzied animal which was determined to wrench them apart. Miriam could feel her clothes being torn from her. She could slowly feel her grip around Dominic slipping, her arms were beginning to ache and numbness was starting to creep into her wearying muscles. She was being dragged away from him she was fighting desperately to hold on. The hurricane was screeching and screaming with all its venom when all of a sudden, shattering the darkness an electrifying fork of light struck the altar. It exploded into a prism of light beams splaying all around it and illuminating the most gruesome sight not even their vivid imaginations could have conjured up.

At the side of the altar, shrouded in a dimly glowing silver mist was the most brutal, frightening and seemingly almost invisible, supernatural creature of immense proportions. And mounted upon the most monstrous ferocious pitch-black bull imaginable. It was almost impossible to make it out, it was disappearing in and out of an any form of an image in the tiniest fractions of a second as if covered by a failing invisibility cloak. It's faintest outline dancing and sparkling with a phosphorous greenish blue tint One split second appearing as sort of a terrifying Leviathan monster from the sea and the next this grotesque monster riding upon its fearsome enormous pitch black bull.. It was one then neither, it was both and then gone, all flickering in the merest time imaginable. It was a Jekyll and Hyde but in the most sickening, formidable guises ever imaginable.

It was neither animal nor beast, nor imagination and nor of this earth. The intense rapid strobing effect seemed to portray the sight of a disfigured head partly hidden behind a shimmering black upper head shield through which protruded two tiny ebony horns. It was not of reality to anything of this earth, if real at all in any universe, but it was here and the threat was immensely real.

The piercing fiery eyes penetrating everything in its sight, glowed deep inside the dark hollows of the mask. Held aloft, clenched in its clawed right hand of its huge black hairy torso was a foreboding awesome spear like weapon. The bull stomping its forefoot onto the stone flags was looking directly at Dominic through its stabbing fearful eyes. The warm air streaming out of its flared nostrils against the frozen night air. And then in the same split moment of time it was the sea monster again lowering its massive tentacled head, revealing the full extent of its horrendous threatening fangs. Un-gritting his teeth for the merest of time from the continuing gargantuan battle with the seething storm Dominic, shouted to Miriam,

"Don't look, you mustn't look at it, keep your eyes closed." It was almost impossible not to. It was hypnotising, mesmerising as if in a trance. They were beginning to hallucinate from the immense rapidity of the strobing effect and the display of its colourful shimmering outline

It was futile against the crescendo of the storm that immediately tried to drown all his words of caution leaving her totally oblivious of his warning. Lowering its head even further, the Bull snorted with anger its foreleg stomping even more vehemently. Then without warning, as the rider let out a mighty roar which shook and reverberated throughout the room, the seething bull leapt forward. With spear now pointing directly at Dominic the animal and rider charged straight for him, the rider still roaring with fury hurtled themselves forward.

Dominic, squeezing his eyes closed and bracing himself ready for the onslaught did the only thing he could thing of and started to recite the Lord's Prayer. He knew it had to cling on to something and how he now desperately sought his help.

"Our Father, who art in Heaven, hallowed be thy name, thy kingdom…." he was abruptly cut short as in full charge the mount and rider hit the blooded chalked perimeter. Thunder clapped all around and sprays of lightning shot out from where the spear had clashed against an invisible barrier that now surrounded them. Dominic glanced up as the bull bellowing with rage and the rider screaming with anger looked down with hatred upon him.

"It works, Miriam, it works," trying to shout above the unbearable noise but his confidence in his statement was soon dispelled. Now in an even more ferocious attack they again charged, hurling themselves against the hidden obstruction that protected their prey but still it held. Dominic, tearing his eyes away from the terrifying battle that was directed at him, forced them closed again and lowering his head started to recite the prayer once more. Again, and again the assault continued never for an instance letting up. The bull streaming with steam from his hot sweating hide and its fuming horrific beast upon its back were not going to give up without their trophy.

Joining forces with the raging howling winds they tore around their enclosure. Faster and faster both the winds and bull raced, incited by their faceless companion. Miriam now desperately trying to hang on with her arms locked around Dominic's waist was being dragged out of the circle by her flaying legs. She was virtually totally drained of all her energy from the overpowering powers that were being generated by the evil that surrounded them, pulling her into their waiting deadly grasp. Her numbed muscles were almost useless now in the fight to hold on to Dominic, and she knew she just couldn't hang on any more. Slowly but surely her grip grew apart, her fingers drained white by the strain of the battle started to let go, she tried desperately to regain the grip but it was too late it had broken and she slipped. There was no way back for her now, from the inevitable terrible onslaught that was grimly and eagerly awaiting her.

Her left foot broke through their guardian perimeter boundary that had protected them for so long, destroying a precious section of it and in an instance the ranting unearthly monster seized upon the opportunity and thrust his deadly spear deep into it. She screamed and writhed in agony as she felt the biting pain searing through her foot. Her captor sensing that victory was now in sight, somewhere under that hideous, hidden exterior a wry smile emerged.

Dominic, somehow amidst the wailing and the screaming that raged all around him felt Miriam lose her grasp. Sensing that something dreadful had happened, opened his eyes saw her sliding out of reach. As if by instinct, his arm shot out grasping hold of her helpless hand and gripping it with all his might he tried in vain to pull her back into the protection of the circle, but the erupting maelstrom was too strong. Miriam was screaming for him to let go but he couldn't hear, he was not going to concede. He looked up and saw the hideous masked Beast of Death towering above her, holding its bloodied spear up high and now sneering with delight at his injured defenceless prey. Spurred on, Dominic gritted his teeth once again and pulled. He wasn't going to lose her not to this creature, and not now and somehow, millimetre by millimetre, started to haul back inside the safety of the circle.

The face of the smiling Demon disappeared into an outrage of fury that exploded across the room as it saw his prisoner slipping from its clutches. Her foot was almost back inside as he raised his spear again and launched another attack. The glint of the spear flashed through the air as it swiftly plunged downwards to her projecting toes, Dominic, seeing the fearsome weapon thrusting down strained with every muscle and sinew in his body to haul her in time, but it was just too late as once again it struck. A piercing agonising cry from Miriam filled the air as the weapon plunged into its target.

It was an immense effort by him, she was safely back inside the confines of the circle but she was writhing in agony from her deep wounds. Dominic knew that he couldn't keep hold of her for too long. It would only be short respite before his last bit of strength gave out and both of them would be pulled out into oblivion.

Miriam had now fallen into a deep unconsciousness, the dark claret red pool of blood oozing from her horrific injuries was growing larger and inching its way towards the meagre protecting circle. Dominic could see it and knew that another breach in their defence would certainly spell the end for them, but there was nothing he could do to prevent it from reaching there. He was so tired now, it was all he could do to hang on to her, the end was inevitable but at least she would not have to suffer any more. There was now no way he could save them. It would only be a matter of just minutes before they would be sucked out into the hands of their eagerly awaiting evil grotesque adversaries.

Bestia Terrae, could see that its prey's bitter fight was drawing to an end, and the sight of the approaching river of Miriam's innocent blood brought a great roar of hideous laughter. Dominic looked up one last time at it and shouted with his last bit of remaining strength, "I hope you choke on us," and then cast his eyes down upon Miriam's face. She looked so beautiful and peaceful in his arms, her swept hair billowing in the rushing air, how he wished that she would open her eyes just one last time and smile at him. He had hardly known her a week ago and yet now she was so precious to him and leaning down he pressed his lips to her forehead.

The room erupted in a crescendo of noise as the tide of Miriam's blood crossed their only defence. This second breach of their priceless defence was too much for the integrity of their invisible impenetrable shield that had protected them for so long, and it totally collapsed. Immediately, Bestia Terrae's enormous black rampant beast tore through the barrier and Dominic, without looking up from their embrace caught the glint of sharp steel as Bestia Terrae readied it, to hurl it through the air.

Will, like Dominic had been desperately racking his mind thinking of an answer to stop this onslaught, when his mind suddenly remembered the parchment that Dominic had shown him when they met at the railway station. Suddenly screamed out with every ounce of strength he had left in his lungs.

"Dominic, do you remember what it said in that parchment, that you had to say something and you'd have the power of the universe, DID YOU SAY IT?" Emphasising as loud as he possibly could to ensure Dominic heard him

In an instance, Dominic's mind flashed back to what was written and with his last remaining ounce of all the energy his exhausted body could manage, whispered the words,

"Lord God, please bless me now with the power of the Universe as Protector to fight against evil and with me it shall remain forever more" and almost in the same very last breath

"Bestia Terrae, in the name of God, I command you to go" were the last words that Dominic managed to utter before the scorching pain of metal tore through his chest.

CHAPTER NINETEEN

ESCAPE

"What happened, where are we?" Will was the first one to wake up and raising his head to look around.

There was nobody there, no hideous creature, no robed priest or worshippers, even the candles seemed friendly. Starting to sit up and feeling his body for the injuries from the battle they had just endured but everything felt fine. It was as if he had dreamt everything.

He looked across to Dominic and Miriam to see that they were in what seemed a state of unconsciousness or deep sleep and began to gently shake them.

"Dominic, Miriam, wake up, you must wake up" and shook them again but with a bit more vigour this time. "Wake up you two, wake up."

Miriam started to stir first and slowly opened her eyes to see Will sitting up next to her. "What's happened where am I?" for a moment remembering nothing of the ordeal they had just gone through. "What's up with Dominic?" Glancing down at his motionless prone figure then turning to Will for an answer.

"Do you remember what's happened, some sort of invisible beast trying to drag you away. It was awful, you must remember?"

Miriam rubbed her eyes for a moment trying to wake herself up properly.

"Yes, I remember now," and suddenly with both arms grabbed Will's waist tightly.

"I was held prisoner by some hooded priests or something and they forced me to lie down on that cold table there," pointing to the altar table. "They gave me something to drink, it was awful and I felt so drowsy"

"I remember better now, you and Dominic rescued me and we had to hide inside the circle we made and then this beast…." And the full recollection of the ordeal flooded back into her mind and before she could finish her sentence, she let a huge scream remembering the horrific ordeal.

As quickly as she screamed, Will acted just as fast and put his hand over her mouth.

"Shh, they might hear us," Miriam's eyes suddenly lighting up with fear.
"You mean it's not over, they are still here?" almost stuttering her words in an effort to get them out so quickly.

"I don't know, Dominic thought they must have gone but we don't fully know."

The scream had now brought Dominic around and he too now started to stir. Holding his head and his eyes remaining firmly closed, he could hear them talking.

"Has that thing gone?" in his feeblest voice ever.

Will was the first to respond as Miriam was too busy checking her body for those terrible injuries that were inflicted on her. Just like Will there was nothing, not even the tiniest sign of a blemish, it was if nothing at all had happened, but she knew it had, it was so real, she was positive.

"Yes, it's gone, everything seems fine, how are you?"

"I'm not sure," feeling his chest. "I was hit with some sort of spear in my chest and I must have passed out with the pain, but I can't feel a thing now."

"We're the same, we have no sign of a fight, no marks, no injuries, nothing, "It's as if we dreamt it."

Slowly to start sitting up himself now, Dominic's memory came flooding back.

"Miriam, are you all right, you're not hurt?"

"Miriam threw her arms around him and holding him tightly.

"You were so brave, the two of you, you saved me from those horrible men, you're my heroes."

At last, all three were now fully awake and starting to make sense of it all and assess the situation.

"The Devil's sect people locked us in and left. I checked the door, I remember, and they were all locked." With that, Dominic unsteadily at first got to his feet and summoned any energy that he had left, half walked and half stumbled across the temple, through the vestibule curtain and to the hallway door.

He'd not forgotten about being careful and put his ear to the door to listen and all was quiet and once again he tried the handle to open.

It opened! Dominic's heart jumped awake with the adrenalin pulsating now through his body with the excitement of a chance to escape. Quickly moving as fast as he could with his exhausted body badly suffering from all the energy that he had used in the battle with the demon he excitingly returned into the temple and in the loudest whisper he dare.

"It's open the door is open" Will and Miriam were on their feet in a fraction of a moment and started to almost run across to meet him.

"You're certain, you're not joking, please say you're not," pleaded Miriam.

"No, it's open, I'm telling you, I don't know why or how. I think it's something to do with what I said to get rid of that beast. When it left everything returned to some normality. But it still may be another trap, we don't know, they could still be in the building so we must be so careful."

"Please don't be here," Miriam almost praying that they had gone.

"Quick see if Randolph is still there," Dominic pointing to Will, "and if he is, grab him and let's get out of here."

Will quickly rushed across to the cupboard where Randolph was hiding. Immediately upon opening the doors, an extremely happy Randolph greeted him with his tail wagging so much with excitement of being let out. Clearly whatever drug that he had been given had now worn off. Luckily, the Devil's Servants had attached a length of rope to Randolph to use as a temporary lead so that they could control him, and Will immediately grabbed it and led him to the others.

They all gathered in a line behind Dominic as he yet again slowly opened the door to the hallway.

There was no one there, no noise no sound of anyone and as silently as they could they paced towards the kitchen door which led to their way out.

Once again lining up behind Dominic, he listened carefully but again no sound so in utter trepidation he slowly opened the door and peered inside.

"India! India!" Dominic couldn't contain his utter surprise and shock to see his sister, even though she was gagged, tied and bound to one of the robust chairs.

"How, what happened?" Questions flowed, as all three of them were getting to grips with rapidly setting her free.

It didn't take long to get India free and soon all four were giving each other briefest of hugs and Dominic turned to her

"India, we haven't time to hear your story about what happened to you. We can talk all about that when we are safe but have you any idea where they all are?"

"Yes, they're all in the church over there," pointing towards the church across the courtyard.

"Do you know why? How long they will be in there? Are they coming back?" desperately eager to know the answers before he opened the kitchen door to the courtyard.

"Well, when I was captured, I was taken to the church where they are now. The person who seemed in charge said, that it was impossible to join you as whatever ceremony was happening to you, they could not be allowed to enter until dawn. That's all I know and I was to be held here until I could be taken to you in the morning. After that they just continued on with some evil chanting it sounded like."

"Brilliant, what a bit of luck," still keeping his voice to a whisper. "They still think that we are safely locked in there, so we should be ok then to make it out. Now everyone, keep quiet and keep as low as possible and stay in the darkest places if possible. Oh! We have to walk past the stable again where that goat is, be especially quiet there, we don't want it bleating and giving us away and we're best crossing it one at a time as well."

"I'll lead and Will, you go at the end so the girls can feel safe in the middle."

Dominic started to open the door, the slowest ever. He could now hear the sound of chanting coming from the church and hearing and seeing nothing else, opened the door just enough to squeeze out just to be safe.

A few moments later they were all in the courtyard with Randolph, and as silently and carefully as they could, started to work their way around the perimeter to the stable and barn.

At last, they reached the stable and Dominic stealthily tip-toed past the stable entrance. Not a sound from the goat and so he beckoned for Miriam to cross. She too managed to accomplish it safely without any disturbance of the goat, next it was India's turn and that too was successfully completed. Now the most difficult to the last, Will with Randolph. Could Randolph remain quiet was going through everyone's minds.

Dominic summoned Will to start crossing and then he and the girls moved into the very dark narrow passage between the stable and barn shielded in between the two buildings.

Will changed hands with the lead so that Randolph was now on the outside of him. Hopefully any sounds or smells from the goat were far enough away not to make him aware. Will took the first step, all fine, then the next, again all fine and the next the same and then on the penultimate step he suddenly noticed the faint red glow of a cigarette from the far outside of the church. It was obviously one of the Devil's Servants keeping a watch on things just in case.

He stopped dead in his tracks and knelt down next to Randolph to be less visible and keep the dog calm. *Please don't look this way*, flashed through his mind, whilst at the same time gently stroking Randolph to ensure he would keep calm and not give him away.

Dominic, now wondering what has happened to Will as he should have been there by now, popped his head back out to see. He immediately saw Will kneeling with Randolph and gestured with his hands holding his palms out to imply, why Will had stopped. Will pointed in the direction of the church and he too now saw the glow of the cigarette and signalled back to Will for him to remain still.

The two girls similarly had now become suspicious as to why they had stopped moving along. Something must be wrong and tapped Dominic's shoulder. Immediately he turned and holding his finger to his mouth signalling to them to keep absolutely still and quiet and whispering.

"There's someone there, we have to wait"

In just the passing of a second the intensity of fear in them went from a moderate level to almost shear panic now. It was off the scale, they were so close to escaping. Pass by the barn and slide back over the stone boundary wall and they were as good as free. But now this, and the fear that they could be held prisoners again was beyond even the worst nightmare that anyone could have.

Has he nearly finished his cigarette? What will do when he does finish it, will he go for a walk around the buildings then? The questions flooded into everyone's minds.

The two boys being more practical minded were thinking, well all's ok so far, just three seconds is all that's needed for Will to be clear and join them and so waited for that one chance.

"**Woof!**" The sound of Randolph's bark abruptly shattered the silence that they had fought so hard to protect. He had picked up the scent from the goat and was now standing to attention desperately wanting to investigate.

As sudden as Randolph's bark was, Will was just as fast to react and clamped his hands over the dog's mouth, whispering in his ear

"Shh, Shh Randolph, shh," hoping that might relax him enough. It seemed to work and Randolph took a slightly less aggressive stance.

Where was the person smoking the cigarette surely, he must have heard Randolph's bark and be coming to investigate. The atmosphere was electric with the tension of it all. Both the boys had their eyes firmly fixed on the direction of the glowing reddish amber of the cigarette. Dominic had already decided that no matter what they were going to make a run for it, if it looked like they were going to get caught. At least there would be some hope that two of them might make it and bring help.

The wait for someone to appear was unbearable, the two girls were doing their best not to cry with the intense worry of what would happen if caught and the boys standing like statues daring not to move a muscle.

But nothing happened, no one came, could it be that luck again was on their side and slowly but surely, they all started to breathe again.

"Do you think we're safe to move now?" whispered Will to Dominic.

"It looks like it, I bet the hood of the cloak blocked his hearing a fair bit. I don't know where he is now, I can't see any glow from the cigarette, I guess he's finished it and thrown it away. I think it's all right to come now as we can't stay here too long."

It didn't take Will any time at all to start to move again and in a few steps, he was at last at the corner of the stable next to him with the two girls standing in line behind lost in the deep blackness in between the stable and barn

"Wow, that was so scary, I can't go through any more of this, we are pushing our luck and just have to get out of here" Dominic nodded in full agreement and turned around to tell the girls when…

Will was grabbed in a vice like grip from behind. Their worst fears had all come true, they were captured. They were so close to freedom but it was all over.

"Don't any one of you move or I'll crush his ribs," a fearsome deep voice commanded.

"I know the girl but who are you two lads?" One of you isn't "Dominic, is it? Own up or else I'll hurt him."

"It's me" answered Dominic owning up.

"Well, I have someone who will be so pleased to meet you, you've caused us a lot of trouble tonight, come with me and don't run off or this lad will be the worst for it" and he started to lead them away when….

"Hang on a minute, where's that girl we caught earlier? She's one of you and we tied her up safe in the kitchen, so you must have untied her.

"Common on tell me, where she is?" Now becoming far rougher and shaking Will vigorously.

WHACK!, The sound of a piece of wood hitting his head exploded, and the Devil's Servant collapsed to the cobbled floor in a heap instantly poleaxed.

"What the heck" Dominic exclaimed in utter shock and surprise. "How" and before he could finish, India appeared from behind with a good sizeable piece of wood. "India, you've saved us."

"You're incredible" Miriam now joining in.

"Now we really have to move fast," Dominic taking back control again. "I've no idea how long he will be unconscious for so we better not hang about."

CHAPTER TWENTY

THE CHASE IS ON

Nearly twenty minutes had now passed since he had been struck by India and although still concussed, he started to get to his feet and began staggering back to the church. A minute later he had reached the entrance and burst through the doors into the middle of the Devil's Servants prayers, collapsing onto the floor.

Everything stopped dead, there wasn't another sound to be heard apart from his attempt to beckon the Master. Then suddenly the whole assembly was in panic and rushed to his aid.

"Stand clear!" a commanding voice rang out, "I said stand clear, let me through." It was the Master, the High Priest.

"What happened?" Kneeling down next to him, demanding in the most threatening tone to know everything instantly

"It's the kids, the kids. I caught them outside and someone hit me over the head," with his blood streaming down the side of his face and over his ear from the nasty wound that India had delivered.

"What do you mean kids, there are only two. The one we tied up in the kitchen and the sacrifice, are there more?" now even becoming more agitated by it all.

"Yes Master, there are four and that dog."

"What that's impossible, no one could have got out of the temple, especially not the girl, who else was there?"

"There were the two girls you know about and two boys, all about the same age. One was that Dominic you've been looking for"

The High Priest almost jumping to his feet, started shouting out his instructions.

"You four, pointing to a small group, go back over the wall and follow it down to the road as that's the way they will have headed. You four, take two cars, I'll come with one of you and follow the lanes around and we should all meet up around the same time at the top of the lane that leads from the scout camp. Now off you go as quick as you can." And with that they rushed out to pursue their prey.

In the meantime, Dominic and his party had already reached the wood and footpath and this time the footpath brought a sign of pure happiness and incredible relief, even for just a second. They were homeward bound and in no time at all would be on the bus heading for home.

Their steps started to lengthen and even the jogging was starting to transform into more of a slow run. They were elated, they were starting to chatter

"This is where they captured me," India shouting out to everyone as they closed in on it. I managed to run away and hide in the woods but there were two of them and it was impossible"

"Never mind India, that's not going to happen this time." Will showing some sympathy for what she must have been through especially all on her own. When Dominic shouted out a stern warning to bring them back to reality and the threat that still hung over their heads.

"All of you shut up, we need to save our energy just in case something else happens. We are not safe until we are on the bus so concentrate, we will all talk about it all back at the caravan."

They all realised, that of course he was right, they were still in danger until all back in the caravan. The talking and laughter stopped and once again all eyes and ears were totally focused on their surrounds.

"I think it's fifteen minutes now to the bus stop, if I remember the directions when we arrived here. When we get there, we can't wait on the footpath as normal just in case the man India knocked out has managed to tell the others what's happened and they come looking. So, we will hide behind that small wall next to it and just peek out now and again to watch for the bus."

"They wouldn't come now would they, I bet it's been nearly half an hour since we escaped," voiced a concerned Miriam.

There was no response, no one dared push their luck and agree that they were now safe.

No matter what Dominic had told them about staying alert and watchful, the elation of being free was impossible to control. Soon they were laughing and chatting again with the thought that they were nearly completely safe and home, just a simple bus ride further after.

They were now excitedly swapping stories about what each had been through as if to boast as to who had been in the most danger.

"I was all alone, and was some sort of a grotesque sacrifice," Miriam adding to the conversation.

"Yes, I have to say, that was the most gruesome terrifying thing, I've ever seen and you were so brave not giving us away as well." Will expressing his support for what she had endured.

"Well, without me, hitting that person over the head, you'd all be prisoners again now," India now trying to score the winning vote.

"That was brilliant and so brave," everyone now agreeing

Now it was even Dominic's turn to add his voice to the discussion.

"Well, I think everyone has done far more than anyone could have ever asked of them and you've all been so brave. I think we can all be proud of ourselves, so well done to us and when we get" ….

Suddenly, Dominic stopped dead his speech as he noticed in the distance approaching them a car's headlights. Now with a sense of extreme urgency.

"Quickly, it might be them, back to the gate we just passed and into the field, quickly," expressing a deep sense of urgency. And everyone immediately turned around and ran back to the gate and into the field, closing it, to hide behind the hedge and wait.

Less than a minute later the approaching car was upon them and stopped just metres from them leaving then engine running and the full beam on.

"Do you think they saw us?" Will whispering into Dominic's ear.

"No, they can't have we were too far away and besides there are bends in the road so it was impossible for them."

"Why have they stopped then?"

And no sooner as he had asked the question, the answer came into view. It was the four men who had come down from the abbey on foot, across the field and past the wood.

The two men got out of the car and soon all six were stood talking, leaning on the gate that Dominic and the others were hiding within a few metres from.

"Did you see anything?" "No, nothing," and the conversation between went back and forth until one suggested they should continue to the bus stop and wait there. There was no way in the time they had escaped, they could have reached there yet and off they went they went as quick as they had appeared.

Being extra cautious just in case they were trying to outsmart Dominic and wait further up the lane out of sight. This time with the headlights off, Dominic held back a few minutes before moving and gathered them all around him.

"Right, we obviously have a problem and that's a desperate shame, but the good news is, we now know where they are and what they're planning. It was too much to hope that they wouldn't follow us, so in a way, I for one am relieved we know exactly where they are and what they are doing."

"But what now?" India asking the question that everyone wanted to know.

"Well, we can't exactly continue along this lane and then along to the bus stop, we'd obviously be caught, so we have no choice but to cut across the fields and hope we come out somewhere after the bus stop and join the road again farther up."

It was an unanimously agreed and off they set across the field, hoping that they were generally heading in the right direction.

Trying to make any sort of reasonable progress across the fields was proving almost impossible. There we just too many humps and bumps and nearly everyone tripped and fell at least once. There was even a stream to negotiate their way across and now they were in some tall dense ferns.

There was no way of trying to maintain any form of silence with so many blind obstacles and sure enough, they were heard by the chasing predators who themselves had entered the fields and were closing in quickly.

It was impossible to outrun them. There were too many of them and they had physically reached their limit of exhaustion, even Randolph was badly struggling to stay on his legs and just wanted to stop and lie down.

The sound of their relentless chasers thrashing through the thicket of ferns was all around them now, they had reached the inevitable end.

"We have to give ourselves up, I just can't go on anymore," Miriam tearfully exclaimed.

"Me neither," even India conceding as well.

Dominic was in a defiant mood though and determined to succeed.

"Well, I'm not! And I'm continuing," his voice now becoming more forceful and emphasising every word. "I will get help and bring them back, so you stay here with Randolph and surrender if you have to."

Will immediately agreed with Dominic, and without even a goodbye or wave to the girls, not wasting a precious moment to lose, the two boys turned and ran the last few metres to the lane. Quickly they climbed over the small boundary stone wall, when almost immediately car headlights came into view approaching them.

"I don't believe it," Dominic angrily shouting at the top of his voice. "Why can't we have some luck at least." Not caring at all now about who would hear him. Even with his determination he had to concede it was all over.

"Wait, Dominic look, it has an orange light on top, look Dominic." Will excitingly shouting for joy at the top of his voice. "It's a taxi."

Dominic had already turned his head as soon as he heard Will say, *"orange light."*

"Miriam, India, there's a taxi coming, quickly come," now also shouting loudly to the girls and immediately shouting instructions to Will.

"Will, we have to stop him no matter what, he cannot pass us so stand in the middle of the road and wave your arms. Whatever happens, he must not pass."

The two boys made their human barrier across the road and it didn't take many second for the girls to have joined them and soon they had totally blocked the road with their barrier.

Moments later, the taxi had reached them and the driver immediately stopped and alighted shouting.

"What the devil do you think you kids are doing blocking the road like that, you'll get yourselves killed?"

It took just moments for Dominic to make up a plausible excuse that would satisfy their desperate measures. After all they could not mention the Devil and sacrifices, no one would believe them and think they were insane. No, he had a better idea.

"Please sir, we're terrified as we're being chased by some nasty looking older lads who wanted to steal or mobiles. Listen," and the driver paused and sure enough he could hear the sounds of the Devil's Servants still thrashing through the thicket fast approaching them.

"See, I told you," keeping up the pretence that they were older teenage boys, "they'll be here in a minute, please let us come with you, Please?"

The driver immediately now understanding the urgency.

"All right, jump in." and they didn't need telling twice and in just a few seconds they were all inside his cab and just driving away as the Devil's Servants reached the wall to see them drive off.

Not a word was spoken by them as they slumped exhausted in the back of the cab, and now the tears really flowed from the two girls from the emotion of it all.

"By the sound of it, you've had a tough time. How long have they been chasing you?" the driver talking to his passengers.

"Since Llangelynin Church," Dominic responding.

"Blimey that is a long way, shall I take you to the police to report it in Conwy?"

"No, that's really kind of you thank you, but would you take us to the caravan park at Bron-y-Wendon Holiday Park where we're staying please instead." And with that, not a single further word spoken until they arrived at the caravan park.

CHAPTER TWENTY-ONE

MADE IT

Following not far behind the taxi had been the High Priest in one of the two cars that had been sent to try and find them. They had been driving continuously up and down a couple of mile stretch of the road, in the hope that they would find them waiting at a bus stop further along the road.

By now his other apostates, were standing in the road thoroughly annoyed that they had just failed by the closest of all margins to re-capture Dominic and them all, when the High Priest's car pulled up.

Immediately winding down the window.

"Did you get them? Where are they?" Not wasting any words or time at all.

"No Master, we missed them by seconds, they jumped in a taxi and went off towards Conwy," pointing in the direction of Conwy.

Instantaneously, the High Priest shouted to his driver in a nasty, angry command.

"Drive!" and almost in the same moment the driver hit the accelerator with the full force of his foot and off they chased in pursuit of the taxi.

The miles were soon eaten up with the speed their car was travelling. The only chance they had, was to catch the taxi before it reached the built-up areas of Conwy. When they driver spotted it not far ahead.

The High Priest had already thought of an excuse of what to say to the taxi driver when they stop him, even if that meant swerving in front of him and breaking.

He had fabricated a story that the children had vandalised the abbey and they had caught them but before they could summon the police, they escaped. Now he wanted them and would take them himself to the police in his car.

The deception seemed highly plausible and indeed with him wearing a robe and looking religious, the driver would probably agree and hand them over to him. All they had to do now was stop the taxi before they hit the rapidly approaching busy town.

Just one hundred meters left before they entered the bustling town all lit up with neon lights and dozens of people and traffic busily going about their business. It had to be now or never and the High Priest's car accelerated to pass the taxi.

Suddenly a t junction appeared and two other taxis appeared from the left and Dominic's taxi saw a clear space and managed to squeeze in between without stopping. The priest's car was momentarily left behind and immediately the road was clear turned to follow them all.

Another junction appeared and then another, they were now in a busy built-up area and one by one the taxi's were peeling off each going in a different direction. It was impossible to see which one Dominic was in and what direction they had gone. The chase was over. Dominic had succeeded in escaping.

"What shall we do now Master, do want us to follow them?"

"No, it's all too late now, if we do anything here the whole of Conwy will be alerted and come running. We will leave it for now and let them enjoy their freedom."

"What if they call the police?" The front passenger quickly responding in a state of anxiety.

"Don't worry, there's nothing they can do or say to hurt us. We will just tell the police, if they do turn up, that we found the children had broken into the abbey and we were about to report them when they escaped, so we gave chase but lost them. We were just doing our civic duty. Who could argue with that?"

"What could the kids say that anyone would believe? They took part in a sacrifice. I don't think so, their unharmed, there's no proof, nothing was smashed. We could even say, we want them prosecuted for trespassing. No, I think we're in the clear, they'll be the worried ones about reporting it, they have a lot more to lose. I'm sure we'll be fine don't worry, just tidy up things as quickly as possible when we get back just in case."

"Next time they won't be so lucky. We now know that Master Dominic is now fully aware of the gift and powers he has, and he is now become a very serious threat to our very existence. He is the one we have to focus on. His power is too great and we must think and plan carefully next time and then take our chance to destroy him permanently when it comes."

And with that the High Priest sat back in the seat with an evil smile on his face as he contemplated his revenge.

Five minutes later Dominic and his friends had reached the caravan park and left the taxi to walk the last short distance. They had escaped, and for the last few miles before Conwy they hadn't even realised that they had been chased for the last mile. They were home, well back at the caravan park and just a couple of minutes' walk left

"Right, we're safe now, so let's just have five minutes to get a story straight so we can tell my mum. Also are we going to involve the police?"

Will was the first one to talk.

"Well, me for one, I don't think we should involve the police. I'm so sorry Miriam, India if you have other thoughts after what you've both been through, it must have been so awful, I just can't imagine. But my thought is if we do tell the police, what can we say? We broke into their chapel and they could even prosecute us. We can't tell them about the Beast, they would think we are all crazy and lock us for being mad, and we have no evidence to show them. We have nothing I'm afraid."

"I agree totally with what Will said," Dominic chirping in. "We have nothing to show and everything to lose. I'm sorry girls but we just have to keep it a secret. Besides we will have great excitement keeping telling ourselves of the story now again. When you think what has happened and what we've been through, no one and I mean absolutely no one could ever have such an adventure as we've just had."

"We just tell my mum, we picked up Randolph from the police station and then went to the fair at Llandudno as we told her in the first place."

Both Miriam and India nodded at the same time and simultaneously spoke out.

"We agree too, it will be our forever secret."

Dominic stared straight ahead and recalled the rite he had read in the Black Book and to which he had the vital missing part. The Incantation of Lucifer; the most deadly and evil ceremony in the whole world of the Black Arts and Satanism. He knew that they would never give up now and that their lives would always be in danger but he couldn't tell Miriam and the others that, not after the nightmare they had been put through.

He would have to be prepared next time and read everything he could about the occult if he was to stand any chance of fighting it. They had been lucky tonight, and that was all it was, but tomorrow......!

Little did any of them realize, including Dominic, just how close they came to being caught again or that the High Priest and his disciples were already plotting their next attempt. This was only just the beginning.

CHAPTER TWENTY TWO

DOMINIC DISCOVERS MORE POWERS

It had been an incredibly exciting year for Dominic, discovering the full potential of the two powers he had been granted. He had honed them almost perfectly now, so that he could control his extra special hearing and telekinetic skills to virtually instant demand, both on and off. He knew that all it required was his total concentration and the more he focused and concentrated the better the results.

Similarly, he had learned that the greater his effort to concentrate, the faster his powers depleted the duration of how long he could maintain that particular power for. It was in effect, a trade-off between the two. However, over the year, it had considerably improved as if it was growing into him.

School and good results had become a formality for him now Although he had through Miriam's persuasion made a reasonable attempt at being more studious himself.

The school year had started really well and even Mrs Pepper never had to call him twice now to get up now for school. He was always up before India and even always the first at the bus stop to await for the school bus.

After a few more practical jokes on the odd pupil who caused him a problem, even the bullying and mockery had virtually all stopped. Somehow, although they couldn't substantiate anything, the other boys had concluded that there was something strange about Dominic, and if you did anything nasty to him, you would somehow end up the worse for it. So almost no one tempted their luck. It was almost the perfect year for him.

The terrifying events of last year had now faded somewhat from their minds. When together with Miriam, Will and India and of course Randolph his pet bulldog they had dramatically managed to escape from the abbey and Satan's Devil Servants. Dominic however, was aware that the anniversary of that horrific day was soon approaching and with it, the same configuration of the planets was already starting to take shape

He didn't want to remind the others of this, believing that it was best not to worry them and so kept it just to himself. But as the days passed getting closer to the anniversary date of the planets' alignment, he was becoming more and more focused on whether anything evil was going to happen. But then just as quickly, he would try convincing himself of how it was impossible for anything to happen this time, as they were never going to the terrifying abbey again as they had no need to.

He still hated football and it was at the last match before the half term school break of the inter form's football competition, when he discovered his next new power. He had been forced to take part in Friday's game to represent his form. Tommy Higgins their goalkeeper, had broken his big toe playing five a side during lunch two days earlier. Despite much protesting about his complete lack of anything approaching any sort of football skill, he was reluctantly forced to become his replacement.

The day of the match against 3C arrived and Dominic found himself wearing the goalkeepers green jersey and some rather large gloves that dwarfed his tiny hands. Mr Skinner, the school's football coach placed the ball ready on the centre spot whilst the two teams formed a huddle at their own ends. Dominic not wanting to join the huddle to hear the pep talk from their captain, instead paced up and down on his goal line muttering about how stupid the game of football was. Why anyone would want to waste their energy kicking a ball around was beyond him, when they could be learning computer coding instead, which was far more valuable.

Second by second, he was becoming more frustrated and looking at the ball just sitting there just waiting for someone to kick it. He hated the ball and wished it would disappear. Concentrating more and more on it with that thought, suddenly it wasn't there, it had disappeared. It had totally vanished. Dominic couldn't believe what had happened, where had it gone?

He stood there in total amazement at what he had just done and tried to logically figure out where it had gone. If he made it disappear, then where had he put it? *Things can't just vanish and go nowhere, but where had it gone?* The thoughts and possibilities were rapidly accumulating in his mind, when there was a loud whistle. Mr Skinner had blown for the start of the match and the two teams separated from their respective huddles and started to make their way to their positions.

"Excuse me Sir, can we have a ball to play with please," shouted Nathan Jones, the centre forward approaching the spot where the ball should be.

Mr Skinner looked across, immediately thinking that it was some sort of a joke. "All right, who's the boy who's taken the ball?" Shouting at both teams on the pitch. There was no response.

"Look, if someone doesn't put that ball back immediately, everyone will find themselves in detention." No one wanted that, especially as it was the last day of that half term before the holidays. Everyone, including Mr Skinner went off looking around the side lines and even back into the changing rooms.

The last thing Dominic wanted was a detention as well and thought, well, if I made it disappear, perhaps I can make it reappear and with that, once again focussed his mind on the ball being there. Sure enough back it reappeared. It was brilliant, he really could make things disappear and reappear, it was too good to be true and couldn't wait to try it again to make sure that it was not just a one-off.

His second chance was to come later that day. It was now usual for him to meet up with both Miriam and Will, his two best friends once a month at 6.30pm at Dominic's local McDonalds. As Dominic was now doing extremely well at school, it was Mrs Pepper's treat once a month to pay for it all.

Miriam had the furthest to travel as she lived in Prestatyn and it was always a rush for her to get there for 6.30pm once a month. She would always stay at Dominic's house for that Friday night and sometimes even Saturday as well. Both Mrs Pepper and Dominic's slightly elder sister India, loved Miriam coming as they all got on so well and could chat about almost anything for hours. It was as if Miriam was now one of the family.

This day though, it was extra special. Not only was it the start of the half term school holidays, but they were also all going on Monday for their annual stay at the caravan park at Colwyn Bay. Despite the troubles last year with Dominic losing Randolph, Mrs Pepper was delighted with how well they all got on together so it was her that even suggested they all go away together.

Dominic set off to meet Miriam from his local train station and following the usual big hugs and smiles off they set to McDonalds to meet with Will.

Will as usual, was already seated at their favourite table when they arrived. He had even ordered two, twenty packs of chicken nuggets between them and three Fantas, so they soon got stuck in.

Dominic had deliberately not mentioned to Miriam on their walk across from the station about his new found power of making things disappear. He didn't want to look stupid if it didn't work and conversely, wanted to see the surprise look on their faces if it succeeded.

First, he decided to try something simple out just for himself without telling them anything. On the table opposite, the previous occupants had just left, leaving their empty coke drinks on the table. Focusing on just one, he put his thought to making it disappear just for a moment and then reappear. Sure enough, it worked perfectly.

Now he could really try it and noticing that not too far away there was a table of three teenage boys on it, and sitting adjacent to their table was another one with two teenage girls sitting there. The two girls were happily chatting away, enjoying a McFlurry each and the boys sharing some French fries with Coke.

Dominic's mischievous mind now working overtime and thought, that he may as well have some fun to improve the effect for Miriam and Will. Acting quite nonchalantly he looked up at them both saying.

"See that table over there with the three boys on it drinking cokes?" Nodding his head in the direction of their table, "and see the two girls sat on the next table having McFlurrys?" Will and Miriam both acknowledged they could. "Just watch then." With that, both Miriam and Will focused on nothing else but those two tables.

The two girls had now momentarily turned their attention to some other girls who had just walked in on the far side of them. Immediately Dominic saw his chance and with all his power, focused on the two McFlurry's disappearing. In an instant they had vanished.

Will and Miriam immediately turned to Dominic in absolute astonishment but he had not finished and told then to keep watching. The three boys were also now engrossed in the girls that had just walked in and without noticing, Dominic not only made the McFlurry's reappear, but he also made them reappear on the boy's table.

It couldn't have been timed more perfectly. The girls had now finished gazing at the others and once again turned to their own table to continue their delicious deserts. They had gone. They weren't there and immediately started to complain to one of the passing waitresses about taking their deserts before they had finished them.

The waitress was profusely protesting her innocence, when the girls spotted the two McFlurry's on the boys table. They knew immediately that they were theirs, as one of the girls had slightly bitten the top of her container and there it was sitting on the boy's table.

The girls angrily stood up telling the boys off for stealing their desserts and to make matters even worse for them, the waitress told the boys to leave immediately. No matter what the boys said about having no idea how the ice-creams got there, the waitress was having none of it and off the boys left.

Well, it was a complete understatement to say that Will and Miriam laughed about it, Will laughed so loudly that the whole restaurant turned to look as to what he had found so funny.

"Dominic, that's incredible, how did you mange that? When did you realise that you had that power as well?" The questions coming thick and fast now from both of them.

And so Dominic explained that it was only today, he discovered that he could do it at the football match he was forced to take part in. Well, that brought on another bout of laughter from Will that once again brought the whole of the restaurant's attention.

The next thirty minutes, the questions never stopped and even Dominic was asking himself them. Could he fly? Could he make himself disappear? Could he talk to animals? The questions were relentless and he realised that over the year, he had done so little to find out.

"Well tomorrow, I'm going to try to discover some new things out so just in case, I might need some help. That was a forgone conclusion. Miriam was already staying the night at Dominic's home and Will was never going to miss this opportunity, immediately ringing his mum for permission to stay. Will was immediately told that it was fine to stay and likewise, Dominic got his mum's blessing for Will to stay over. So, everything was set for Saturday.

Saturday morning turned out to be a beautiful day, with the sun spreading its abundance of warmth and happiness all around. Even the sparrows were busy twittering away, as if eagerly awaiting what magic Dominic was going to perform. It was the perfect day for Dominic to see what other powers he had in his arsenal.

All three were up early in eager anticipation of the day ahead and thinking of all sorts of things for Dominic to try. Will wondered whether Dominic could talk to animals or better still change into one. Miriam wondered whether it was possible to fly. They were busily chatting away just as India was coming back from the bathroom and overheard them all talking.

Not to miss out on anything this time, after her late joining of their terrifying encounter with the Devil's Servants last year, she knocked on Dominic's door and entered.

"I can hear you all talking about Dominic's powers and what else was possible and you're not leaving me out this time. After all, I helped save everyone last time." No one could argue just how brilliant she was saving them and immediately they agreed she should be there right from the start.

After one of Mrs Pepper's ginormous cooked breakfasts, which no one had ever fully finished yet, off they all trundled to Dominic's shed at the bottom of the garden.

Dominic reminded them again that each time he uses his powers, it drains some of his energy, although it's getting far better than it was a year ago. If it's something simple then very little is used up, but if it's something that requires serious concentration then his power is drained quicker. Once his power is depleted totally, he has to wait until it re-charges, a bit like a rechargeable battery This can take seconds, minutes to even a few hours, he didn't know.

He'd realised over the year, that this magical holy gift needed to be part of him. It was something that he didn't even need thinking about, it was an automatic reaction, just like moving your hand. Things that took minutes before, were now instant There seemed to be no set rule, so they had to be very aware of that until it fully developed to be a natural part of him.

With this in mind, they had decided that he was going to start with his telekinesis power. This was easy now and was instant with no energy loss at all. He had done this many times before but had never tried it over a reasonable distance.

Dominic's shed had everything a boy could conceivably want in it. Electricity, water, cooking utensils, a variety of tools, everything and even some tins of baked beans for when he got a bit peckish.

"Perfect," he exclaimed picking up a tin, "I can use this." And with that, placed the tin on the grass next to the shed and focused on it. A few seconds later, the can rose up and was gently placed down again just a metre away.

"Right, that's my warm up, now for something harder," and started looking at the houses around theirs. "O.k. See that garden shed over there, the black and white one, with the flat roof", and pointed to a shed some fifty metres away, "I'm going to place it on there."

The others now keenly focused on the tin of beans, and sure enough and at a speed which made it invisible, the tin was sitting on the shed roof. Everyone, although they had witnessed his telekinetic power before couldn't believe it. They were in astonished at what they had just witnessed.

"Can you bring it back then?" Miriam asked. "If the people in the house see a tin of beans on their shed, they'll faint,". Even by the time she had finished her sentence, Dominic had the tin of beans back in front of them.

Will picked it up to make sure it was real and to test if it was hot and confirmed that it was exactly the same, no difference, Well the requests of what to do next flowed thick and fast until Dominic interjected.

"Look, I don't think that used up much energy, if anything at all so I'm still fully charged if you like, so let's do something that really pushes the boundary. After all, this is not a toy gift, it is the most serious and important thing in the world, so we should treat it with the utmost respect and find out truly what it can do."

Everyone totally agreed in the seriousness of respecting it and finding out its full potential. For the next thirty minutes, suggestions after suggestions flowed, until Miriam reminded Dominic about something.

"Dominic, last year when we were at your caravan and before we went to see those Devil's Servants, we had a walk along the beach." Dominic nodded his head. "Well, we were dreaming up what to do with your power then and you said, it would be great to go back and see the dinosaurs, so let's see if you can create that."

"What you mean, time travel or something?" Dominic instantly replying. "How do I create that then?"

Will, now eager to join in on this exciting prospect.

"I know, create a portal, a wormhole, I think they call them, that you walk through and instantly you're there." That was it, everyone was in on the discussion and ideas were flowing thick and fast.

Eventually, they had decided which would be the best way for Dominic to tackle it. He'd have to create not only a portal but also create a whole different world the other side of it. What this new world would look like, he needed to know in order to create a vision of it in his mind. Third, if they were going to try this, could they all go. Last and most important, about getting back. How long would it take his power to recharge so he could create a portal the other side.

The decisions were enormous, both incredibly exciting abut also terrifying daunting. They need to plan properly and be prepared if they were going to try it.

In the end and after a lot of debate, Dominic summed it all up.

"Look, we all know that this power is real and is a gift from God, so we have to find out what powers it's capable of. Miriam's just brought up, Satan's Servants and what we went through last year, so just in case we're ever faced with them again, we just have to try some immense things." No one needed convincing further and the decision was unanimous to at least try it.

Dominic immediately sprang into action and started to organize things.

"India, can you and Miriam go and grab, two backpacks and put some food and water in them with a torch in case we're there for a few hours. Oh! And tell mum we're all going out until dinner tonight, just to be safe. Will and I will research the internet in my room and find about life and what the world was like during the dinosaur period."

"Will, you better ask your mum can you stay tonight as well, just in case we're delayed and India can you just check with my mum that it's ok for Miriam as well."

With that, everyone shot off to sort out their respective jobs. The girls were busy collecting everything and Mrs Pepper was happy for Miriam to stay Saturday night and if they were late back, she would keep their dinners nice and warm in the oven.

Forty minutes later they were all back at Dominic's shed. Mrs Pepper was fine with them going out until dinner or even later. The two boys had settled on trying to go back in time to one hundred million years ago, as that was a nice round number and there were certainly dinosaurs around then. As a bonus, they would also not need coats as the climate in that period was warmer than today.

CHAPTER TWETY THREE

WILL CAPTIVE BY A PTERODACTYL

That was it, they were ready, and all grouped tightly together with Dominic and Will at either end to protect the girls in the middle. Will, at the last moment grabbed his mobile phone deciding to bring it along. Although of course no internet there, it would come in very useful to take pictures to prove where they had been. Gripping each other's hands extra tightly with everyone extremely nervous at what was about to happen, Dominic shouted out his instructions.

"No talking now until we get to where it is we end up. I have to concentrate really hard on this, as I'm doing two things. One is creating a portal and the second, I have to keep focused on a picture in my mind of an area that we need to be teleported to, it's really difficult. Remember, keep tightly together so we end up together, and with that Dominic started to imagine a portal and an area of landscape back in time one hundred million years ago.

Ten seconds passed and nothing happened, then twenty seconds, still nothing and then at thirty seconds, in front of their eyes, the trees in Dominic's garden started to go blurry. Dominic's focus was becoming even more intense now. Forty seconds passed and almost imperceptible at first, a three-metre diameter circle slowly started to appear in front of them. It was rotating anti clockwise, slowly at first but with each passing second gathering speed.

Almost a minute now and the rotating circle had taken the shape of a sphere, rotating at such a speed it was impossible to tell if it was even moving at all and totally opaque. No one could tell what was on the other side, not even if it was in the middle of an ocean. It was an immense leap of faith into the unknown.

Then, without any noise or warning the faintest light green glow started to appear around the sphere's perimeter. With each passing second it grew brighter and brighter and a few seconds later the glow had become a solid volt green continuous line encircling the sphere. Instinctively, Dominic knew that this was the time to start moving forward to walk through and took the first step pulling Miriam's hand along with him.

Miriam repeated the same, pulling India with her at the same time and similarly India pulling Will's hand. When suddenly, Will dropped his phone. In the same instance that he bent down to pick it up, he let go of India's hand for the tiniest fraction of a second and at the exact moment they all walked through the spinning portal.

"Are we here? Dominic, do you think we are here?" India immediately asking him.

"I don't know, how could I, I've never been before." Dominic irritated by the question as he was totally exhausted from the effort and energy it took.

At first, apart from India's question, everyone was trying to individually focus on what had just happened and trying and come to terms with it. No one had even taken account of the landscape such was the incredible realisation of their time travel.

Several minutes later, they slowly began to notice their surroundings. The first thing was the air they were breathing. It was heavy, warm and moist and almost immediately they all began to sweat. The sky made a stunning backdrop of a hazy golden hue as the light, filtered through the drifting clouds. They were standing on what appeared to be a flood plain with a lazy meandering crystal clear shallow river in the middle ground and following which, bordered clusters of dark green ferns.

In the background gently rising were some shallow undulating hills covered with conifers with an odd outcrop of a couple of sharply rising peaks showing some evidence of earth's violent past.

At last, they were now relaxed enough to talk. They had taken in the wonders of it all but the one big question remained, India's. Were they back one hundred million years ago? It all seemed too perfect. Even today you would happily live in this setting and a landscape gardener couldn't design a more perfect place. There was not even one dinosaur to be seen in the huge panoramic vista that was displayed in front of them. It was too perfect, and then India screamed.

"Where's Will?" and Dominic and Miriam immediately turned around. There was no Will, he wasn't with them, he couldn't possibly be hiding, as there was nowhere to hide within just a few seconds distance. "I remember he dropped his phone just as we were entering the portal, so do you think he's still back at home?".

"I don't know and we can't go back," Dominic replied. "Look, the portal has totally disappeared now and I think I will need a bit of time to recover from that exertion before I could even try again. Although I've been getting far better at being more efficient with my use of the amount of energy I use, it lasts a lot longer now and sometimes the whole day. I think the more it becomes second nature to me, like an integral part of me without thinking, the longer it lasts. It's the same with needing to recover. When I do exhaust it, sometimes I recover in just seconds, but anything immense like I've just done, taking four of us back in time, it could take anything, seconds, minutes even hours. I just don't know and I don't want to take the chance for a while in case it may be a day, and then we are in a mess then." Dominic continued on....

"I guess if he's not hiding, which is impossible to, he must still be back there. All we can do is wait until without any risk, I have recouped enough energy to try again. In the meantime, let's enjoy being here, that's what we wanted so we may as well scout around a bit."

With that, the three of them moved off towards the meandering river to inspect their new world. They had only travelled ten minutes when once again India, still puzzled that no one could answer her question as to why there were no dinosaurs asked…

"But don't you think it's strange that there are no dinosaurs?" addressing both of them more forcibly this time. Dominic was just about to try and answer her, when Miriam screamed.

"Look, look, over there, it's a huge flying bird." And immediately Dominic and India spun around to see a pterodactyl flying some four hundred metres away heading for a hundred-metre-high rocky peak just behind them.

"See, we are back a hundred million years ago. My calculations, ok my thoughts must be correct, as they all became extinct sixty-five million years back." Dominic now proudly boasting about his newly acquired time travelling powers.

"Are they dangerous?" India joining in, deeply worried about this enormous flying reptile being so close to them.

"Well, yes." Dominic really not able to hide the fact and thinking it's best they should know. "I read about them earlier this morning with Will when we were deciding how far back in time to travel. They can grow up to a wing span of over ten metres, so they can be quite massive. I can't tell from here but that one looks about half that size but it's certainly big."

"Look, it's landing on top of that small peak there," India pointing to what looked a landing spot right at the very top. "That must be where its nest is. See, you can see the top of what looks like small branches sticking in the air." With that, the large pterodactyl fluttered majestically down to land, carrying in its mouth what seemed to be a small animal, the size of a sheep.

"Oh my God, look it's Will." Miriam now screaming in utter shock. "It's Will," and all of them were completely mesmerised at what they were seeing. Will had stood up as the pterodactyl was landing as if to fend it off but he was no match for the fearsome predator. With a quick waft from one of its wings he was soon knocked back down again, out of sight.

"What's he doing there? How did he climb that peak so quickly without us noticing? Do you think that thing is going to eat him? So many questions, were fired at Dominic by the two girls so rapidly, that he didn't even have time to think.

After a moment's pause, really to take in the shock of seeing his best friend standing next to, what must be the picture of the century. No, the millennium, no since the birth of Earth, Dominic realised what must have happened, and turned to the two girls.

"I think I know what's happened. In the split second that Will dropped his phone, when we were just about to pass through the portal, he let go of India's hand and that broke the link to me. So he's ended up in that nest. Otherwise, he could never have climbed to the top of that peak so quickly."

Dominic, then burst out laughing and the two girls couldn't understand why in such a desperate situation. "I know it's a bit mean, but you have to see the funny side. The pterodactyl, probably thinks he's one of its babies and is looking after him, trying to feed him all strange bits of meat. I bet the pterodactyl is thinking, surely, I didn't have such an ugly baby."

With that, all three burst out laughing at the thought of Will being mothered by such a creature. Dominic's sense of humour now in full swing.

"You've heard of Crocodile Dundee, I think we should call Will, Pterodactyl Will from now on." That was the final straw and they all doubled over in laughter.

The laughter, although a welcome break didn't last long and the major issue of rescuing Will soon came to the forefront of their minds.

India, suggested that they all would find some decent long sticks, climb the rock peak and attack the Pterodactyl to chase it away and rescue him. But Dominic thought that it was far too dangerous. The reptile could just fly around to the back of them and attack each individually from behind. On top of which they would be balancing on rocks, with a significant drop.

No, Dominic felt that the safest way was wait until it flew off again and then he would climb up and rescue him. Besides, girls are nowhere as good as boys when it comes to climbing. So that rescue plan was decided upon and until the animal flew off, they would just keep watch waiting for their chance. Besides, they still had to wait for sufficient time to allow Dominic to regain full use of his powers.

Dominic still liked India's idea though, of getting some decent long sticks just in case they have to do some fighting against it. So, whilst they had time to wait until it flew away, off they went to hunt for some decent sticks. They couldn't travel too far as they had to keep a close eye on the Pterodactyl, waiting for it to fly off and then immediately start the rescue of Will.

They walked upstream of the meandering river for about six hundred metres always keeping the nest in sight. It was beautiful to see the water so majestically clear and sparkling in the sunlight. Not one slightest miniscule piece of litter was anywhere to be seen.

"Oh, wouldn't it be so wonderful if our world could be like this today, free of pollution and debris." Miriam really appreciating the pureness of it all. "Why did everyone destroy it?" Following it up with a rhetorical question.

"I guess that's the price you pay for progress," Dominic chipping in trying to be a bit philosophical. "But I agree, they should have done a far better job of taking care of our world though, instead of leaving us with the problem. Anyway, we have bigger things to concern us at the moment, rescuing Will and finding some decent sticks." So on they kept searching.

Two hours had nearly passed now and there was still no sign of movement from the Pterodactyl's nest.

"What are we going to do if it stays there all night, or it flies off in the middle of the night and we can't see it?" Both girls voicing their concerns and becoming increasingly more worried now. Gone was the excitement of being in a totally different world and it was now replaced with the harsh reality that they were in serious trouble.

"Well, no matter what, or however long we have to wait, we cannot leave without him. He would do the same for us and we are a team." The two girls quickly agreeing with Dominic's firm comments.

Then into view about two hundred metres away they spotted a copse of small trees and hurriedly they all dashed off to see what they could find to fend of the Pterodactyl if necessary.

Luckily, two perfect sticks of a decent length and size were laying strewn on the floor under one of the nearest trees and Dominic managed to break off another decent one from one of the branches,

"I guess, I'm the first person in the history of all the world to become a vandal." Dominic proudly boasting his claim to fame. "That will never be beaten in the Guiness Book of Records" with a chuckle to himself.

Now they had everything they needed, and off they set to walk the short distance to the nearside base of the small peak which Dominic had to be ready to climb for Will's rescue. It was well hidden from the nest but had a decent view if the pterodactyl flew off and so they settled down to wait.

"I'm certain that my energy is fully restored now. I think it has been for a while now but I just needed to be absolutely certain as it's my responsibility to get you all home safely. As I said, the more comfortable I get with this gift of power, the more it becomes part of me without even thinking. I'm sure then, I will be able to perform anything instantly and forever."

"Well, if you have your powers back, why can't you destroy the pterodactyl then, what are you waiting for? India posing a good question.

"Two reasons, I'm scared to waste any energy to make sure we get back as quickly as possible. Secondly, we shouldn't destroy it, it's his world not ours, we have no right to interfere. It's one thing defending ourselves but we're trying that in the gentlest way possible."

Neither the girls could disagree with that and so they continued their wait.

Another hour passed and still no movement from the nest and then the next hour, something stirred high above them. Bits of twigs and an odd small branch came cascading down, landing close by them.

"Something is moving up above us and I bet it's from the nest," exclaimed Dominic excitedly, peering out from their hiding place. "Yes, it's the pterodactyl, it's just flown off." And with that, Dominic picked up the best long stick from what they had just collected and immediately started the climb up to rescue Will. It wasn't the easiest of climbs with one hand holding on to the stick, just in case it came back but after thirty minutes he had reached the nest.

It was enormous, with hundreds of small branches and twigs forming an almost perfect circle, standing over one and a half metres high. A master builder would have been proud of such workmanship, but it was all silent, there was no sound at all coming from inside it.

Terrible thoughts were now going through Dominic's mind. *Was Will still alive? Had he been eaten?* There was only one way to find out and standing on his tip toes he slowly and quietly peered over. There was no Will, he wasn't there. Dominic's heart started to race and even he was beginning to panic.

What do I tell his mum, my mum when we get back. He's been eaten by a dinosaur, no one will ever believe that and his thoughts continued.

Trying to calm himself down, he started to think logically. *Well, the bird's not carried him off or we would have seen it. We never took our eyes off the nest once. So, the only other explanation, is that he's been eaten, and if that's the case there must be bones scattered around and I didn't see any. I need to look properly as there must be something there.*

With that, Dominic stood back up on tip toes and again peered in. No, there was just a mat of twigs and small branches, blanketed by feathers and bits of ferns covering the whole area but no bones. He couldn't work it out. For a moment he was totally stumped by it all and started to lower himself back down, when he caught something move at the other side of the nest, from under the ferns. It was a foot, it must be Will, he's here and still alive.

"Will, Will!" Dominic whispered just in case there were young pterodactyls lying in there with him. Nothing moved. "Will, Will," now raising his voice and then a movement from underneath the ferns and a dirty coloured mass of red hair appeared covered in foliage.

The relief for Dominic was as much as when they managed to escape from the Devil's Servants last year. To say he was elated would be the understatement of the century.

"Dominic, is it really you?" Will, starting to realise his rescue.

"Of course it is you fool, who else would be so stupid to be up here rescuing you?" And with that, a huge grin appeared across Will's face.

"Right, we need to get you out of here quickly before that thing returns. The girls are waiting at the bottom."

Will didn't need telling twice and in no time at all he was up and over the top of the nest hugging Dominic.

"Hey not too close, you smell awful," as Dominic tried to at least keep a bit of space between them. Will just laughed.

"Yes, I do smell a bit putrid, but so would you, having bits of an animal's stomach dropped on you." With both now chuckling about it, they started their descent.

It didn't take long to reach the bottom and Will was greeted with the biggest hugs ever from the girls. Well, they did their best but the aroma was just too much for any human to get too close to. So they settled for jokes and laughter instead.

"You look so cute Will," India was the first to trigger of the bout of jokes. "Will mummy miss you?" Even Will had to join in laughing about that one.

At last, Dominic brought back the seriousness of it all into the conversation.

"Look, that thing could be back any second and will be furious seeing it's new baby missing," Still not completely resisting to joke Will. "So we have to hurry and be ready. Although my energy has been restored now, I don't want to use any testing it. I'm just being extra safe to make sure we get back and I think this is as good as spot as any to stay. I'll create a portal in front of us here. If that bird comes back, here is better than being out in the open as it offers us protection from our backs."

With that, they made ready their return. Will and India on the outside carrying the sticks as that would be the likely area they would be vulnerable to the pterodactyl. Miriam would hold the other stick just in case it tried to come from above and go through the portal with them. Miriam, joking commenting,

"Wouldn't it be funny though if it did come with us. Can you imagine it flying all over the country, it would be incredible to see?"

Will, as quick to respond. "If that thing comes through, then it's ending up on my plate for dinner," which brought out the biggest laughter of the day.

"OK be quiet now, I need to settle and concentrate again. If the pterodactyl comes back, you will have to take care of it yourselves, just do not disturb me or it will all be wasted. And do not forget, especially you Will, we don't want another adventure like this one. To hold hands and not let go ever!"

Everyone fully understanding the importance of Dominic's instructions and then they were completely quiet, allowing Dominic to focus.

Five seconds passed and nothing happened, then ten seconds, still nothing and then at fifteen seconds, the dust on the ground started to slowly be blown around and the three-metre diameter circle slowly started to appear. As before, it was rotating anti clockwise, slowly at first but with each passing second gathering speed. Forming the portal was certainly far quicker this time as Dominic became more comfortable with his new power.

It was fascinating to watch the sphere being formed in front of their very eyes, a passage to other worlds and they were fixated on it slowly forming.

"Watch out"! Will suddenly screamed. They had been so focused on the magical appearance of what was happening in front of them that, they forgot to keep a close eye on the sky around them, and especially for the pterodactyl coming back. It was fifty metres away to the side of Will and coming in fast. The fury in its eyes was hideous but was equalled matched the terrifying scream it made as it came in to attack.

But nothing could distract Dominic's attention to the forming of the portal and the vision of their destination, his garden back home. The rotating circle had once again taken the shape of a sphere rotating at such a speed it was impossible to tell if it was even moving at all and totally opaque.

It was just seconds away now from being fully formed and ready for them to pass through when the pterodactyl swooped in attacking Will. It was really impossible for Will to do much, as his left hand was tightly gripping Miriam's hand so he had only one hand to wield the stick. The reptile wanted its baby back and nothing was going to stop it. Thrashing about with its fearsome talons try to get hold of anything of Will's clothing so it could drag him away.

The faintest light green glow was starting to appear again around the sphere's perimeter. It was rapidly growing and brighter and then into its familiar solid volt green continuous line encircling the sphere.

Dominic knew that this was the time to step forward and walk through and pulling Miriam's and India's hands along with him commenced the few steps walk to the portal.

No matter what, Will had learned his lesson and was not letting go of Miriam's hand. Although trying his best to fend of the pterodactyl at the same time, he simultaneously began the walk with them.

The reptile was getting more furious by the second at seeing its baby moving away, and in one last desperate lunge made a grab for Will's bottom and caught hold of his trousers. It started to pull Will backwards and Miriam was doing her best to hang on to him and pull him though the sphere with them. But the reptile was winning the tug of war and centimetre by centimetre Will was moving backwards.

Dominic was now just half a step away from passing through and somehow, despite keeping his concentration on the portal, sensed the pulling of Miriam on his hand and pulled her with all his might. It was an immediate chain reaction and she too gave Will's hand a huge yank and they were through.

All four ending up on their knees back in Dominic's garden. No one could say anything as they all collapsed prone onto the grass.

It was several minutes before any of them started to stir, slowly starting to kneel back up again.

"I've never been so pleased to smell grass again," were India's first words.

"I have to admit that was some experience," Dominic joining in. "I wonder what happened to the pterodactyl. Did it come through with us?" Then Miriam screamed out laughing.

"Look at Will's bum, you've got a huge hole in your pants Will." The others quickly turning to see and now they burst out laughing so loudly that it brought out Mrs Pepper to investigate.

"What are you all laughing about, what is so funny?" And then she saw the state of Will. Covered in bits of ferns and twigs, his hair dishevelled and then the huge hole in his pants.

"What the devil have you been up to?" joining in with the laughter.

"Ahh, it was just an upset mum losing her baby" Dominic adding to the laughter and for the next minute no one could move with the laughing.

"Will, go and get a shower and I'll find you a pair of Dominic's trousers which should fit. The rest of you get cleaned up and then we can then all have dinner."

India couldn't help having the last laugh,

"Hurry up Mummy's boy, Pterodactyl Will," which brought another round of laughs and a thoroughly embarrassed Will.

CHAPTER TWENTY FOUR

MIRIAM WORRIED ABOUT HER DREAMS

Getting cleaned up didn't take long at all as they were absolutely famished from their extraordinary day, and Will was like new again. This time, in a pair of trousers without a huge hole in them. Despite Mrs Pepper asking every two minutes over dinner, how Will got into that state and where had they been all day, they skilfully managed to keep the truth secret. Always one of them would try and change the topic and then she would forget for five minutes.

Dinner didn't take too long at all as they were both hungry and, in a rush, to analyse and discuss the day's events over what had happened. They stayed a little bit longer at the dining room table than they really needed to, not to be rude to Mrs Pepper for her kindness, and then off they all shot to reconvene in Dominic's bedroom.

Dominic, as usual started things off by saying what an achievement. What an adventure and well done to everyone for playing their part so well.

"Just think, we are the first people in the history of the world to travel in time, we're the first to see a live free roaming dinosaur, ok a pterodactyl, but close enough, and Will's the first to be adopted by one." Which brought a cheer and a giggle from everyone. "But it's such a shame we can't tell anyone and even if we tried no one would believe us, but what an adventure."

"I think we ought to keep a record from now on of all our exploits." India adding her thoughts to the conversation. "Perhaps one day we might be able to publish them." They all agreed that it was a great idea and as India suggested it, she would record it all with Miriam's help.

Next, Dominic brought up, probably the most important topic of safety.

"In future everything we do has to be properly planned and meticulously executed. It's far too dangerous to have something go wrong, like today. We could have easily lost Will forever, it really was that close. It's not as if we can just ring the police or ambulance, we are totally reliant on ourselves. So, we must never break the rules we set in future. Does everyone agree?" Which was unanimous.

"What about trying something else now." Will eagerly keen for another adventure and for the next hour they all discussed what might be the best for Dominic to try.

Miriam's idea won the day. She suggested to see if Dominic had some form of super weapon, a bolt of lightning or something and their memories instantly flooded back to their encounter of the Devil's Servants. Miriam continued on.

"I've been meaning to tell you all something but I wasn't sure whether I was just having bad dreams, but they're not going away, if anything they are getting stronger." Everyone now intensely listening.

"I keep dreaming that I am being called by that High Priest to go back to the abbey. I know it sounds ridiculous and it's the last place I would ever go near again, but the dream is getting more intense every night and I'm getting scared."

Dominic now saw his opportunity to own up about having concerns about the Devil's Servants as well.

"Well, I wasn't going to mention this in case it started you to worry you all, but I've been watching everything closely about them. Do you remember Will, in the book we read that was in the temple, and when the Incantation of Lucifer can occur. It mentioned that it must be when there is a configuration of at least five planets. Well, next week, we have six, Mercury, Venus, Neptune, Saturn, Uranus, and Jupiter and its exactly one year next Thursday."

"Now it could be a coincidence and Miriam's dreams could be her remembering last year because it was hugely stressful. I do think though, we better be on our guard. I don't want to scare anyone but we must be ready. I knew last year that these people would never give up, I just kept it quiet."

Miriam was beside herself now becoming more terrified by the minute but Dominic continued on.

"The last thing I want to do is worry you. I wasn't going to mention anything, but now you've mentioned strange dreams seemingly trying to entice you away, we have to face things. It's better we understand and prepare now and if hopefully it's all nothing then great, but at least we are prepared just in case."

"How can they possibly do that if we stay here," Will puzzled by the conversation.

"We don't know what they did to Miriam for the ceremony last year. They could have hypnotised her so when a particular phrase is said, or if she reads a certain word or phrase, it awakes her subconscious and she has to follow exactly what it's telling her. I'm just guessing but perhaps I'm right, we'd be stupid not to have a plan, especially for Miriam's sake."

So, they all started to immediately plan what precautions and safety measures they could put into action just in case. Luckily, it was just for tomorrow after she got home. On Monday, they were all going away together to the caravan and there was no way anything could happen with them all there. After Thursday, there should be little risk as the planets will have moved from their perfect alignment for another year.

Although Dominic believed that she would be safe tomorrow, a half an hour later they had at least the outline of a plan to protect her until they collected her for the holiday on Monday morning. Catching the 1pm train tomorrow, she would probably arrive home by 2pm.

Every fifteen minutes in between, up to 11.00pm, Miriam would text them all, *"I'm', fine"* and if she ever missed sending one, then everyone would immediately text her. If no reply to anyone was received within ten minutes, then Dominic and India would immediately start the search for her, keeping Will updated.

There was nothing more that Dominic could do, unless Miriam was to stay at his and India's house for all day and night tomorrow as well. That was impossible this time, as she needed to go back home to prepare for the holiday on Monday, when Mrs Pepper and the three of them would be collecting her.

Dominic, after his time travel power, was now even believing that perhaps his powers were almost unlimited and was considering whether he could put some sort of a protective barrier around her. But it was all too late now to start experimenting as he didn't understand his powers well enough yet. So, they all agreed that this the best they could do.

India brought the problem up, how would they know where they have taken her, perhaps it wasn't back to the abbey. Once again, they chatted about various solutions and in the end decided that Miriam had to wear a tracker at all times. She can secure it around her waist and if the Devil's Servants discovered it, it would be too late. They would then be at the place where they were holding her and Miriam's movements would be safely recorded on Dominic's laptop and mobile.

In the morning, before it was time for Miriam to go home, they would rush out to the local Curry's store and purchase one, setting it up back at Dominic's before she left to catch the train.

No one had noticed the time was fast approaching midnight with everyone's thoughts being focused on protecting Miriam and today's astonishing visit back to a time one hundred million years ago. But now they had settled on everything their exhaustion set in and it wasn't long before they were all fast asleep.

CHAPTER TWENTY FIVE

A CHANGE OF PLAN

10am Sunday morning found everyone still deep asleep, no one had moved a muscle except for Mrs Pepper, who had already been up for two hours. Knowing that Will and Miriam had to go home soon and she wanted to get on cooking their favourite English breakfasts and gave them a quick knock on their bedroom doors.

"Kids, it's gone ten o'clock and I'm cooking breakfast." Well, with the smell of bacon percolating its aroma through the house, it didn't take long at all before they were all sitting around the kitchen table tucking into a delightful breakfast.

Although the breakfast was as delicious as ever, everyone's minds were on Miriam and keeping her safe. As quickly as they could, and after thanking Mrs Pepper off left Dominic and Miriam to go to Curry's to buy a tracker with Will joining them as it was on his way home.

Two hours later, with Will now at home and Miriam sporting her new tracker, which was now linked to Dominic's mobile, Dominic walked her to the station.

"Don't worry, nothing is going to happen, I'm certain they won't even try anything before Thursday, we are just being really safe."

Miriam managing a small smile but clearly, Dominic could see the fear in her eyes. "I know you will take care of me and tomorrow we will all be together again." And with big hugs Miriam departed on the train.

Although, Dominic, really believed that the risk was negligible and as did the others, all day long everyone was watching their mobiles for the fifteen minute messages from Miriam. By 11pm everything was still fine but Dominic was fixated to his mobile and he was still watching it until gone past 2am, to be sure that she was safe.

It was the same the next morning, he was awake by 6am for the first time ever in his life and checking his phone but it all seemed well. She should be safe now, as her dad was always up early and they were picking her up around 11am with Will to go off to the caravan. So, one night was safely behind them.

The next few hours were as usual pandemonium whenever they went on holiday, lots of running around finding things and packing everything. It never took Dominic long though, it was always his mum and India with their huge bags of make-up and cosmetics. He never needed much, just really his laptop, phone, spare trainers, a few clothes and toothbrush.

But his mind was all the time on the problem of how to protect Miriam. After thinking of numerous options, he decided that one would be the best, but it carried the most risk.

He'd decided that to try and keep such a tight contact with her, texts every fifteen minutes, was impossible and anything could go wrong. Her phone might have a temporary glitch, her battery could go flat, on top of which everyone was constantly glued to their phones.

"No, that is just not going to work," muttering to himself. On top of which what was to stop the Devil's Servants trying to lure her away next, week, next month and so on? He didn't know enough about astrology, astronomy or their rituals to be sure when something could happen. Secondly, it was impossible to keep monitoring her for a whole year, even worse, year on year possibly.

His conclusion was although with risk, attack was the better part of defence. His plan was to enter the abbey in the early hours and try and locate where the High Priest kept everything of utmost importance. He knew from his research into the Devil's Servants that various old abbey's had secret rooms or hidden chambers for housing priests during times of religious persecution, or for safety, even a means of escape. It made sense therefore, that given they were practising some really evil things in the occult, they would probably have one.

If they could locate it, hopefully, they would uncover lots of secret things about them and especially their weaknesses.

"Yes! That's what we will do," quite loudly speaking to himself in a now determined voice.

Thirty minutes later with the car all packed, off they all set and of course with Randolph, the pet bulldog who had really caused the problem last year with the Devil's Servants. First, was to pick up Will but as he was on the way to Miriams in Prestatyn that was simple enough and with the cursory ten minutes of chatting between the parents off they left for Miriam.

As she only lived twenty miles away, they were soon there and with the courtesy's between the parents over with, they were soon continuing their way to the caravan. They were desperate to talk about Sunday and what happened to Miriam and what lay in store ahead for them. But with Mrs Pepper in the car that would have to wait until later.

It was only a short drive now, just ten miles to the caravan park from Miriam's house but it gave Dominic enough time to reflect the past few days. It was incredible how fast things had moved on since Friday evening at McDonalds and showing his new power. Then on Saturday, going back in time one hundred million years and fighting with dinosaurs, well almost. To now preparing to fight with the High Priest and the Devil's Servants again. All that in a little over two days seemed inconceivable now.

And now, what lay ahead for this week, what was going to happen, what new powers would he discover he had. It was whirlwind of non-stop events one after another, never stopping even for just a moment.

And the next moment, he realised that they were already parking up at the caravan. It didn't take long at all to get the caravan ready, especially as they had all stayed last year and basically it was a duplicate of that. An hour later and a cup of coffee with Mrs Pepper, they were ready to get some fresh air and discuss yesterday's events. Mrs Pepper was delighted to get some space and peace for herself and after telling them to be back no later than 5.30pm for dinner off they went taking Randolph with them.

Dominic was the first to start the conversation.

"Look about yesterday and all this messaging every fifteen minutes. I don't think it's going to work," and continued to outline his reasons. Summing up with.

"It's impossible to keep texting possibly for months even years, we just do not know, so I think we should find out everything about them and so we can defend ourselves properly or even attack them."

India in particular was very vocal about it all and totally agreeing with Dominic.

"Look, it's not fair that Miriam is carrying the brunt of it all. After all, all she was doing was helping Dominic and now she has this hanging over here head possibly for years. I'm all for attacking them and giving some others a whack over the head." Referring of course to her knocking out one of the Devil's Servants last year.

That at least brought a good laugh from everyone.

"I totally think it's the right thig to do too and I'm all for it," Will quickly following up. "But how do we sneak in and how do we find this secret room if there is one?"

"We will have to go the same way as last year, but at least we know our way around now and the rooms they may be in," were

Dominic's first thoughts. "With regards the secret rooms, I must admit that could be a problem, we will just have to hope we're lucky."

"I think I may know", India responding. "When they tied me up in their kitchen, I heard the High Priest tell one of his servants to fetch some document from his private office at the back of the dining room."

Then Miriam hit upon a brilliant idea and turning to Dominic, "Why can't you use your powers and create a portal to get us in. After all, you did it for a hundred million years. Surely this must be far easier."

That was it, everyone was suddenly talking excitedly offering suggestions and where the portal should take them.

"Look, firstly it's a great idea but I've only done it twice. Admittedly, I was quicker the second time but I'm not sure what's the fastest time I could do it in or how long my recovery would be. Getting there should be fine because we can create the portal from here somewhere and I can get us landing in say the barn, not the stable where the goat is, just in case. We can then easily get to the dining room from there."

"Well at least that's something, "Will being encouraged by that.

"What if the door through the kitchen is locked, which is the only way in?" India now throwing a spanner in the works.

"All right I've heard enough," Dominic taking control again. "This is what we will do. I will teleport us straight into the dining room. From what we saw last time, I don't think they use it, preferring to eat in the kitchen by the look of things. But to be safe that no one is there when we reappear, we need to do it early morning, say 7am. Is everyone happy with that?"

Although the risk of it all was significant, it was better than trying to try another way and so everyone agreed.

"As you know, the most likely day for them to try anything with Miriam is Thursday so we have to do this in the morning. We need to tell my mum a reason for going out so early, say 6.30am otherwise she will think it strange so has anyone any ideas?"

No one could think of a perfectly plausible excuse, but India suggested that it was to go to a car boot that they had noticed and they always start very early. You have to be there at that time to get the best buys. So, with that as an excuse off they set back to the caravan to gather things for tomorrow. They would need torches, a backpack and definitely their mobiles so they could photograph everything.

Mrs Pepper totally understood their keenness to be away early and even cooked them all breakfast. They avoided taking Randolph this time saying that with so many cars around it would be a bit dangerous and with that, at 6am they departed.

The only suitable place for Dominic to create the portal which was at least out of sight enough, was behind the toilet block on the beach about four hundred metres away and a few minutes later they were all lined up ready. They all knew the routine now and gripped each other's hands tightly and Dominic started to concentrate.

This time, the light sand covering on the ground started to quickly be blown around and even the sphere quickly started to appear. Once again, it was rotating anti clockwise and the forming of the portal was just mere seconds. This time things were happening so quickly that even the faint light green glow was unnoticeable as it went almost immediately to the solid volt green continuous line encircling the sphere.

And they all stepped forward.

CHAPTER TWENTY SIX

THE HIGH PRIEST SECRET IS UNCOVERED

Virtually in the same moment, they were standing in the abbey's kitchen and their luck was in, no one was around. Although not quite sunrise yet, it was still sufficient enough to see reasonably well.

Dominic wasted no time reiterating his instructions from the night before.

"First, we are looking for a handle, a lever, a button or something like that to find the secret office. Looking around, the office opening must be in the floor as the walls don't seem deep enough to hide an office. Two things, whisper only and anything you move or touch must be put back exactly, as we don't want them to realise that someone has been here. Each person focus on just one wall at a time."

With that, off they set on the search for the secret lever or whatever it may be. One wall was totally bare with no appliances, furniture nor even pictures, it was completely, just a flush boring wall. In no time Miriam had finished checking it, running her hands over it without finding anything, except for a few old cobwebs in the corners.

India was next to quickly finish, as her wall only housed the door leading from the hallway. The two girls then immediately joined Dominic who was searching in the most likely place. The wall against which stood an old disused old fireplace, and its large heavy over mantle. Their hands rummaged everywhere, pulling tugging, banging virtually almost everything you could do with your hands and just as they had given up with finding anything, a hole in the floor behind them started to slide open.

All three immediately spun around to see what the noise was and Dominic immediately whispered as loud as he dare in a forcible voice.

"No one move, stay exactly where you are. India, turn around exactly to where you were, now look just at the place you were touching and touch it again just in that area." Mirriam turned and started once again to touch everything around that area, but nothing happened.

"Miriam your turn. Again, turn slowly around so you keep the exact spot you were before and do the same." Miriam had been searching the over-mantle and once again feeling around, touched something and the secret door began closing.

"That's the spot where the secret access button is then." Dominic now at the side of her and feeling the underside of the mantle discovered a small lever. He pulled it again to make certain and once again the access in the floor started to open.

Wasting no time at all, he descended the few steps into the secret office with the two girls, leaving Will in the kitchen as a safety precaution in case it closed again. Once again Dominic issued his instructions.

"I want a photograph of everything; pictures, documents, artefacts, everything. There's no need to read it, just photograph it and we will look at it all back at the caravan." He was just about to photograph a hideous picture hanging on the wall, when he noticed the sacred black occult book that the High Priest had used in the ceremony previously. This was by far the most important thing he could have wished for. "I'm going to photograph the whole of this book, if you two can do everything else. "Remember, whatever you move or pick up, it must go back exactly where it was."

With that they started their examination and recording of everything in the room. Page by page he photographed the book being extra careful not to miss anything at all. He knew that the high Priest's power lay within this room and it was their chance to find his weaknesses.

Thirty minutes later, they were all complete and started to climb back out when Will, in a state of urgency whispered.

"Quickly, I can hear voices in the hallway."

Five second later they were all out and Dominic immediately pressed the lever to close the secret access. The voices were outside the kitchen door now. They were trapped in the kitchen, it was impossible to get out in that time or even create a portal.

Domnic suddenly remembered his power to make things disappear, like the football on the pitch and immediately ushered them all into the furthest corner away from the door. Immediately he focused his thoughts on them all being invisible when the kitchen door opened and in walked two Devil's Servants.

For a few seconds he had no idea whether they had seen them, or had his power worked. How could he know, he was on the inside. His heart racing, as they walked around the room to the side of the fireplace and looked straight into the corner where they were standing.

The first servant, walked closer looking exactly into Dominic's eyes and as he was just about to step into the corner where they were,

"Look, there's nothing here, I don't know what made that noise, it must have been the wind somehow but there is nothing in here at all; Let's go." Voiced the other apostate, and after one more intense stare at Dominic as if he knew there was something there, the first servant turned around and left with the other.

Immediately there was a huge sigh of relief from everyone.

"That was too scary, so weird, so surreal," were India's first words. "It's unbelievable, we can see them as well as I can see all of us as normal, but they can't see us. It's terrifying, as you're thinking there's no difference but there is. I know it saved us, but it's just too frightening for me." Everyone, now joining in with India's thoughts before Dominic stepped in.

"We can talk about all this when we get back, but there's not a moment to lose now. They are obviously all up and about so we need to get out of here and with that Dominic started the creation of a portal to get them back to the caravan. A few moments later they were back outside the toilet block where they started from.

The whole journey had taken less than one hour, and it had turned out as perfectly as they hoped but what now. They had told Mrs Pepper that they were going to a car boot which would have taken hours to go there and back, as well as have a look.

"Look, we just have to get back to the caravan as quickly as possible as we have loads of pictures to read and examine. The book alone will take hours and every day is critical before the planets fully align. We tell my mum that India", pointing to India, "that you have stomach ache, so we turned back. She'll believe that as you're hardly ever ill and also it gives us an excuse to stay in the caravan all day."

Mrs Pepper was full of sympathy for India with her stomach ache and felt so sorry for all the others for such a disappointing start to the day that she made them all, excluding India, nice bacon and sausage sandwiches. Although Mrs Pepper thought it a bit unusual, they all managed to squeeze in to Dominic's and Will's bedroom so they could closely study the photographs together on Dominic's laptop. Of course, they also took the sandwiches with them as well, and needless to say shared them with Olivia out of Mrs Pepper's sight.

The next few hours they had analysed everything they could but nothing jumped out at them which would give them any clues as to how they could defeat the High Priest. Eventually, they were down to the photographs of the occult's black book. There were a couple of hundred pages. Many with detailed drawings, pen and ink paintings as well as a multitude of satanic rites. Although gruesome and horrific in what they depicted, they were so carefully and finely detailed by the finest of craftsmen they were the finest of art.

Page by page they carefully examined, looking for the slightest clues and some at times, so gruesome in their depiction of sacrifices that the two girls had to look away. Page after page they continued reading the sickening prayers and rites and then.

"Here's something," Dominic shouted out and pointed to the heading of the page and the following Latin prayer.

Prayer to Lucifer for Magic and Psychic Powers

Lucifer, magicae princeps, potentiae dominus,
Da mihi artes arcanae, viresque animi bonus.
Mens mea sit aperta, ut videam ultra,
Virtutes tuas capiam, et potentiam multa.
Secretorum custodem, me facias fieri,
Ut possim vires magicas semper invenire.
Da mihi claritatem, conspectum inter mundos,
Per te, Lucifer, crescunt potentes immundos.

"I have no idea what that means but it must mean something as it's a prayer to Lucifer for magic powers and quickly copied and pasted the Latin prayer into Google's translation.

Lucifer, prince of magic, lord of power,
Give me arcane arts, and good strength of mind.
May my mind be open, that I may see beyond,
I may receive your virtues, and much power.
Make me a keeper of secrets,
That I may always find magical powers.
Give me clarity, a view between the worlds,
Through you, Lucifer, the powerful unclean grow.

"Look, on the opposite page there is a painting of; I guess it's supposed be the Devil, placing something around a priest's neck with flames shooting out from it." Will adding to Dominic's remarks.

"That must be the High Priests source of power then, he wears something around his neck that's been blessed by the Devil. I guess it's a bit like me and the silver needle I injected myself with. At least with me, my power is inside me now, part of me but his is something that he has to keep close."

"Well, that's the answer then." India now becoming excited that there may be a solution. "All we have to do is destroy whatever it is."

"I remember something now," Miriam too now joining in. "It was when I was in the altar room on that horrible table. I saw, I think, although it's all a bit hazy now, that High Priest remove a small pouch from around his neck and remove a jet-black stone from it that had a strange glow to it. He mumbled a few words and kissed it and then put it back in the pouch."

"Well done Miriam," Dominic praising her. "That seems to confirm it then, his power is in that stone and as India says, somehow, we have to get that from him and destroy it. The trouble is, if his powers are unlimited, and I have no idea how we do it."

"I saw that pouch on the shelf in the secret office," India adding to the conversation. "I took a picture of it, you passed it earlier with the other photographs."

"Did you see the crystal inside?"

"No, I didn't want to open it in case they might notice as you told us to be careful. But there certainly was something more or less round and very hard inside."

"It doesn't matter we know now anyway, but at least that's a bit of good news. My guess is that he must have no powers unless he has that crystal on him and he probably takes it off at night, that's why it was in his secret office. I imagine that he only wears it now and again as wearing it permanently would not only be uncomfortable but might affect him in some negative way. We just don't know but it gives us some hope at least."

"I bet that's why he couldn't do more when we escaped, he wasn't wearing it," Will joining in as he turned over the next page photographed which made things even worse.

"Oh no, if it wasn't bad enough, read this."

Prayer to Lucifer for Protection

Lucifer, custos meus, defensor noctis et diei,
Protege me ab omni malo, tuus servus fidus.
Circa me sit tua lux, me custodias in pace,
Ut in tuis manibus securus semper sim.
Angeli tui vigiles, me circumdent semper,
Ut ab hostibus occultis tuear, nec timeam umquam.
In nomine tuo, Lucifer, sit mea salus certa,
Ut sub lumine tuo vivam, sine cura vel meta.

Again, they translated it to see what it meant.

Lucifer, my guardian, defender of night and day,
Protect me from all evil, your faithful servant.
Let your light surround me, keep me in peace,
That I may always be secure in your hands.
May your angels always surround me,
That I may protect from hidden enemies and never fear.
In your name, Lucifer, may my salvation be certain,
That I may live under your light, without care or goal.

"Well, we certainly have a battle on our hands to defeat these people and as I said, I have no idea how. The only thing I know is that somehow, we just have to." Dominic now becoming a bit despondent for the first time. "If only we would have known about the crystal when we were there, we could have taken it and this would be all over."

"Don't worry," Miriam trying her best to console him. "You've beaten them every time so far and just because we now know his powers now, why should there be any difference?"

With a gentle smile and squeeze of her hand.

"You're right, we can beat these people." Now becoming more positive and upbeat again. "I think we have to draw them out of the abbey first. They are totally familiar with it and we really no nothing about it, so the first thing to do is get them out into the open. I'm not sure what then so we need to think really hard."

Little did Dominic know that problems were already arising back at the Devil's Servants Abbey.

CHAPTER TWENTY SEVEN

THE HIGH PRIEST PLANS HIS REVENGE

The High Priest had entered his secret office to get prepared for Thursday when the stars would be in full alignment and for the sacrifice of Miriam. He'd only been in there for a few minutes when he came rushing out into the hallway from the kitchen.

"Who's been in my office?" There was no answer. Once again, his voice boomed out but this time, more screaming with anger in it. "Who's been in my office, answer me?" but still no response. The High Priest knew that no one would dare lie to him as their punishment would be the worst imaginable.

But still no one came forward. He was fuming and loudly thinking to himself. *Where has it gone? I know it was in the chalice I placed on that shelf but it's empty. No one here would take her hair, they can do nothing with it, so that's not the answer*, when suddenly it all became clear

"It's Dominic Pepper, of course it is, he's been here." Now his brain starting to whirl away rapidly with all sorts of possibilities and explanations and shouting again to his servants,

"Who was first in the abbey this morning?"

"I was Master," came back a timid response from one of his apostates.

"Was the door still locked when you came?"

"Yes Master, why?"

"It's nothing, just carry on with what you were doing," and with that the High Priest went back to his office.

What had gone was a locket of Miriam's hair which he had cut from her, whilst she lay on the altar at the ceremony last year and he needed it for this ceremony on Thursday.

It was starting to become clear to him now. And sitting back in his chair stroking his chin thinking through things. *So Master Pepper, you're learning your new powers quickly. You have a power to unlock obstructions or become invisible to walk among us unnoticed, possibly even teleport yourself. Hmm, if you think you can challenge me, your very mistaken. I will teach you a very painful lesson before I destroy you. First let's see if you can stop me taking your girlfriend to my Master*

Then taking the pouch from his shelf and removing the blackest of the deepest, black crystal, which had been blessed by Lucifer. He rubbed it between his fingers with a twisted smile on his thin pale lips and started to plan his revenge.

Meanwhile, Dominic and the others had pretty much exhausted everything they could find about this evil satanic cult, and they too had started to think of what next to do.

"Look, let's lay out what we know and what we have," Dominic suggested, now keenly focused again. "The most important thing of all is to protect Miriam. We know that the alignment of the planets take's place on Thursday, so the greatest risk to you is..," and looking deep into Miriam's eyes for a second, "..is I'm guessing anytime from Thursday after lunch onwards." To take you too soon would mean that they risk us and possibly even the police on their tail longer than they want. So, I can't see them risking anything before then."

"The next thing is how we protect you every second of the day on Thursday. Once Friday arrives it's too late the alignment has gone, so we have one day of complete protection for you with at least two of us. You must not be left alone for one second without two of us watching over you. Ok, when you're in the bathroom, standing on guard outside of the door." Which at least brought a faint smile from Miriam and a giggle from Will.

Dominic continued with his thoughts about it all. "I will try and place a protective shield around you but I don't know how to really do it or whether it will work and for how long, so we need to try that out later. I think what the High Priest will do, is use that hypnotic thought he's placed in your mind and will somehow send you a signal which awakens it. So, we all need to watch if you start going into a trance and if necessary, restrain you I'm sorry," gently squeezing her hand again.

"Last but not least, is how we defeat him for good. From what we believe, his power comes from that crystal. The enemy is not so much him, it's the crystal. We have to get hold of that and destroy it."

"Why don't we just go back early in the morning again like we did this morning and take the crystal? As you say, it will probably be there again because we didn't remove anything and we put everything back exactly as we found them." Suggested Will.

"Well, I'm sorry but that's not strictly true," Miriam starting to sob whilst managing to quietly admit to something." I took something, I'm sorry, I know I shouldn't have, but I just couldn't stand the thought of that creepy horrible person have a locket of my hair." before bursting out crying.

India immediately threw her arms around her trying to console her with the boys also joining in on one big group hug. "I would have done exactly the same too, that dreadful creature." And seeing the support for her from everyone, Miriam started to smile and the tears stopped flowing.

"We're going to destroy them all for what they've done to you, we will I promise you," Will showing his bravado making everyone laugh.

"Well, it's now too risky to go back there again then. He has probably discovered it's missing by now," Dominic continuing the discussion thread. "The only way is to try and draw him out or as I've already said, we wait for Thursday when we know he has to act.

Little did they know that the High Priest, because he was aware that they had been in his office and taken Miriam's locket of hair, had decided to try and take Miriam tonight and not wait until Thursday. He'd guessed that with Dominic breaking into his office, he must also be aware of the planet's alignment on Thursday and that any attempt to take Miriam would most likely be then.

Leaning back in his chair and staring at the ceiling, he gleefully thought. *What a surprise for clever Mr Pepper lays in store for him, a*nd a grotesque laugh burst out.

There was no more Dominic could do now except wait and be patient. They had a plan all sorted out, well except how to get hold of the crystal but that would have to wait until an opportunity arose. So off they went to test if he had any power with creating a protective shield.

Finding a quiet area on the beach, where it was unlikely anyone would be watching, he shouted to Will.

"Will, since you're so brave about destroying them, you can be the target first."

"What do you mean, target?"

"I will create, well I hope so," with both the girls bursting out laughing, "an invisible shield around you. And because I will be focusing on that, the girls will throw things at you." The girls were now in stitches laughing along with Dominic but the worried look on Will's face showed he wasn't happy at all about the proposal.

"Don't worry, the shield should work and if it doesn't, we have lots of plasters in the caravan," Well, that was it. The girls were doubled over in hysterics and Will was storming off.

"Will, I'm only messing, it's been such a serious day and it was good to have a laugh for a moment. Please come back, it's all back to being very serious again." Will paused for a moment and then turned back.

"Right girls, find something small and light to throw and we will start with that first." With several litter bins around that didn't take too long at all and soon they were ready.

"Will, keep still now, whilst I create a shield. Girls, count to thirty to be safe and throw at Will's body, not his face, Go!" And Dominic immediately started to imagine an impenetrable invisible shield around him.

The countdown was soon reached and India and Mirriam started to throw the objects they had found. It was an incredible sight watching them almost reach Will within a few centimetres and then just fall to the floor. Dominic let his imagination of the shield collapse.

"Did you feel anything Will?" eagerly waiting the answer, like the girls were.

"It's really scary, seeing objects come at you and you brace yourself for the pain but nothing, you feel absolutely nothing. You actually see them fall to the floor."

"Shall we try properly now then with a few large pebbles?" and although with some trepidation, Will agreed.

The two girls gathered three or four pebbles each and waited for Dominic's countdown signal again.

"Now!" Shouted Dominic again and the girls immediately started the thirty second countdown. This time the pebbles were thrown as hard as the girls possibly could and even at Will's face, but again the same result. The pebbles got within a couple of centimetres and fell to the floor.

Dominic again collapsed the shield. "Anything Will?"

"Nope, nothing at all. Mind you though, it really is scary to watch these things come hurtling at your face and try and not move but you just have to be brave." This time, Will's bravado had returned.

"Brilliant, we know it works but for how long? An hour, two, ten, a day? We need to know so Miriam is protected. "I think we should start right away as the sooner we find out the better." Are you ok with that?" Turning to Miriam.

"Yes, I suppose so if it protects me against that evil creep. One question though, how do I eat my dinner or go to the toilet?"

"That's a good question, I never thought of that, I don't really know. I don't think you will be able to logically but I guess we will find out back at the caravan."

"Well, if you don't eat or drink, you won't need to go to the toilet, so that solves both things." Will getting his own back on them from before and laughing away.

"Miriam, I don't think you will be able to. When we get in, try cleaning your teeth and that will show us. If you can't break through the barrier, then I suggest we start it when we go to bed."

A short time later they were back in the caravan and Miriam quickly went to try cleaning her but found the barrier prevented her. She could pick things up and everything else was normal apart from nothing could touch her body apart from her own body.

Dominic, on being told this, "I thought as much, so when we go to bed tonight, I'll put the protection on and then we can see if it lasts until the morning."

After a delightful Mrs Pepper's dinner, Dominic called them together for a meeting in his bedroom.

"I'm sorry Miriam but there's no way we can avoid this now. We have to assume that the High Priest is probably aware now that we've been in his secret office, so we can't take the chance that he might come at any time now, even tonight so it's essential we are all prepared." Miriam went completely pale thinking she didn't have that worry until Thursday but tonight came as a complete shock to her.

"Look I know it's a shock and a huge worry but we are all here around you so nothing will get past us, I promise." Although Miriam tried her best to put on a brave smile, everyone could see that she was terrified.

"This is what I propose, India you're sleeping next to Miriam anyway, so it's up to you to be alert throughout the night. If anything happens just bang on our dividing wall, which is only a light plywood and we'll hear it instantly and come running. The caravan door will be locked as usual but I'll keep hold of the key tonight just in case. The only way she could possibly get out is through your bedroom window. I don't think that's a problem with three of us holding her."

"Do you think I will dragged out as brutally as that?"

"No, not at all. He's probably thinking we won't bother doing anything until Thursday and hope that you will just walk out calmly without anyone hearing or being aware. We just have to be ready for anything that's all I'm saying."

The time to go to bed quickly arrived but they were all so much on edge, especially Miriam that no one except Mrs Pepper was going to sleep.

"I'm off to bed now kids, so don't stay up too late or you will be too tired in the morning." and with that Mrs Pepper went into her bedroom. Dominic waited ten minutes to be sure she was settled and then checked that the caravan door was locked and removed the key, putting it in his pocket.

"Miriam, go and get ready now in the bathroom and we'll stay outside and when you come out, I'll put a protective shield around you. I'd rather do it now just to be extra safe."

CHAPTER TWENTY EIGHT

THE HIGH PRIEST ATTEMPTS TO TAKE MIRIAM

Five minutes later, Miriam had finished and within a few moments Dominic's shield was in place.

"It's strange, I can't feel anything at all, it's just like nothing has happened, can someone throw something at me please." and no sooner had she said it, India threw her hairbrush at her. "Wow, that's so cool, I felt nothing at all."

"Well let's see how long it lasts now, it's 11.30pm so we will try again in the morning."

For the next hour, no one was going to sleep, they were far too nervous about what dangers lay ahead. To even try and take their minds off things, they even tried talking about where in the world Dominic could take them for a holiday, the Seychelles, the Caribbean but nothing worked from distracting their minds.

Eventually they just couldn't keep their eyes open any longer. It had been a long day with their early start searching the High Priest's secret office and even the worry of what lay ahead couldn't keep them awake, and they were soon all asleep.

Oger, the High Priest, had no such problem staying awake. He had to not only capture Miriam for his Master, Lucifer but also, he wanted his revenge and teach Dominic a painful lesson. He guessed that Dominic and his friends, would be on their guard now and would try and stay awake until late and had planned to wait until 3am before attempting to kidnap Miriam.

It had now gone 2am and was time for him to get prepared. The first thing was that he commanded two of his servants to take one of the cars and drive to Bron-y-Wendon Holiday Park, near Colwyn Bay. This was the caravan address he forced India to reveal the year before of where the children were staying.

"You two, take one of the cars and drive it to Bron-y-Wendon Holiday Park and park up close to the entrance but out of sight. We don't want to cause attention. Ring me as soon as you're there and I will bring the girl to you." With that, the two servants disappeared.

2.45am arrived and the call came that they were parked up ready. Immediately the High Priest left his office and carrying his black satanic bible under his arm walked across to the Temple and up to the altar. Placing the book on the large circular black table he had used previously when invoking Lucifer, he read out loud, the prayer to command Miriam to come to him.

"Expergiscere, Miriam, expergiscere.
Lucifer te vocat ut surgas.
Prode, et nemo te impediat.
Magister tuus Lucifer tibi imperat.
Veni nunc, Miriam, expergiscere et veni.
Ad introitum stationis caravanarum venire debes, ubi currus te exspectat.
Veni nunc, Miria, veni ad Magistrum tuum."

And following which he chanted

"Oriens splendor lucis aeternae
Et Lucifer justitae: veni
Et illumine sedentes in tenebris
Et umbra mortis"

And again and again repeated the prayer and the chant. His mind was starting to become one with Miriam's and she was starting to stir. Slowly at first but soon becoming more restless as the High Priest's prayer and chanting started to take more effect.

The prayer and chanting was relentless and the Priest was speaking them louder, he could feel her moving more and more and starting to stir from her sleep.

Miriam's sub conscious was fighting, she was fighting with all her subconsciousness to refuse the commands to go but slowly but surely, she rose from her bed. The shield had failed, the High Priest's power was more powerful and he was winning. When India, suddenly deep down in her sleep, heard Miriam tossing and turning and moaning.

India immediately shouted at her and threw her arms around her in an effort to stop her trying to leave. But the Priest's calling was too powerful and in desperation, India banged on the dividing wall to Dominic's room. They'd half been ready for something to happen and in no time at all were out of their beds immediately and rushed into the girl's room.

Immediately, Dominic could see the glazed look in Miriam's eyes, she wasn't hearing anything they said such was the power of the evil commands. She had become immensely strong and threw off India's hold on her as if she was a rag doll and India went crashing onto the bed.

"Get her onto the floor Will, do a rugby tackle around her legs and I'll push her over," shouted Dominic. It was an almighty struggle, Miriam was as strong as the two of them but with India now joining back in, over went Miriam onto the floor. The two boys immediately jumped on her pinning her down but still she refused to give up fighting.

The High Priest could sense that something was wrong. He could feel her energy being exhausted and he had to do something quickly or she would be lost to him and he invoked the prayer to deliver the terrifying monster, Bestia Terrae.

"Princeps Tenebrarum, audi me, Baphomet,
Domina Terrae, audi me!

Audi me, Satan, quaeso mitte nuntium tuum Bestiam Terrae ut ad te
humilem oblationem nostram perferat
quam alii prohibent. Praecipe Bestiam Terrae ut eam afferat"

The black candles in the Temple started to flicker and the room stated
to get colder, the air started to encircle the room, imperceptibly it
seemed to be gaining in strength and speed and flowing around the
table. The flame from the Temple candles were now distinctly being
bent over in the direction of the wind.

The Bestia Terrae was here and beckoning for the High Priest's
command.

"Progredere, fidelis servus Luciferi.
Progredere et ad me Miriam ex ulnis Dominici adduc.
Progredere et ad me Miriam
adduc ut eam Domino tuo, Domino nostro Lucifero, offerre possim.
Progredere nunc et ad me eam adduc."

And with that, the Temple fell silent and the wind had disappeared.
Bestia Terrae had left to fetch Miriam.

The struggle to hold down Miriam was still continuing, it was a
relentless battle with all three of them pinning her to the floor but still
she continued to struggle such was the power of the Priests command.

"What do we do, Dominic, do we keep her here all night?" India
shouted, becoming considerably out of breath.

"Yes, if we must, if she escapes, I'm afraid she's gone forever so no
matter what, that's not going to happen."

"Why didn't your shield stop it?" Will now joining in.

"I don't know, perhaps it's worn off because we didn't actually know
how long it would last. Or else, the shield is only good for physical
protection and perhaps it can't stop thought waves, which is what is

happening to Miriam. We will have to sort that out after she's back with us."

"It's funny, I should be really warm with the struggle holding Miriam but I'm quite cold," voiced India.

"Me too," Will joining in and also Dominic agreeing.

"Will, do you remember when were in the altar trying to fight off that beast last year, do you remember how cold the room went firs?"

"Don't say that Dominic, it's not funny. You're getting me scared."

"Will someone tell me what you're both talking about, as you're getting me scared as well," India now too beginning to panic.

And Dominic quickly explained the horrific battle with the Devil's messenger, Bestia Terrae.

No sooner had Dominic finished explaining then, a definite cooling draught had now entered the caravan, swirling its way through a veil of icy blue light and soon a wind started to develop. It was continuing to gain in strength as each second passed and a discerning whistling sound was beginning to develop as it rushed around the caravan.

With each speeding revolution of the rushing wind, the whistling was becoming more acutely audible. Louder and louder, it was growing, the breeze now developing into a biting gale. Both Dominic and Will, instantly recognised what was happening but more importantly what was about to happen.

The wind continued accelerating and screaming its way around the caravan and outside the bedroom where they were. They were trying everything they could to keep Miriam with her super human strength pinned to the floor. But with the ferocity of the wind, which had now developed into a tempest acting like a vortex trying to pull her out, they were quickly becoming exhausted.

"Dominic, you have to do something, we can't keep holding her down for much longer," screamed Will.

"I'll try to put a shield around the four of us, I just hope it works." And Dominic closed hie eyes and focused his mind on an imaginary protective force around them.

Almost immediately the hurricane force winds stopped and there was complete calmness. Even the icy blue air had frozen still as if it was painting the background picture for something hideous that about to happen.

The High Priest could sense the new barrier that Dominic had created and screamed in fury at him. "How dare this child challenge me, who is he to defy our Lord Lucifer," and this time commanded that the creature must not fail.

"Serve fidelis Luciferi,
Dominum tuum Dominum nostrum Luciferum
non deficere debes. Exhauri omnem vim tuam et eam ad me adduc."

Dominic sensing something really awful was about to happen shouted. "I don't like the feel of this, just be prepared, and whatever happens just keep a tight hold on everyone. India, what's about to happen is frankly terrifying but we beat it last time and we will again, just keep tight." And with that, Dominic braced for what was about to happen.

Then, as before, a dimly glowing silver mist developed inside their bedroom and surrounded the four of them. The faintest outline of an almost invisible monster took shape, sparkling with a phosphorous greenish blue tint. One split second appearing as the terrifying tentacled monster from the sea and the next some sort of evil monstrous Leviathan. It was impossible to tell what it was, it was fading in and out of view in the merest of a fraction of a second.

From within the eerie silver mist appeared two venomous piercing, fiery eyes which penetrated everything. in its sight and which glowed deep inside the dark hollows of its mask. In its clawed right hand of its huge black hairy torso was a foreboding awesome spear like weapon.

The beast wasted no time and with a blood curdling scream, immediately thrust its three pronged trident straight at Will's chest Will immediately fell backwards as the trident hit with such force his chest, but nothing had happened, he was unharmed, the lethal trident had stopped the merest millimetres from his chest. Dominic's shield was working.

"Dominic, your shield is working. I felt nothing, I just fell back as it was just an automatic reaction, but I felt nothing."

"Hang on Will, we don't know how long my shield will last, so don't relax for one second."

The most terrifying supernatural creature imaginable had paused for a moment, as if in shock that something had dared to defy Lucifer. Fiery glowing red-hot air streamed out of its flared nostrils revealing its anger at being repelled. Once again it readied its tortuous spear and then thrust it with all its might, accompanied by an horrendous roar it's spear at Will's chest.

Yest again, Will was knocked backwards but the barrier had held yet again. The enraged monster screamed in anger, its fluorescent greenish blue tint now changing to one of an orange reddish colour as if changing with its anger.

It was relentless in its attacks and again and again, it charged, in a frenzied fury, changing its body in the blink of an eye. One moment, a sea like monster with a massive tentacled head and horrendous fearsome fangs and the next, a terrifying bull like beast with a huge black hairy torso. Mounted high in either form was its masked rider, with its piercing fiery red eyes, and holding in its clawed hand a trident spear which glowed red with fire. Nothing could break the barrier of the invisible shield.

It was almost 5.30am now and the brutal assault had been going on for over two hours when Dominic suddenly remembered what he did last time when they were exhausted and on the brink of giving up.

And repeated the last sentence of the potion again.

"Lord God, please bless me now with the power of the Universe as Protector to fight against evil and with me it shall remain forever more." And commanded the Beast to go. "Bestia Terrae, in the name of our Lord God, I command you to go."

At that exact moment, India screamed out. The hideous Monster had caught her eye full on and came charging straight at her with its trident blazing in flames. She could see the hatred in its eyes as the trident flew at her chest...

Then everything fell silent, the coldness of the air had disappeared, everything was as it was before the Beast's arrival.

No one moved, no one was sure whether it had gone and no one spoke. The anticipation of what was about to happen next was over-whelming, when Dominic spoke.

"I Think it's gone and we're safe now," and Dominic stood up releasing Miriam. India was in a state of complete shock, putting her hands up to her eyes crying. Dominic leaned across and put his arms around his sister.

"You were brilliant Sis, you were so brave," When all of a sudden Mrs Pepper came dashing in the bedroom, thoroughly annoyed at being woken from her sleep.

"I heard a scream, what are you kids up to? Why are you all on the floor and why are India and Will sitting on Miriam, are you playing a silly game at this time of the morning? Get this place tidied up and you two boys get back in your own bedroom." And stormed off slamming their door shut.

"India, Dominic, I want a word with you two later," shouting as she walked to the kitchen to make herself a coffee.

Dominic looked at Will and India, "We need to sort out what we're going to say," when Miriam, started to move and turned over to see the other three standing around her.

"What happened, why am I aching so much, it feels like an elephant has been sitting on me? Did they try and come for me last night?" and one look at everybody she knew and burst out crying.

That started India off again and the two girls hugged each other tightly and sobbed away.

"I saw that terrifying beast, it tried to kill me with a huge sort of spear. Is this what you went through last year?" Miriam couldn't speak instead just nodded her head still sobbing away.

Will looked at Dominic, "we have to stop this Dominic, once and for all. We can't go on like this every day not knowing if it will come again., especially the girls."

"I've been thinking the same, at least this time by attacking him and finding out about the High Priest's powers we were ready so we need to think of some way to get him out in the open.

The girls had now stopped crying and joined in the discussion with India asking, "What are we going to say to mum Dominic, we can't say we were playing a game, she will never believe that?"

"Yes, that is a problem. I'm thinking of telling her the truth. If it comes again, she might become involved and I don't want that. Luckily last night that Beast left her alone and with mum sleeping like a log as usual, she never realised but probably not so lucky if it happens again. Also, if we decide to tackle the Priest away from here, we could be gone for a day or two, even longer perhaps so there's no way we could keep that secret."

"Let's make some coffee and have a think what's best."

CHAPTER TWENTY NINE

DOMINIC'S SECET IS REVEALED

At the Temple, the High Priest was furious having failed again. Lucifer was not known for kindness or a forgiving nature. The only good thing, was that by attempting to take Miriam now, still left enough time to deliver Miriam but if he failed do that by Thursday then the consequence for him could be catastrophic.

He too needed some way of over-coming Dominic's powers and skills. He had treated Dominic so far as an irrelevant child who could easily be brushed aside but not anymore. He would not be over confident again and would treat him from now on with the respect of almost his equal. The High Priest left the Temple to prepare for his next attempt.

Meanwhile back at the caravan, the children were in deep discussion over what do next and what to tell Mrs Pepper.

Dominic started off, "Well, we have three problems. One easy, but the consequences could be anything, telling our mum and…" looking at India's reaction. "…She could involve the police but as we've said before, we have no proof and she certainly won't want to look stupid but you never know. But if we decide to challenge the High Priest away from here, which I think we have to, as I want to keep him away from mum then she has to know. We just can't say, we're going away for a few days"

Everyone agreed that it was best she was told and after all Dominic could prove they were telling the truth as he could show her a demonstration of his powers like he did with the others.

Continuing on with his thoughts to everyone, "How to beat the High Priest and where? Let's rule out three things first which is the easiest. It can't be here, we've just seen how dangerous that is. Two, it can't be at the Temple as that is where he is in control and last it can't be obviously at our homes. So where? We just can't book an hotel, we don't have the money and we don't know anything about it. I don't even think at our age we even can. I think we have to fight him somewhere totally different where he won't know."

"Where do you suggest," Will asked.

"In another universe, another planet in another universe to be exact. It will be totally different to what anyone knows, even us but there are four of us and I'm sure collectively we will be quicker and better at taking advantage of it."

With that, everyone joined in with questions. "How do you create it, it was fine going back to the dinosaurs because you had a mental picture from Google to shape your thoughts but what do you do for this?"

"I was thinking of creating a mental picture where everything is jumbled up, perhaps the sea is the sky, mountains go down not up. Somewhere where it is totally confusing."

"How will the High Priest know how to find us?" Will asked

"I'm hoping that he can reach through Miriam and can use her like a homing beacon," and on the discussion continued.

"India, Dominic," Mrs Pepper's voice shouted breaking their meeting. "I need to talk with you both please."

"Look, I think it's a good idea we all go." India taking the lead for once. "I think that when we all tell her she will be at least more prepared to listen." And with that all four went to see Mrs Pepper in the sitting room.

"Will, you and Miriam are fine, it's just India and Dominic I want to speak to".

"But Mrs Pepper, we are all in this together and we have something desperately important to tell you." Responded Will.

"Well, if you must then, let's hear what you have to say about last night," and Dominic with the help of everyone joining in, explained what had been going on.

Needless to say, Mrs Pepper being a very level headed woman, where black is black and white is white didn't believe a word. Even with Will and Miriam trying their best to convince her, nothing was working. It all came down to a demonstration of Dominic's powers.

"Mum, we will all go outside and close the caravan door and you go in your bedroom and whisper, covering your mouth with your hand so it's impossible to see anything or lip read and whisper three words of anything and one number and I will tell you what you said."

Like everyone before, when Dominic came back in and told her what words and number she said, she was in utter disbelief thinking it was some sort of a trick and insisted Dominic repeated it but this time she put her head under her duvet in her bedroom when she spoke. Once again, Dominic correctly told her what she said. Although still not totally convinced, thinking it was some sort of a magician's trick she was now starting at least to waiver.

"Dominic, show your mum how you can move things and make them disappear." Will voicing a suggestion which should finally convince her.

"Mum, put your handbag on the table and keep watching, don't take your eyes of it." Mrs Pepper did as Dominic asked and few moments later with Dominic's telekinetic and psychic power it disappeared. Mrs Pepper tapped the table everywhere, even looking underneath it but there was nothing there. All the kids fell about laughing at the bewilderment and puzzled look in Mrs Pepper's face.

"Mum, now go and have a look in the shower."

"You're being serious, it's in there?" and Dominic nodded his head whilst all the others continued giggling away. A minute later Mrs Pepper was back with handbag in her hand and of course checking its contents.

"I need a coffee," were the first words she said and sat back down at the table, whilst India jumped up to make her one.

The next hour was taken up with telling Mrs Pepper the whole story from the start. She was astonished that such things went on and such evil terrifying things, let alone now trying to deal with the fact that her son had magic powers from God himself.

Eventually when she had fully grasped the situation, Dominic explained the deadly dilemma they now faced. How to destroy the High Priest and where.

"Mum, we have two days before he has to take Miriam," and Mrs Pepper, looked at her. "Come here" and put her arms tightly around Miriam.

"If he touches you again, no matter who he thinks he is, he will have me to answer to," which brought out a chuckle of laughter from everyone.

"Mum, I'm being serious, this is going to happen and we have to be ready and somewhere he's not familiar with."

"Well, you could go and visit Aunt Enid up in the Lake District, she'd love to see you and you'd be fine there."

"We can't do that, we'd only bring the danger there. We have to go to a different world."

"What do mean different world?" They had forgotten to tell her of Dominic's powers to go literally anywhere and their adventure with the pterodactyl a hundred million years ago. That was enough, she'd already had to take in, Demons and the Devil, Dominic's magic powers but now dinosaurs and different worlds as well.

Even a coffee was not enough this time and out came the brandy which was only ever used on very special occasions.

"Are you telling me, that you have to go to a different world to beat this monster?" and all four nodded.

"Mum, it's the only way, we have no choice. We don't want to, we just want to get back to some normality but if we don't do something then this, the most horrific monster you could ever imagine will come for Miriam."

"Mum," India now joining in. "This is the most evil, terrifying thing you've ever seen. It's grotesque and utterly ruthless. It's a monster from the sea with huge fangs one moment and then it's a hooded demon sitting on top of a ginormous huge black beast the next. It's the most terrifying thing you could ever imagine. We just can't sit here waiting. None of us could rest for a second knowing it could come again at any time, even at school or home. We have to do something now."

Mrs Pepper fully understood and agreed with what they said. She too was now terrified about keeping the children safe and what to do. There was no good answer. She had to trust their judgment, they were sensible children and with Dominic's powers at least they knew far more than she did. But she had a responsibility to Will and Miriam's parents, it would only be right to tell them.

Eventually, they had exhausted all options. It was too late now with Thursday fast approaching to try and arrange to meet with Will and Miriam's parents, as they too would need to be convinced of the situation and that could take easily a day again, which would mean Thursday would have arrived. In the end, they decided they had no choice but to keep it secret and hoped everything would work out.

It was time to plan where to go, when and what to take to last for a few days and so on. At least with Mrs Pepper involved now, it made things so much easier. Mrs Pepper took control of organising enough supplies to last at least three days and the food would have to be able to be eaten cold. It was quite a task, especially with clothing and of course essential things such as matches, torches, binoculars and of course knives. At least they all had backpacks to carry everything.

Next came the question of when. They agreed to have a light early dinner, more a late lunch and leave. Rather than take any chances of when the next attempt could happen. Perhaps next time, the High Priest would send Bestia Terrae early evening and catch them off guard. The risk was just too great to take.

Next was a plan at least of some sorts as so much was unknown. It was one thing hoping the High Priest would follow but what to do when he arrived there. Dominic was the first to forward his thoughts.

"The High Priest has really two sources of power. That Satanic Bible and the crystal around his neck. I propose to tackle the book first. We know that he leaves it in his secret office when he's not using it, so I'm thinking of teleporting back to their kitchen again, the same night as he arrives to where we will be on the new planet. It might even be tonight or early in the morning again. If we have that, he is definitely weaker as there are so many rites and prayers in there, he surely can't remember everyone. Plus at least we will have a bargaining tool if we ever need one."

The others fully agreeing that it would be a good idea but Miriam stressed not to be gone for too long as they would all be stranded on this new universe not knowing anything without him.

"I should be back in less than an hour at the most, so no need to worry." At least that brought some comfort to Miriam as she knew that although the others would do their best, without Dominic really everyone else could do little.

Last but not least, was how to defeat the High Priest and which was the most important issue of all.

"We know now that his power comes from the crystal he wears around his neck most of the time, except probably at night when he goes to sleep, so then would be our chance.

"We have to go to a planet somewhere strange, completely different from anything he's ever experienced so he's unsure about anything and everything. We need him confused and distracted so whenever he removes it, we can make a grab for it. It will have to be somewhere where what we know here may be the opposite there. It has to be somewhere totally confusing."

"There are four of us and that gives us a bit of an advantage, and we're all reasonably smart enough to conjure up some forms of distraction to give us a chance of getting it. The binoculars will come in handy and they're infra-red night ones too, so if we can find a discrete place to hide and watch him, we can see when he takes it off.

"Outside of that idea, I can't think of anything better, so I'm open to suggestions of anything better."

"We can always tell the police and have him arrested." Voiced India,

"We've talked about this before several times and we always come up with, what proof is there? The police would think we are insane. Besides, even if they did lock him up, he still has the power and can really do anything he wants. The police are no match for him."

No one else could offer any other suggestions as to what would be best, and although not happy about taking the battle to somewhere where no one knew anything there was no other choice. The plan was agreed, even with Mrs Pepper's reluctant approval but she had one final question

"How will you know, you can survive there, what about the atmosphere, oxygen to breathe?" It's one thing going back in time on Earth which you know all about its history and suitability to sustain life but there, you know nothing."

"I've thought of that, I'll travel through the portal first and test it and then travel back and if it's fine, go back with everyone."

With that all agreed, everyone went away to finish their final preparations and packing, whilst Dominic checked through Google for where to go. It didn't take too long for him to decide that the galaxy Andromeda would be best as it had many planets within it that could support life and one in particular which he named, "Wilmindor," as it contained at least three letters of everyone's first name. They were all delighted with that name and particularly having a planet named after them.

Thirty minutes later, they were all set and standing in the same place that Dominic created his portal to take them into the Abbey's kitchen, at the park's toilet block. Everyone and especially Mrs Pepper, giving Dominic huge hugs and wishing him good luck. Everyone was on edge and particularly Miriam as if he was stranded there and couldn't return then there was nothing to stop the High Priest taking her. The risk was enormous and tears streamed down her face with the consequences of what was about to happen.

"Look don't worry," Dominic, shouted trying to put on a brave face as the portal started to develop. "I'll be back in no time at all, just wait there and see." And with that walked forward through the portal.

CHAPTER THIRTY

TAKING THE BATTLE TO PLANET WILMINDOR

Moments later, Dominic was there standing with a handkerchief over his mouth, try to breathe in the tiniest sips of air, in case it was a poisonous gas of some sorts. The first sip seemed fine and then a slightly larger one and that too seemed acceptable. It smelled and tasted a little metallic with a flavour of a very small pinch of elderberry but it was acceptable and so he took away he handkerchief and took a few normal size breaths. Thank goodness it was fine, he could breathe reasonably well, good enough for a few days there at least.

He didn't want to stay there too long as he'd promised the others that he would come straight back and besides he had to make sure that the return through the portal worked. A quick gaze around showed the most bewildering picture he had ever seen.

The clouds were not like on Earth, fluffy white and grey, looking like cotton wall balls that you could walk on, these clouds consisted of billions of tiny shards of mirrors reflecting the landscape and spinning and rotating constantly. It was a Kaleidoscope of images and colours that you couldn't take your eyes off.

But he'd seen enough and although extremely brief, it was good enough to bring the others back with him.

He was now an expert at creating portals and in no time at all, he walked back through the other end of the portal behind the toilet block. Mrs Pepper was the first to throw her arms around him followed in the merest second by everyone else.

The questions were instant, everyone was on tenterhooks waiting to hear what it was like.

"Ok, stop squeezing me and I'll tell you. Well, as you can see, I was only there for less than five minutes as I knew you'd be worrying, so I didn't see hardly anything. The first thing though was the air, I could breathe in it."

"It smells and tastes a little metallic with a flavour of a very small pinch of elderberry but it's fine and I'm sure we will get used to it very quickly. The only other thing I noticed were the clouds. They were like a kaleidoscope of mirrors, millions and millions of them. All spinning and rotating with the reflections of the landscape, it was stunning to see. That's all I had time to notice, but the main thing is that it's safe for us to go. Well, let's say hopefully, as there may be lots of hidden dangers there, I just didn't have time to check anything else."

With a big hug and kiss each from Mrs Pepper, who was still in shock from seeing Dominic walk through the portal he had just created out of thin air. And all this on top of his magic demonstrations and the story of the Devil and a monster chasing them, all in just half a day, was enough to finish off the whole bottle of brandy when she returned to the caravan later.

With a funny parting comment from Will to help break the tension and cheer everyone up, he shouted to Mrs Pepper,

"Mrs P. U.S.A. astronauts depart in glory from beautiful places lake Cape Canaveral, and that's just to the moon. We're going thousands of trillion times further, to a different galaxy and we have a toilet block send off!" At least that brought out the loudest burst of laughter from everyone and with that, they entered the portal.

Just like Dominic's teleport, within just moments, there they were standing on a strange mysterious planet in another galaxy. Surreal wasn't the word, it was something possibly even greater than even going back one hundred million years to see the dinosaurs. It was different world and no one had any knowledge at all about it and probably wouldn't for hundreds of years to come.

As Dominic had first experienced, everyone's eyes were immediately taken with the cascading kaleidoscope of mirrors that made up the clouds. They rotated and spun in a spectrum of colours and reflections, that constantly changed. It was daylight, in as much as you could clearly see, but it was also night. You could see countless thousands of sparkling, dazzling stars in a rainbow of colours, spreading across like a cloak of sequins behind the kaleidoscope of clouds.

The ground upon which they stood was not solid and firm. It was slightly spongy, something like walking across a blanket of moss. With their first few steps, they sank down up to their ankles releasing a small puff of slightly pungent air but shortly after the ground recovered back again.

Will, sat down on a nearby rock to take in this wonderous new world. The rock was warm and felt like sitting on soft rubber which, as if alive, adjusted itself to nestle snugly around your body encouraging you to lie back into its body.

"I've found my bed for the night. Come and try this, it's incredible," and as he went to stand up to let India have a go, the rock gripped him even tighter. "Hey, I'm stuck, this thing won't let me go," But with a pull on each arm from the two girls, the rock gently released him and he was soon up.

"It didn't take you too long to find a girlfriend," grinned India laughing away.

Everywhere was an abundance of plants. A floral spectacle of colours, shapes and sizes. Some towering the height of trees with huge luminescent pods coloured in an array of orange and gold hanging from them. In the distance to their far right there appeared a lake which shimmered with the colours from the dazzling display from the clouds above it. Surrounding it was what looked ice white sand and the fringes of it all peppered with what appeared to be a forest of immensely tall plants. Their stems as thick as the trunks of trees on Earth and the colours ranging from the deepest emerald to burnt amber.

To their left appeared to be a vast area of desert, dotted with an oasis of plants and small dunes

"let's take ten minutes and put some sort of plan together," Dominic calling them to his side. The first thing is we need somewhere we can use as a base, where we can shelter and sleep and ideally two places in case we have to give up one. We need to find water. We brought enough for three days if we are very careful which should be long enough as the alignment of the stars is past then and we can go back home. But just to be safe, I think we head in that direction first, where the lake is," and pointed to their right.

"Next, we need to find some nasty surprises for the High Priest. I guess it's a case of trial and error, finding which things are deadly here or at least can totally distract him enough to give us a chance at snatching the crystal. We need to keep an eye open for anything we can use." And off they walked, heading towards the forest and lake.

Time was useless here as they had no idea what a day was, how many hours. It could even be years, was there a night and day or did it remain like it is? Everything single thing was different to any concepts they had back on Earth. Gravity was less than on Earth and they all found that thoroughly enjoyable. A single stride was three times the distance and jumping three of four metres high was no problem. It was a playground of fun, it was like having your own fair until Will's hand accidentally struck one of the huge luminescent pods hanging from one of the huge plants.

Down it fell immediately bursting open, releasing thousands of tiny black flying antlike insects. These were nothing like anything on Earth. Their wings were of the lightest metal-like fabric with razor sharp edges which could inflict the most painful damage. Immediately they swarmed at the intruder as if one body and launched a ferocious attack on him.

Will screamed as the first few flew past skilfully slashing and creating tiny painful incisions along the side of his head. Dominic totally unaware of what happened as he was the lead person, immediately turned and saw the immense danger Will was under and instantly threw a protective shield around him. Luckily, his powers held good for this strange world as well.

"Well done Will, you've discovered one weapon pretty quickly," which brought giggles from everyone except Will who was looking the worse for wear. On they continued to stride, the distance was no problem with this lower level of gravity and each step was enormous compared to one on Earth. They soon reached the edges of the forest which peppered around the fringes of the lake and decided to check the lake out first.

The iced white sand looked so inviting dazzling their eyes with its brilliance.

"I wish we had sunglasses and deck chairs," shouted Miriam. "It makes the finest beaches on Earth look bland compared to this," and took her shoes off jumping on to it. "Oww," she screamed. It wasn't sand at all, it was completely made of the finest ice crystals and quickly jumped back off again to the amusement of others.

"Try the water Miriam," voiced Will, "it must be freezing with so much ice around." And putting back on her shoes, walked the short distance across and dipped her hand in. "It's warm, it feels brilliant. It was crystal clear, the ice crystals covered the entire lake floor reflecting the colourful kaleidoscope of the clouds and yet somehow the water remained warm.

"I'm having a quick paddle," and before Dominic could say anything, in she went.

"Miriam, be careful, you have no idea what may be in there,"

"It's fine, I can see everything, it's crystal clear, it's so nice."

"Hang on there, I'm coming in too," as now India rushing to join in, threw her shoes off and ran across and with one huge leap landed alongside Miriam. "You guys need to come and try this, it's incredible," and Will started to take his shoes of when Miriam screamed out in pain.

"There's something here, I can't see anything but look my legs bleeding, it bit me," shouting at the same time as running out with India following soon behind.

"Are you sure Miriam, I can't see anything," voiced India. "Could it have been from the ice somehow?"

"I can't see how, look how high up my leg the cut is, it's near my knee." Peering intensely into the clearness of the water. "Look, look there, what's causing that movement in the water." And they both stared intensely at the wave that was moving with some speed towards where they were standing. They were completely mesmerized by the bow wave heading for them, waiting for it to stop and turn as it came close to the ice crystal beach. But it didn't stop, just the opposite it accelerated and leapt from the water onto the beach pushing aside the crystals as it sped along. The two girls instantly turned and ran screaming off the beach with it following closely on their heels. As soon as the creature hit the end of the crystals, it immediately stopped and headed back towards the lake.

"Did you see it, did you see it?" shouted the girls simultaneously to Dominic and Will who had been watching it all happen.

"I saw it but there's nothing there." shouted back Will

"There has to be, something has to cause those waves and bite me."

When Dominic suggested the answer. "It must be some sort of an invisible fish. It is not even translucent, it must be completely transparent, and you just see right through it. Not only that, it must also be amphibious if it can come out of the water onto land."

"Well, that could be good news, as it's just too dangerous to try and cross it. If we camp around here somewhere, we will have our backs protected a bit at least. In the meantime, let's check out this forest of plants to make sure nothing nasty is going to come running out at us," and off they set into the forest of plants.

What a sight and noise greeted them. It was a cacophony of sounds, from the countless thousands of insects which flew and crawled around everywhere and which deafened the ears. From the outside, it gave no indication that it would be anything but quiet and yet just one metre inside it was deafening. Somehow the forest held all sound captive.

Huge stems rose to one hundred metres and more, hollow and ringed with apertures that open and close as if breathing. Tendrils that extended horizontally, weaved together to form vast living canopies for the abundance of luminescent insects. And which allowed the canopies to glow faintly in the forest's constant twilight, casting the ground below in an underwater-like radiance. Droplets of viscous liquid dripped constantly from the tendrils, falling down onto the spongy ground and feeding a carpet of smaller fungal like growth of radiant blues and reds mosses.

The insects were the masters here and the plants were their food source providing all the nutrients they needed from the sticky viscous liquid that fell.

Dominic threw a protective barrier around them and walked further into the forest to see if they would attack, but nothing happened. The insects had no reason to, they hadn't disturbed their harmony or food source and he let the shield disappear. Still nothing, the insects remained calm, seemingly uninterested in this new species that walked amongst them.

Then Dominic had an idea and picking up a small piece of an old decaying stem and threw it as far as he could deep into the forest. Immediately swarms of insects sprung alive and attacked it completely cloaking it with their bodies. At first believing it to be an unwanted intruder before realising it was part of their forest and returning back again to their canopies.

Dominic turned to the others. "I think we've gone far enough to give us a good idea of what this place is like now," and with that they turned back to where they entered the forest. "I think the forest is pretty good protection as well. All we need do if the High Priest or anything comes that way is throw a stick near it and the insects will attack."

"We need to find the best vantage places around here then," and everyone started scouting for the best vantage points. "Don't forget we need at least two places, even three would be better. The Priest will automatically home-in on Miriam, so he will immediately know that one. I'm hoping that as soon as he's aware where Miriam is, he will disappear somewhere close by to hatch some sort of a plan. That's when our other hideouts will come in handy, so we can watch him with him thinking he's watching us, and when he falls asleep and removes his crystal, we can take it."

"Remember though, everything is new here. We have no idea, what powers he may have, he might not even be able to get here, but I doubt that with Lucifer's crystal. Perhaps he will come with that terrifying beast, and if it does come, what do we do then? I don't even know if my powers are restricted, we have no time to try anything so be ready for things going wrong. We wanted to confuse it all and we've certainly got that."

It didn't take them too long to find three suitable places. The first was the throw-away one, which would effectively be their decoy one and where they would first stay until the Priest's arrival so they settled down to eat some of the food that Mrs Pepper had packed for them whilst Dominic again repeated what he was going to do.

"As soon as he's here and settled, I'm going to teleport back to the abbey and hopefully steal his satanic black book. If it all goes well, I should be back here in less than an hour, probably just thirty minutes. Try not to worry too much Miriam, I promise I won't be long and won't leave until he's settled." With that, India gave her a big hug to try and comfort her.

"We've beaten him twice now Miriam, so your safe with us." Will's hopefully reassuring support joining in.

CHAPTER THIRTY ONE

DOMINIC GETS HELP FROM SOME STRANGE FRIENDS

Dominic looked at his watch noticing that back on Earth it would now be 9.30pm.

"I'm just going into the forest for a few minutes to try something but you all need to settle down now as it could be a long night ahead. Miriam, as I said before, I'm guessing he will read your mind to find out where you are and teleport to here, so be prepared for some strange dreams and thoughts entering your mind. Hopefully we will notice a change in you but tell us as soon as you can anyway. Don't worry about it, it's just the only way he can find out where we are, he's not the type to try anything before he's weighed things up and planned." And with that Dominic wandered off into the forest of plants and insects, whilst the others settled down hypnotised by the memorising sky in their wonderous strange new world.

It took Dominic no time at all to cross the two hundred metres to the forest edge with his huge strides on this lower gravity world. As before, it went from complete silence to an ear deafening crescendo of noise in the space of just one metre, it was incredibly difficult not to find it completely confusing.

In walked Dominic to about one hundred metres in complete peace and acceptance from the millions of the strange inhabitants and sat down. Leaning back against one of the enormously tall plants with its huge pods overhanging him, he closed his eyes and focused his mind on trying to communicate with the life of the forest.

Slowly but surely the crescendo of noise started to quieten, each passing second the forest was becoming quieter. They were starting to listen to him. The countless thousands of pods were starting to slowly peel open releasing millions upon millions of strange luminescent looking flying insects with razor sharp, silver teeth gleaming in the constant twilight of the forest.

Insects of all differing shapes and sizes were streaming down every stem in the forest from their overhead canopies. They were far too numerous to count. The forest floor was fast becoming a dense, deep mat of injects. Everywhere a mass of insects was forming as far as the eye could see around Dominic and they were listening to him.

He was asking for their help to protect them against the evil that was coming to their planet. Even the plants appeared to be listening as their tall trunk like stems were twisting themselves towards where Dominic sat. The insects and plants lived together in a beautiful symbiotic relationship, each helping the other. The plants were taking the nutrients from the rich undergrowth and the insects would pollenate the flowers to become pods and which in turn provided shelter and protection for the insects. Each one relying on the other for their existence.

Together the whole of their world acted as one voice and thought now and understood what he was asking them. A few moments past and once again the forest burst into its normal pinnacle of noise before falling again in total silence. The forest had agreed to help him and the others. It explained that their world lived as one body, the lake which the girls had entered was the living home for the invisible fish-like creatures that lived there. To them, it was not water it was the very life blood of their existence. The warmth in the water was from their energy of life and to enter it would harm the whole of their being. Dominic, apologised for their recklessness in not finding out first but they certainly would never have entered had they understood and back on planet Earth, water is not like that, it is something to enjoy and play in.

They accepted his explanation and apology, explaining that everything on the planet was a living being and could act as one when necessary. Even the lake and its inhabitants were in tune with what was going on and had heard Dominic's apology which they accepted. They had never fought anything before, there was never a need to on their planet but they understood the need to protect any world from evil and Dominic returned back. He now had a whole new world on his side and returned back to tell the others.

It was just a brief few minutes before he was back to find them all huddled together and apart from the danger that was about to befall them, it was the most serene setting. Beauty surrounded them wherever they looked. Everything was so calming, the whole planet was about living together in harmony and peace and it was rubbing off on them too.

"Wake up guys, I need to tell you something really important. I've got some great news, we have the whole of the planet helping us." Everyone immediately jumped up in total shock at what Dominic had just said and he went on to explain what had just happened.

"What, you mean everything?" Will being the first to ask.

"Yes everything, from the creatures in the lake and the lake itself to every plant and insect, everything."

"How does it all work then If we need their help, what do we do?

"They can read your minds, so all you need do is ask for their help in your thoughts when you need it."

This news cheered everyone up, they were elated knowing that a whole planet was on their side whenever they needed. As quick as their smiles appeared, they disappeared when India shouted.

"Look at Miriam's head it's rocking back and forth, the High Priest must be contacting her."

Dominic looked across and agreed. "Yes, he's on his way. No need to panic though, I'm sure she will be fine for a while at least once he's here. "What we have to do is try and locate where he going to rest, but we have help from the whole of this new world which will let us know, which is a brilliant help. As I said before, as soon as he's settled, I will go and find his satanic bible. For now, all we can do is just wait."

A few minutes later, Miriam's restlessness relented and she became calm once again, even opening her eyes.

"I feel strangely tired, what happened, has he controlled me again?"

"Yes, but only to get here and now he's here somewhere," Dominic keeping his voice low. "I'll wait fifteen minutes to make sure he's relaxed and confident and teleport back. Remember what I said, every living thing on this planet is here to help, and you only need to ask them with your thoughts and they will be there for you."

Fifteen minutes soon passed. "I must go now, so I'm back in time before he does anything. Our friends have found where he is, he is over in that direction," pointing to some large rocks about five hundred metres away. "Now he is settled, his mind won't be on Miriam and so you should move to the second spot we found. Hopefully, he will still be automatically thinking we are all here. Good luck, I'll be back soon," and with that Dominic was gone.

CHAPTER THIRTY TWO

DOMINIC FALLS FOR THE HUGH PRIEST'S TRAP

Virtually in almost the same instance as Dominic left Wilmindor, he was standing in the kitchen of the abbey. It was in total darkness and not a sound could be heard, even with his super hearing. Excellent he thought, they must all be in bed asleep somewhere and quickly located the lever again on the underside of the mantle and pulled. Once again, the floor slid open revealing the High Priest's secret office and down Dominic descended into his room.

It didn't take him long to search everywhere and no satanic bible was to be found. He knew that the High Priest wouldn't have taken it to Wilmindor as it was just too bulky, but where was it? The only other possible place it could be, was in the altar room where their evil ceremonies were conducted and closing the hidden trap door behind him, off he went to search there.

Remembering his way around was easy, how could he forget after his last traumatic encounter there and was soon into the temple. This time though it was strange and not like before, it felt colder and for some reason more ominous which was bad enough then and lit by just two black candles. Putting this distraction out of his mind, he noticed something resting on the ceremonial black oak circular table and went across to see.

It was the satanic book but why would it be there and not in the High Priest's secret office, something was wrong. When the moment his hands touched the book to take it, the candles started to flicker and spit. The room was starting to become even colder and a blue tinge started to circulate around the temple. From past bitter and painful experiences, Dominic knew what this meant. The Bestia Terrae was about to make an appearance.

Immediately Dominic went to snatch the book and leave as the last thing he wanted to face was that horrific monster again and besides, he had to get back to the others before the High Priest attacked. But the book wouldn't move, he couldn't lift it up. It was as if glued to the table, it wouldn't even budge the meetest fraction on a millimetre. Clearly this had all been planned.

The High Priest had outsmarted him and had made him look foolish. He had counted on Dominic coming back for the book, as now he had Dominic out of the way taking Miriam would be easy.

The High Priest made his move and crossed the few hundred metres to where they were. But they had gone, he had not bothered to communicate with her again taking it for granted that they had not moved. At least this time, Dominic's planning had outsmarted him. But this was just a mere inconvenience, a short delay which would soon be rectified and the priest focused his mind on Miriam once again.

His telepathy was far too powerful for her to resist and a few moments later she revealed where they were. They were just two minutes away and immediately he sprang into action taking giant leaps towards them.

Will and India had been keeping a close eye on Miriam waiting for something like this to happen, and the moment her actions became distant as if trance like, they took immediate action. Snapping her out of her dream state they pushed and pulled her as fast they could run and jump into the forest.

They remembered exactly what to do and rested some fifty metres in against some plants and focused their minds on contacting the inhabitants of the forest. Once again, the crescendo of noise started to immediately quieten down and countless millions of insects started to quickly descend from their pods and canopies forming a throbbing mass of life all around them and growing deeper and deeper by every passing second.

They had heard them and understood the danger the high Priest presented and soon there was a wall of insects three metres high all around them with numerous of the closest plants bringing their leaves to form a barrier above them.

This new world was ready and communicating as if one. Outside of the forest, every living thing that could move was moving towards them to help. The ground was alive with their movement, pulsating as if the lungs of the planet as they marched towards where Miriam and the others were waiting. The air too was vibrant with the sounds of insects their wings rapidly beating as they too rushed to help.

The next moment the High Priest had arrived at their new location and sneered at the seemingly feeble attempt this world had made to protect them.

On this planet the High Priest appearance had altered. Seemingly the planet strips all signs of pretentiousness in anything living, preferring to expose the real being in all its humility. But not the case with the High Priest. Although his appearance had been exposed to show his true self, this was such an evil person who could never ever show any degree of humbleness.

Here, he was tall and skeletal, still draped in black woven robes of an era past His face was smooth like polished bone, with no eyes, only two burning pits that smoked like red hot coals. His hands stretched long and spidery, each finger tipped with a black finger nail that curled like a claw.

He swiftly set about clearing every being from his path but the more he did the quicker it was replenished by the enormous army rushing to maintain their protection.

He was seething with this wasted futile attempt by these feeble beings. He wasn't sure that without his help the Bestia Terrae could destroy Dominic. He hoped that at the very least it could delay his return enough to allow him the unrestricted time to capture Miriam., but nothing was certain so he had to hurry.

A panic was soon beginning to set in and more ferocious means of clearing a pathway to Miriam was at last starting to show some progress. Centimetre by centimetre he was slowly progressing but at such an horrendous loss of life to this harmless planet who were willingly sacrificing themselves to save these children from Earth.

Back at the abbey, Dominic was still desperately trying with everything he knew to remove the book but without even the slightest of success. Without the full knowledge of what powers he possessed and which could possibly assist, it was just impossible.

The Bestia Terrae had finally arrived in the Temple. The room was plunged into total darkness as the two candles were sucked into the tornado which was twisting its way around the walls of the temple as if imitating a spinning top. Jagged bolts of lightning tore through room, exploding into a terrifying display of light followed immediately by the most deafening claps of thunder. Once again, Dominic's old adversary shrouded in a dimly glowing silver mist appeared, dwarfing him with its enormous presence just a few metres away in front of him.

Even now, with its piercing fiery eyes glowing deep crimson red inside the dark hollows of its fearsome mask made Dominic take a step back in awe. It presented the most spine-chilling sight that no one could ever imagine. Mounted once again upon its monstrous, ferocious pitch-black bull, sparkling with its phosphorous greenish blue glow. One split second appearing as sort of a terrifying Leviathan monster from the sea and the next this grotesque monster riding upon its fearsome enormous pitch-black bull. It was one then neither, it was both and then gone, all interchanging in the merest time imaginable It was almost impossible to make it out as it was disappearing in and out of an any form of an image.

This time though it was different, it had come as if prepared. If it couldn't defeat Dominic, it at least could secure him to give the High Priest time to capture and bring Miriam back to the temple. In its clawed hand it not only held its three-pronged trident spear favoured by the Leviathan part of the beast but also a net, forged by materials not of our world but by Lucifer himself that no one could break.

This time though, Dominic had discovered more powers than the last time he was in the temple and readied himself for the inevitable impending attack by quickly creating an invisible shield around himself.

The monster, its warm air streaming out of its flared nostrils against the bone chilling air, understood what Dominic was doing. Its hideous rider let out a mighty roar which reverberated throughout the temple, and the seething bull leapt forward. With the trident spear now pointing directly at Dominic, the animal and rider charged the rider roaring with fury as they hurtled themselves forward.

Dominic's invisible shield held, it was impenetrable as flashes of lightning shot out from where the trident had clashed against his invisible barrier that protected him. Dominic glanced up to the hideous rider who was screaming with rage looking down with hatred upon him.

Attack followed attack, it was relentless but still noting could penetrate the shield. Dominic was virtually helpless. The swirling tornado constantly accelerating around the inner wall of the temple was so powerful that it had created a vortex of immense strength. It was a maelstrom and Dominic's attempts to form a portal for even the merest fraction of a second were proving impossible as the vortex destroyed everything immediately.

The hideous faceless rider, its deeply recessed piercing red eyes deep inside its horrific mask now in an even more ferocious attack charged again, hurling themselves against the invisible shield. This time though it was different. The fearsome trident was not thrust at Dominic but instead the charging beast let out an enormous roar and threw the demoniac net with all its force at Dominic.

The net encircled him in a tight bind as if possessing a mind of its own. Although Dominic felt nothing because of the barrier he had created, the net secured the barrier and anything inside, including Dominic was its prisoner. There was no way out, he was bound, the vice like net was immovable and he was now its prisoner.

The monster seeing its prisoner now held captive, slowly paced forward and the massive bull placed its nose almost to Dominic's touching the shield stared intensely at him in a sign of conqueror and satisfaction. At last, it had if not conquered him, had him trapped and the faceless rider shrieked with an evil fearsome laughter at his defenceless captive.

Try as he may Dominic was trapped. He tried everything to break free but it was useless against the supernatural net and the awesome maelstrom that encircled him. Dominic could only think of what was happening to his friends on Wilmindor and especially Miriam now they were on their own. They stood no chance on their own now against the powerful High Priest.

The children's fate was sealed although they were not aware of Dominic's capture, they had realised with each passing minute that something was wrong. Dominic should have returned long ago and it was not like him to say something and not fulfil it. There was nothing they could do except sit and wait for their inevitable fateful end. It was up to the beings on this new world to save them now, if they were to have any chance at all.

But outside their protection was becoming less and less as the High Priest ruthlessly swept their protectors aside. The forest had tried its very best but it was no match for the powers that the priest possessed. Countless upon countless of lives were viciously annihilated by the evil that was amongst them and yet still they never gave in. The priest could sense he was close and could now even smell their fear.

They were his now and nothing could stop him from seizing them, certainly not the pathetic creatures of this planet. With one more sweep of his hand brutally casting aside those who had fought so valiantly, he was through the barrier. In front of him sat his prey, the three children huddled tightly together.

"Your mine now, you sad urchins and where's your Master Pepper now to help you?" letting out the most evil laugh.

Will jumped up, not frightened by this evil skeletal of a monstrosity, his cloak now covered in the deep darkest red from the blood of so many who had given their lives to protect them.

"We will never be scared of you no matter what you do to us, try fighting us without your magic powers."

The priest laughed even louder knocking Will down to the floor as if swatting a fly.

"You're of no interest to me, you're far too insignificant" and reached out to grab Miriam by her hood with his long spidery fingers which gripped her like a claw. Immediately she bit down on his fingers with all her might which made him quickly recoil.

"My master will enjoy your spirit, enjoy your last moments of freedom," grabbing her more forcefully this time and dragging Miriam to her feet. Will and India tried in vain to snatch Miriam back but it was futile against his power and he turned to walk away back out of the forest.

Miriam was screaming their names and they too hers as he started to take her away when suddenly he let go of her screaming in immense pain. He was clutching at his neck and shouting in immense anger.

"What have you done? What have you done?" Trying his best to kick every creature around him. But now the tables had turned they had the upper hand and he was the pathetic individual.

Cleverley, the forest had listened carefully to what Dominic said and to where the evil priests source of power came from, the crystal in the pouch around his neck. They had deliberately sacrificed so many lives to keep him distracted whilst several of them had been gnawing their way through the strap that held the crystal close to his body. It had fallen to the floor and in all the melee when he captured Miriam, it had fallen to the awaiting army below.

Now he was powerless and they were attacking him as ferociously as they could. Blood was streaming down his legs from the hundreds of painful bites they were inflicting. He was now totally vulnerable without his crystal but despite the horrendous pain being inflicted he had no choice but to scour the forest floor searching for it.

Instantly Miriam saw her chance and with Will and India they started to run out of the forest towards the lake they had their encounter with earlier. They knew from what Dominic had told them that the fearsome invisible creatures of the vast lake would now help just like the forest did.

They had just reached the ice crystal shore of the lake when an almost inaudible humming sound accompanied by a faint blue glow in from of them appeared.

"Oh no!" Screamed India, "he's found his crystal and he's here, we're too late to get into the lake for their help." Thery had no escape, no one to protect them now. They had tried their best and such a heavy price had been paid. There was nothing they could do to stop this evil High Priest take Miriam now and huddled themselves together with arms tightly around each other, waiting for their inevitable fate.

"What are you guys doing just standing there?" a voice rang out in front of them. Instantly recognising it, they looked up and standing there with a huge grin on his face was Dominic. With a collective enormous scream of delight, they immediately all rushed over knocking him down with their excitement onto the beach crystals.

No one could speak fast enough, everyone wanted to talk at once and tell Dominic what had happened and ask where had he been, why had he not returned earlier as promised. They were so many questions from everyone.

Soon everyone had relayed their stories. It turned out that as soon as the crystal had fallen from the High Priest's neck, the powers that controlled the Bestia Terrae immediately vanished and Dominic's binds disappeared along with the beast.

They were now faced with a dilemma. Assuming the High Priest recovered his crystal, should they return home? If they did so then they were back to square one not knowing when he would try to take Miriam again. Even with Dominic's powers he could not remove or destroy the embedded command in Miriam's brain, to do that they had to destroy the crystal.

The other alternative was to remain on the planet where they had the whole of this new world on their side and try again.

"Why can't we beat him to finding the crystal and go back now?" Will offering another possibility.

"I thought of that but it's quite possible that he has already found it now and is thinking the same, planning for us to do exactly that." We would be in real difficulty then. I think our best option is to remain somewhere else on this planet and try the same again. This time though, I will remain here with you and not go and try retrieve that satanic bible.

They all agreed and with that they started their move to find a suitable different area on the planet and await for the high Priest to come. They had defeated him again but they knew that a war consists of many battles and more battles would need to be fought before it would be finally over.